CoverBoys & Curses

He prays for prey.
His prayers have just been answered.

By
Lala **CORRIERE**

ISBN: 13: 978-1490558486
Copyright © 2013 Lala Corriere

Here's what the Master of Suspense, **Sidney Sheldon**, said about the Mistress to Romantic Suspense, Author Lala Corriere—

"Her writing is provocative and fast-paced, with vivid descriptions and skillfully crafted dialogue. Real page-turners."

A thrilling suspense that will keep you guessing to the very end! I loved every minute of this story and couldn't put it down until THE END. Corriere is THE author to read. K.T. Bryan

Although not the type of book I normally read, I couldn't put this one down. Creepy, did I say that? And complex. I don't want to give too much away, but get yours today! You will want to find everything this author has out and devour them! D'Ann Ludlum

I had to stop reading this book. Because I was home, alone with my 3 year old and I kept hearing bumps in the house. Turned out it was only my imagination... :) Seriously, loved CoverBoys & Curses - but if you have a vivid imagination and/or you scare easily, read it in a crowded place so you don't freak yourself out. The characterizations are very good, the dialogue snappy and the twists and turns will leave you breathless. A definite, fun, weekend read! Kristina Knight

I don't know of another author who can strike the high notes every time with their beginnings and their endings. She takes risks

many authors wouldn't dare, and comes out brilliant. Quintessential Corriere!   Peg Brantley

This book is dedicated to my personal hero,
Chuck Corriere.
You make me giggle. You make me whole.

In loving memory of my mother, Shirley Jean.

Posthumous thanks to Sidney Sheldon, the Master of
Suspense, for his guidance and mentoring.

Editing Acknowledgement:
Bonnie Lewis

Back Cover:
Patty Henderson

"Beauty is as summer fruits, which are easy to corrupt and cannot last; and for the most part it makes a dissolute youth, and an age a little out of countenance; but if it light well, it makes virtue shine and vice blush."
–Francis Bacon

Chapter One
3 Women & a Funeral

THEY SAY WOMEN DON'T KILL themselves with a single bullet to the head.

They're dead wrong.

The entire funeral screamed of blasphemy. Payton Doukas's father, of fierce Greek Orthodox persuasion, insisted that viewing the body was a necessary ritual in the institution of a proper burial. As self-proclaimed host of the event, he was none too thrilled that his daughter had decided to blow her brains out. In compromise, Payton's casket commandeered a corner of the chapel veiled behind cranberry colored sheers. I kept trying to peer through the fabric while knowing I would avoid any sight of what might be left of my best friend.

Divorced, Payton's mother left a much different thumbprint on her daughter's final service. She did this theme thing. The altar in front of me brimmed with potted plants, buckets of cut daisies, and an odd assortment of gardening tools, sunbonnets, gloves, and clunky looking black rubber shoes. I guess it could have been nice if Payton had lived to love the garden, but she couldn't sustain the life of a Christmas cactus. I knew better. If Payton had a theme it was the little foil package of not-so-clunky black rubbers, also known as condoms, she kept tucked inside her fake crocodile purse.

1

I hadn't spent much time in the desert. It must have been Payton's final laugh to go and kill herself in Tucson in June. At 109 degrees, the historic church didn't have air-conditioning. A few floor-stand fans blasted out hot air. The tired looking surroundings offered a splintered cross, suspended above the altar and impressive in size. It seemed to be the only adornment other than the temporary garish gardening exhibit and those wretched cranberry sheers.

Carly Posh sat next to me. A gifted Los Angeles interior designer, she preferred to dress as if she'd just returned from some combat boot camp. Always organized and in control of both body and mind, Carly was the fine stitching that kept our tapestry of friendships woven together.

To the left of Carly, Sterling Falls constantly adjusted the miniskirt that seemed to be sticking to the wooden pew. Late to arrive, she'd wedged her slim body toward Carly from the opposite side of the church. I didn't see her face, but there was no mistaking who she was. Sterling's trademark wardrobe was skimpy and bright, but not as shiny as her long lacquered fingernails adorned with even brighter gemstones. Her fingers looked like popsicles with giant chunks of lime and cherry ice swirls clinging to the sticks. When her dad became the legendary jeweler to the stars, Sterling was quick to partner up with him. Their sign on Rodeo Drive simply read, *'Falls & Falls'*. Falls of cascading diamonds, rubies, and emeralds, that is. Fair to say that Sterling was the shellacked gold threads embedded in the fabric of our friendship.

Payton's father rose to the altar and conveyed his final goodbyes to his *Petroula*—Payton's given name and one she loathed. The heavy Greek accent made his words difficult to understand. Instead his grieving eyes, red and swollen against an ashen face, communicated his story of deep loss.

I had been witness to this type of grief far too many times. I admit my mind was drifting from the service when Sterling shoved the latest issue of my magazine across Carly and into my lap.

The sound of her voice carried loud enough the family members in the pew ahead of us turned and shook their heads in disapproval. "What's up with this, Lauren? Are you asking for death threats? These types of stories are going to get you killed."

I shrugged my shoulders in an attempt to shun the conversation. Between the glossy images of male models, my articles solicited an abundant readership of both sexes. *CoverBoy* would become known, if not respected, for presenting in-your-face current world events based in fact not commonly known or believed, or even conceived. The stories pushed the edge and this time, maybe, I had gone too far. A death threat is pretty far.

Who knows why I loved Sterling. She fell into the obnoxious and self-centered and rich and drop dead gorgeous category. She was just pissed to be the last one to know I was moving my magazine to Los Angeles. And that meant I was moving, too.

We were four. We had become friends when we were only eleven years old. Now we were three, and I wanted to be alone. I wanted to be one. I wanted to sit in the back of the church away from everyone and out of earshot from the minister's words and all the other people that had to stand up and drone on about something irrelevant regarding my friend behind the cranberry sheers. I'd feel safer in the back. *Safer? Safer if you're a bowling pin, maybe.*

Who needed protection? Not me. But anyone and everyone who had ever loved me had died. My loved ones were not safe. This much I knew. And apparently I was not safe either, but I hadn't mentioned this to my friends. I hadn't mentioned it to my own self.

Chapter Two
An Empty Pew

THE DARK AND HANDSOME man had a spy planted at the services. Just to make certain all the details were neat and tidy. A mere kid, but good at blending into any crowd of mourners. Dressed in black. Good boy.

FOLLOWING THE SERVICE we moved across the church grounds to a noon gathering of Greek food. The three tables offered grape leaves, *moussaka*, unidentifiable fish replete with metallic eyeballs, and flaky baklava dripping with golden syrupy butter.

Sterling, lanky and lithe ever since I met her in fifth grade, devoured her second chunk of baklava. Between gulps she asked me, "So, what gives? Why the tell-all story on one of the most famous ballplayers in the country?"

Why not, I thought, even though I felt the knot in my throat pulsing while knowing someone out there was ready to kill me over it. "I stand by my work," I said. I had the facts. Steroids. Steroid sales. Steroid cancers. One could call it an old story, but I took a spin on it with the big money bribery.

Carly looked on and attempted to hide the concern that seized her eyes. She tried to blink away the tension.

Oblivious to Carly, Sterling changed the subject. "What do you say we ditch this place? Go back to the resort and splash around in the pool. Hang time. Payton would have wanted that."

Sterling was right. But it didn't feel right.

"You guys go ahead. I'm going to stick around here for a bit. Maybe take a walk," I said.

Sterling tossed her long blond hair to the side, "Yeah, right. 109 degrees and Lauren wants to take a walk."

I grabbed a bottle of cold water from a nearby barrel. "I'll catch up with you soon."

I walked, all right. Right back into the already emptied church. Where had all the mourners gone? And Payton's casket? The flowers, the tacky garden crap, even the cranberry sheers were gone. I took my preferred seat at the back of the church.

And I made the mistake of turning my phone back on and checking messages. Three of them were from the identified person in my article accepting bribes. One was from the identified briber. All were irate. Screaming they were going to get me. Shit.

I'm twenty-nine and I've lost too much, too soon. My mother died of a heart attack when I was away at university. My father and my fiancé perished together in the family jet that was bringing them to me the day before my wedding.

And now, Payton. She's one of my best friends. Why didn't I see this coming? Suicide? Could it be I had no idea that Payton was suicidal?

Distance separates no one in today's world of instant communication. Sure, Payton and I talked. Phone, emails, texts, even webcam chats, but over the years I admit the contact became less frequent. We sold out to careers and endless promising futures.

Yeah, right. Futures. Mine was just as secure as any futures market. Nothing but speculations and hedging bets. Who would start up a glossy magazine when they were folding like origami and sinking like forgotten treasure chests in reckless seas? My future and my past seemed to die and I couldn't let go of the bullet. Perhaps that's why I still held on to my own box of the dead—the first thing I had packed to make the move from Chicago to Los Angeles.

Tucked inside the box, I'd wedged the envelope in between a copy of *The Prophet* and a box of tattered and fading family photographs. The gold ribbon on my own wedding invitation stuck out, curling around the top of the box like golden angel hair growing out of a hastily covered grave. The very good and the very bad. My own personal dichotomy of life.

I grew aware of the stale air in the church and took a deep breath. Almost historic and in need of restoration, I thought. Aging wood bled of life from the rays of sunlight streaming in from the clerestory windows, I watched dust particles sway and settle in the unseen movement of space.

Remorse and regret overwhelmed any grief. An old familiar guilt consumed me. Payton Doukas died because I loved her too much. The Lauren Visconti Curse. But there was a different feeling this time. A certain angst that went beyond the shock of an unexpected death.

They found Payton at her home and slumped over her computer soon after she hadn't shown up for work. Her method of choice, the .357 Magnum, had fallen to the tile floor. The pooled blood had been tracked through every room of Payton's house by the tiny paw prints of her cat, Teddy.

I wasn't the last person to see Payton alive, but I was the last one she had emailed. She was my best friend, and yet her typed words made no sense to me.

Saguaro National Forest. CAC. 3 Skeletons. Import

Chapter Three
Case Closed

DEATH IS ABRUPT. ALWAYS. It is impossible to digest. Even though it may lie in propinquity to your heart because of some terminal illness—a death expected, even then after any attempt to prepare for it—there is still no reconciliation of lost time. It is always stolen from us.

As for the unexpected, is it worse?

Two days after Payton's funeral my phone rang again. The caller had identified himself as a detective. I was stupefied.

"Is this Lauren Visconti?" he asked.

"Yes."

"I'm from the Pima County Sheriff's Department."

"Pima County?" I asked.

"Southern Arizona," he said. "Tucson."

My palms grew moist. "This is about Payton?"

The detective told me he was just wrapping things up. He wanted to know what Payton's final email to me might mean. I told him I had no idea and asked him why.

"Just routine when someone so young dies. We never found a suicide note. Would you know anything about that?"

I had never thought about *that*.

"Nothing to worry about, I'm sure," he continued. "It happens more often than you think. Some people get so wrapped up in their final intent they actually forget.

8

Sometimes they just have nothing left to say. It's when we get a case of a female with no suicide note, and—," he cleared his throat, "—well, her means of death."

"You mean a gun?"

"Yes, ma'am. Firearms aren't usually used in a female suicide. There's no need for alarm. We did the background work and everything is as it appears."

"You mean the suicide?"

"Ms. Doukas had no enemies and not too many friends, either. She worked for some national lecturer. She worked out of the elderly man's home with his wife of almost fifty years. Not exactly any love triangles going on. Doesn't seem she dated much. Besides a nine-to-five job in a quiet home she lived almost like a recluse. Does this seem about right to you?"

Sadly, it did.

"And there was no evidence of a forced entry to her home. We want things nice and tidy before we close the case."

I didn't know there was a case. And now it looked like it was closed.

Why didn't Payton sign the email to me? She always did. A joke of the day, usually. And then her trademark way of signing off. BFF, I love you. Payton.

It was a bad case of nerves, I told myself. The rash extended down my inner arms and the back of my legs. What did I expect, for crisakes? I had just returned from a funeral.

HARLAN COAL WAS ANYTHING but satisfied. He was so close. He could smell it. He could reach out for it. He could grind his molars on it and taste the juice, but the meat and cartilage remained just outside of his clenched jaw.

Coal studied his image in the mirror while adjusting his Brioni tie, appreciating the fact his looks opened doors for him. He was those three little words. Tall. Dark. Handsome. At six-foot three he towered over most people. His frame was slim but athletic. He used his physique to his full advantage, not unlike most Hollywood types on the big screen or not. He had perfect white teeth. Coal's imposing smoky eyes hosted deep crevices at each side making it appear as if he had a friendly wink and a perpetual smile. His hands were gentle, but with a firm handshake he'd practiced over and over again before he was even twelve years old. That was after his mother's boyfriend *du jour* told him he had the grip of a limp pussy.

Beyond his good looks, Harlan Coal knew his mind would keep those doors open just as long as he didn't make any more mistakes. He'd earned his way. A Rhodes Scholar, he was so much more. Coal had a rigid plan that would launch him into fame and fortune. He was well on his way to becoming the leader of a revolutionary frontier in psychotherapies.

He thought himself to be a patient man who simply used his resources to his advantage. Resilience was his next of kin. When things didn't work out in New York he was quick to relocate to Tucson. The incident there wasn't really his fault. Perhaps he let his desires put him in harm's way when it came to getting caught. He would not let that happen again.

Coal was smart enough to pick-up and move, again, to Los Angeles where the pulse of the city was hard and fast and no one ever really knew what was beating.

Chapter Four
The Welcome Mat

PHOTOGRAPHER SUKIE FIELDS was getting up there in age. I was lucky she didn't retire. Instead, she gifted me with her skills and exuberance behind them. As *CoverBoy's* new head photographer, Sukie sat with me at the O'Hare gate awaiting departure to Los Angeles. We finally boarded the last flight of the day—one that should have never left Chicago. Despite a late hour snowstorm gathering strength across the Rockies, the plane landed in Denver to wait out an even more dangerous rainstorm that had LAX shut down. I white-knuckled through both legs of the trip.

Sukie slept through most of it. She'd just returned home from Antigua, her last assignment for *Earthly Wheres*, my first magazine I was turning over to good hands. While I had been planning the move for months, Sukie's schedule gave her about four days to pack in between travels. I admired the gentle smile she wore while sleeping. Sukie welcomed the change.

"I'm too old for the travel business," she told me. When I worried she might retire, she quickly added that she became bored easily. That's exactly what she was when photographing more landscapes, villages, and exotic dishes of glow-in-the-dark scorpion soup and rattlesnake pasta. What she wanted was a challenge. The opportunity to jump into portrait photography, she said, would

11

complete her life's mission. I promised her carte blanche to create and produce, including choosing her own models.

Also making the journey was Geoff Hayes, our IT guy. I heard plenty of whispers after I made that announcement to our team at *Earthly Wheres*.

"I don't get it," someone at my Chicago-based *Earthly Wheres* offices said. "Geoff's a good guy but why would Lauren take on the expense of moving him?"

"Something's up," another had answered. "Techies are a dime a dozen in California."

My former staff was unaware I assigned my IT guy the role of top model before I even got his consent. Correctly pronounced with two syllables and lovingly coined Queen Geoff, he was everything fabulous about the letter G. Geek. Guru. Genius. Gentleman. Gorgeous. Everything G was Geoff except going for any G-spot. G was also for gay. Geoff wore gay pride the way a Tiffany lamp wears its fine stained glass. It was a damned shame, though. Geoff was a captivating African-American male specimen. Women constantly tried to be the lucky girl to change his sexual orientation, if only for a night.

God, did he have fun playing it straight. He held my hand throughout much of our long flight, well aware he had captured the heart of every female flight attendant. Queen Geoff confided in me, as he always did whether I liked it or not, that he could almost feel himself growing hard. Not for the women pining for him, of course, but for the infusion of misplaced attention he received while harmlessly playing the game. My new magazine would launch with him gracing the cover and he'd devour the spotlight. Los Angeles would suit him well.

Our plane landed in turbulence, two and a half hours late. As we entered the terminal I said my goodbyes to both Sukie and Geoff.

"Not nice of you to leave us at the airport, sweetie." Geoff looked at me with mock despair.

"I hardly call a limo and reservations at a five-star hotel grounds for grievance," I answered.

"Who is this guy picking you up, anyway?" he quizzed.

"I've already told you. His name is Brock Townsend. I've known him since I was a kid. Now he's a famous sports star."

"There you go again, attacking my lack of macho sports trivia knowledge," Geoff whined. "I just worry about you, Laurs."

"Seems to me you're the one that told me I needed to loosen up and find some sexy thing. You said something about me finding rock candy, if I remember correctly."

Sukie trailed behind saying nothing, which is not atypical for her. We made our way to the baggage claim, where the limo driver I'd hired would be holding up a placard with her name on it. It was clear she wanted nothing more than the sight of the limousine and the key to her suite, and I didn't blame her one bit.

Spotting Brock two carousels over, I pecked both Geoff and Sukie on the cheek, promising to meet them for breakfast at their hotel first thing in the morning.

Brock's big eyes fixed on me and he started to run. In seconds I found myself wrapped in my old friend's arms.

Brock Townsend relished life as a baseball legend. The New York Yankees reluctantly traded the pitcher to the Dodgers for a reported twenty-something-million dollar contract, not including the signing bonus, deferred payments, and incentive clauses. Brock wasn't indifferent to the money. He respected it. He welcomed his achievements but not so much the notoriety that accompanied it. That was probably why he dressed as he did. I could get the trench coat and the wide-brimmed hat, given the rain, but sunglasses? At midnight?

13

"I'm sorry you had to wait for my flight," I whispered, still engulfed in his hug. "I could have caught a— "

"I wouldn't miss the opportunity to welcome you to your new home, sweetie. Besides, the sight of you is worth any wait."

I felt myself blush. Not a Visconti thing to do.

Brock grabbed my luggage, all but my smallest bag, and led the way to the parking lot.

"Son of a bitch!" he yelled.

Three young thugs were hovering over his car. Two peered into the darkened windows while another stood guard. Brock dropped my bags at my feet, giving full chase to them. I stood in horror, thinking only about .357 Magnums.

Chapter Five
Ecstasy

THE SIGHT OF THE MUSCULAR six-foot-plus pitcher charging after them sent all three boys racing off in the opposite direction only after one final attempt to detach the Jaguar's vintage hood ornament. The screeching car alarm blared throughout the parking level, although in Los Angeles no one seemed to take notice.

As I struggled to schlep luggage toward the car, Brock sprinted back to help me.

"So, is this the infamous Los Angeles Welcome Wagon?" I asked.

Brock was fumbling through his jeans pockets for the key remote to silence the alarm. "Are you telling me they don't have car thieves in Chicago?"

I was the first to notice the three nylon gym bags the would-be car thieves must have left by the passenger side of the car. "What the hell is all this?" My voice quaked.

"Well, I'll be. Guess those boys really were the Welcome Wagon," Brock said, tossing the gym bags into the trunk on top of my luggage. "Little bastards. I swear, if they had a dad around to teach them baseball they'd never hit the streets like vermin. They'd be out at a ballpark."

"Brock, should you take those bags? Don't you think we should call the police?"

Brock only laughed. "If there's something in the bags that can identify them as thieves, maybe then. But they didn't exactly steal anything, did they?"

"In other words, I guess you don't think it's an airport bomb. And we're the ones stealing."

"Let's get you to your hotel," Brock said.

"You're right," I acquiesced. "No harm done. And yes, they do have car thieves in Chicago."

THE JAG ROLLED DOWN Sunset Boulevard and glided to a smooth stop in front of the hotel. Brock instructed the bellhop to deliver the luggage to my bungalow, escorting me into the lobby lounge after I picked up my room key.

Spotting the waiter approaching our table, Brock asked, "What will it be, sweet Lauren? Chardonnay, or maybe some Dom?"

"I'll have a *Tanqueray*. Number Ten. Dry. Two olives."

Brock scowled at me in disbelief.

"Oh, Brock. Don't look at me that way. Payton went and killed herself. I've just spent six hours on a damn airplane—something I swore I'd never do again, and traveled half way across the country no less in nothing but rain, hail, sleet, and snow."

The hysteria in my voice turned to a whine. "Now I'm in a strange city and I'm presumptuous enough to think I'm going to take it by a storm with a new publishing venture while the entire magazine industry is on its ass."

Brock looked up at the waiter who was patiently waiting for my outburst to clear. "Better bring me one, too," Brock said.

We slugged down the first martinis and tried to order one more round while being told we'd barely made the last call with our first drinks. It was late. I should have been exhausted, but neither of us wanted to say goodnight. It seemed innocent enough when Brock requested a bottle of champagne be sent over to my bungalow. All night room service, after all.

YOU KNOW, BROCK," I'm sure I slurred slightly as I eased out of my dress and fell back onto the four-poster bed, "I don't think friends are supposed to fuck one another. And I'm still grieving the loss of Payton, and I'm in the middle of a major move. I'm trying to make a new start and I'm just too—"

"That's the best thing about friends with benefits. Only with you it's more like rapture. Besides, my friend needs a jumpstart into her new world."

"And by jumpstart you mean jumping my bones?"

Despite my feeble verbal protests, Brock Townsend rightfully understood he was the one being seduced. I lay naked as he uncorked the champagne. I reached for the bottle to pour, skillfully filling the flutes with one hand while working open the metal buttons of his 501 jeans with the other. Multi-tasking.

Three years had passed since the two of us had been together in bed. Or in the back-seat of a limo. Or on the bleachers in the deserted baseball stadium. I felt the old familiar feeling. I knew I was wet with desire long before my mouth was wet with the vintage champagne.

His soft denim jeans fell to the floor and Brock lifted off his cashmere sweater to reveal rippling rows of muscular abs. I wanted him inside of me and I'd learned a long time ago how to get exactly what I wanted, especially when it came to Brock Townsend.

I became a tease in need. I bit his nipples and sucked at his neck. I pulled at him and guided his movements, slowing him down, or pushing him faster and faster, depending on my pleasure. I flung myself on top of him

17

and rode him. My words were nasty and my breasts swayed wildly above his body, rocking and taking what I needed. I collapsed upon his chest and moaned in satisfaction.

"We never did it, you know," I whispered.

"Yes, Lauren. We did it. We're doing it. And we've done it before."

"Off the record. I have to protect my reputation. Keep my name off your list of conquests."

He pulled away from me, faking a frown. We started bantering; we always seemed to get along best when teasing each other. My cell interrupted what might have been left of any lucid conversation after all the booze. An unidentified caller.

"Lauren Visconti?"

"Yes. Who's calling?"

"Sorry I missed you. It wasn't a suicide. Remember Mike? You're messing with trouble, Missy."

"Trouble? Missed me where?"

It was too late. The caller hung up. I turned to Brock. He was sound asleep.

Chapter Six
The Dream

MY WEDDING DRESS IS understated elegance. Low-cut in the back and with braided silk pulled tight across my waist, the gown cascades to the floor in layers of scalloped edging. The chiffon sways and billows with every step I take.

I can't make out who is walking me down the aisle. My father is dead. It can't be him. Who is it?

The music is too loud. The first notes don't end as yet others begin. Fierce sounds of chanting begin to clash with an incendiary noise. It was the sound of warriors igniting blood.

The man that leads me by my arm stops in the middle of the aisle. He's staring at my gown with pity drawn across his eyes. The exquisite fabric is fraying, metastasizing into paper. My wedding dress is made of paper!

Gusts of wind roar down the center of the church. The paper scallops of my gown ripple and begin to tear, shredding into sheets. The tang of smoke fills my lungs. The funneled wind fuels the flames. My escort drops my arm and screams as he falls away from me, engulfed in a bonfire of human flesh, bones, and hair. The screams of my loved ones lining the pews overpower any other sounds except for the spitting and crackling of bodies. And the ear-piercing clash of musical notes.

I glance down at the remains of my dress. I am all but naked. Why am I not burning? Why am I not melting in pain with the others? Dear God, take me! While everyone else falls into clumps of pugilistic attitude. I remain standing.

I'm not even singed. I am left, alone.

Chapter Seven

The Morning After

MORNING LIGHT FLOODED the quaint bungalow. Brock stirred from under the sheets, arching his back to glance up at the clock.

I'd already showered and dressed in my standard office couture, ready to go.

"You're making me feel cheap, my dear," Brock said.

"What are you talking about?"

"You aren't even going to let me finish what I started last night? How about you at least buy me breakfast?"

"Sorry. I have a working breakfast."

Brock sat up, looking pale and tired. I could see the fast pace of his pulse ticking on the side of his temples. "You know, Laurs, I'm still grieving, too. I feel like shit that I didn't make it to Payton's funeral. She was my friend, too. That girl had no reason to die."

I elected not to tell him about the phone call. Or my dream. A disturbing thought crossed my mind. I was sure Brock had slept with my friend, Sterling Falls. Had he done Payton, too? "Look, Brock, I just have a lot of things on my mind."

Brock went to the bathroom. Any jealousy I did or did not feel ended when I looked through the window and across the hotel grounds. Two men stood near the side of

21

another bungalow. One was on a cell phone. The other had a huge camera zoom lens aimed right at me. They fled when they realized I'd spotted them. I think.

Or maybe I was crazy. Maybe I only imagined they fled. Or that they were there at all.

Chapter Eight
Roots

AN IMPULSE SEIZED ME on my way to breakfast. I phoned the detective in Tucson. I told him about the call. I reminded him of Payton's missing brother.

"Don't you understand?" I urged him. "The caller said it wasn't a suicide. I believe him."

"Ms. Visconti, you don't even know who *him* is. The case is closed. It was a suicide, and from what you've just told me about her missing brother she must have never gotten over it. The suicide serves to confirm it.

"With all due respect, these things happen all the time. People with nothing better to do read something in the paper and get off on stirring things up. And you have quite a name out there that makes you a special target for weirdos."

"It's not like I'm a celebrity."

"No. But you have a reputation. People know your name. If you need further assistance, I suggest you contact your local police department."

LOOKING OVER MY SHOULDER all the way, I stormed toward the restaurant for breakfast, still wary about any intrusive intent behind the men and their camera. It certainly wasn't the paparazzi. unless they mistook me for some Hollywood starlet. I was already used to the buzzing of low-flying helicopters trying to cop

23

a million dollar photo of anybody who is somebody around the hotel grounds, but that wouldn't be me. *Maybe they were only photographing the stunning buildings and landscaping. I just happened to be square in the middle of their photo shoot.*

The phone call was another story. The caller *knew* my name. Was it a warning or a threat he delivered? Why?

By the time I entered the café, Sukie and Geoff were already gobbling down French toast and asking for coffee refills. Sukie's beautiful Asian face, sprinkled with powdered sugar from the brioche, glistened in the dappled morning sunlight.

"You guys certainly adapt well to foreign land," I joked as I took a seat in the booth.

"It's all about learning their customs," Geoff said.

We each had a full day ahead. Sterling's real estate friend had already sold me a beach house. I was waiting for Carly to work her design magic on it before moving in. I liked the agent, Gabriella Criscione. She may have been a little over-the-top, but she knew Los Angeles and Malibu real estate and she knew how to kiss ass. It worked for me. Gabri, as friends called her, had now lined up commercial properties for me to tour. Out of her list of seven, I had zeroed in on four. The pressure for me to find space and find it fast could have overwhelmed me, if not for Gabri. Key staff planned on working from hotel rooms and street-side bistros until I could find us corporate offices. Cash is king, so said my father. If a property had a clear title I could close on it quickly.

"Earth to Lauren," Sukie said. "That's not just stress drawing your face up into a knot."

Sure, I had angst about buying an office building. But Sukie made me stop and ask myself why my stomach felt like I'd swallowed a live Long-jaw Mud Snapper.

"Geoff, let me ask you something," I said. "You know all the email texting lingo stuff, don't you?

"What do you mean?"

"The shorthand. Like LOL and JK?"

"It's not exactly technical information, but yes, I guess I do."

I had memorized Payton's email.

Saguaro National Forest. CAC. 3 Skeletons. Import

"What does CAC mean?"

Geoff shot a glance at Sukie and they both shrugged. "I haven't seen that one," she said.

"Let's see. There's CAS. Crack a smile. CAAC is cool as a cucumber," Geoff said.

I grimaced. No good.

"It's not texting, but what about the Paris Bourse? The CAC-40," Sukie suggested.

The Paris market index? That didn't make sense, either. Not that I knew. Payton resented anything French, probably only because she thought the French resented anything American.

"Does 3 Skeletons mean anything?"

"Not in the land of the living texting. Not that I know. Why?"

"Someone sent me an email I don't understand."

"Ever think of calling them up and just asking them?" Sukie grinned.

I turned to her. Her voice came off as sarcastic, but I quickly realized she didn't know *them* was dead. "What would a seven—maybe nine-inch lens do for a digital camera?"

"Hard to say, but it's a big boy's tool. You might as well open up a planetarium."

Geoff laughed, "Oh, dear God, don't use that on me when I have a zit coming on."

"What's with all these questions?" Sukie asked.

I shuffled papers around in front of me, opting to change the conversation rather than think about the camera lens pointed my way. "Sukie, how many interviews do you have lined up?"

She raised her almond eyes, framed with thin brows beginning to gray. Her eyes served as a constant reminder of what Sukie was. A private woman. Gifted behind the camera, I knew little else about the mysterious photographer. The only thing I really understood was that she was even keeled and dependable. Since most artists of her caliber were temperamental, eccentric, and erratic in their performance, at best, I counted myself lucky.

Sukie said, "I've lined up a baker's dozen, all with ample studio time to shoot them once you tell me where. They're seasoned print models and I have about fifty more if I need them. This town's flooded with hunk-of-the-month wannabes."

"Hey, Laurs," Geoff interjected. "Just how much longer are we supposed to keep our new project a secret? You know I don't do good secret."

"Not much longer, Queen. I'm organizing a press party gala for our grand opening, assuming we have a place to cut the ribbon. With a little luck, when we do come out of our closet the whole country will know our secret overnight."

Geoff smiled.

I was still thinking about the email I had received from Payton. The police told me that typing the email and sending it to me was the last thing Payton did on this earth. Before blowing her brains out.

What did that last word mean? Import? Import what? And why didn't she sign it like she usually did? And why was it so cryptic?

I should have mentioned it to the detective again.

Payton always signed her emails to me. Always. It was

a programmed signature.

Chapter Nine
Riches, Roses, & Robberies

GABRIELLA CRISCIONE KNEW she was one extraordinary real estate agent. She did it all. Residential, commercial, land and sand. As long as they were million dollar deals, she was your woman.

Well connected and a pro at client interviews over orgasmic pasta lunches, it didn't take her long to figure out Lauren Visconti wore deep pockets. She only had to show the girl four homes on the beach, knowing exactly what she was doing when she saved the best, and by far the most expensive one, for last.

Four must have been her lucky number, because that's exactly how many showings it took to sell Lauren Visconti her new corporate offices. Gabri probably didn't fool the girl when she threw in some real dog properties to solidify the buying decision. Showing Lauren Visconti a couple not too perfect alternatives only proved that she needed to spend a couple million more than she had planned on in order to get what she needed. Gabri considered herself Master Enabler in all of it.

Gabri worked hard. And smart. Maybe she was a little pushy, but she liked it that way. And she always remembered her manners. She had to think of some way to express gratitude to Sterling Falls for referring the Visconti girl to her.

I DON'T THINK IT was buyer's remorse eating at me, even though my purchase offer on the twelve-story building was signed and off to the seller without much blinking on my part. *CoverBoy* had a home. That should have left me thrilled.

Maybe the seclusion of the hotel bungalow was too quiet after the taxing day. I looked around at its living room and bedroom. I shouldn't have been surprised that all traces of Brock were gone. Did I expect to find him in the reading chair or out on the patio? Was he supposed to stay in bed all day?

No red roses. No yellow roses. No yellow sticky note, for that matter. I took in a deep breath, well aware that I was trying to pick up the scent of his musky aftershave. Fresh bed linens and the lemony fresh smell that follows the maids, as thick as contrails of a jet, had removed any lingering waft of the salty sultry man-smell from the night before.

I functioned on autopilot, finding myself exhausted and exhilarated at the same time. I opened the bedroom entertainment armoire, then peered through the wood blinds to make sure no cameras were aimed my way, then laughed at myself for the paranoia. I lunged onto the empty bed with the TV remote in hand. After mindlessly surfing the channels for a few minutes. I settled on the local evening news.

A bleached-blond bimbo advertised her new line of jewelry. Instantly I felt a pang of guilt. Damn. She reminded me of Sterling. I needed to call her. I promised her I would as soon as I arrived into town. I can't explain my friendship with Sterling, except that everything outrageously over-glitzed about her seemed to be matched by the songs of heaven's laughter.

When I reached for the phone to call her I spied the three athletic bags the would-be car thieves left behind.

29

The bellhop must have brought them in by mistake. They sat beneath the luggage bench with my half-opened cases on top.

Chapter Ten
Stolen Goods

CURIOSITY KILLS THE CAT. I jumped off the bed, grabbed the bags, and zipped open the first one, heavy but also almost empty. Auto parts? The only pieces I could positively identify were a small CD/DVD car component, a GPS, and a couple sets of car keys. One had the familiar Jaguar emblem and another one, Porsche. I presume the thieves had a productive night. And excellent taste.

Unzipping the second bag, I pulled out two brand new shoeboxes. Running shoes. If I remembered the ads in the newspaper, they ran about three hundred dollars a pair. No receipts, of course.

Crumpled newspaper filled the inside of the third bag. Reaching deep inside, I pulled out three wallets. The little bandits weren't just in the auto business.

It appeared they hadn't yet rummaged through the wallets. Cash, credit cards, and drivers' licenses all seemed to be intact.

"Just great," I mumbled aloud to myself. "I've been here less than 48 hours and I've witnessed an attempted car heist, engaged in mindless sex, and now I have three stolen wallets in my possession."

Brock was right. The police wouldn't consider it a high priority. I'd mail the wallets to the addresses listed on the licenses in the morning. I tossed the shoes back in the bag and zipped it closed, wishing I could do the same with Brock Townsend.

31

The stresses of the day gnawed at me, and sometime after the early evening news I drifted into a deep sleep. The phone stirred me to consciousness. I couldn't believe the time. The sunset was casting shadows of orange on the wall; its light show competed with the muted news broadcast still running on the television.

Leave Brock horny, I thought. He'll come running back for more, every time.

"Hey there," I answered.

"Hey there to you. Forget about me?" The sharp soprano voice drilled my ears.

"I'm sorry. Who's calling?" I mumbled.

"Jeez, Lauren. It's Sterling. As in Sterling Falls. Supposed to be a dear friend of yours. At least any time you want to borrow some ten-carat bauble."

"Sterling. I meant to call. I just got into town and I've been slammed."

"That's not what Brock said. He told me you came in yesterday."

"Brock told you that?"

"We went to the theater tonight, decided we were hungry, and grabbed a bite to eat over at Crustacean. Your name came up over dinner."

I felt like a coiled serpent, circling and circling with no one near enough to strike with my venom. Crying, screaming, kicking—all viable options. Brock goes to bed with my friend the very next night after having sex with me? Okay. She didn't say they went home together. But it's Brock. And Sterling. I don't think they wrapped up the night chatting over a game of Mahjong.

"It's late," I stammered. "I should get some sleep."

"Man, you sound cranky. Get your beauty sleep."

"Yeah. I'm tired. Real tired. I'll call you in a couple days after I get settled."

Sleep fought me all the way, refusing to offer sanctuary. When finally I drifted off, the Technicolor nightmare seized control of my night's slumber, again. The church was the same. My gown turning to paper, and the loud music, and the fire, and the man walking me down the aisle—they were all the same. But this time, Payton stood in the corner, waving at me. And she and I were the only two not succumbing to the flames and smoke. Payton was very much alive. Resilient to death's fury.

The sweat soaked my pillowcase. Tears, as well. I sat up and took a sip of water from the nightstand. I don't know what was worse. The nightmare or the remnants of my true history creeping back into my mind.

There had been no wedding for me. On the eve of the marriage, a knock on my hotel door interrupted the celebration with my bridesmaids. The uniformed officers informed me that a freak storm had taken down the Visconti family jet. On board: the pilot, copilot, my beloved father, my fiancé, plus a couple of his groomsmen. No one survived impact.

From a second room in the suite, Sterling had heard my wails and rushed in beside me wearing nothing but a green thong and a T-shirt. A damn Dodgers T-shirt.

Memories. Nightmares. Reality. I understand sadness. I even understand fear. But jealousy is an odd emotion, isn't it? I closed my eyes and shut out any last bit of feeling I might have left residing in my heart.

Chapter Eleven
Easy Money

GABRIELLA HUNG UP the phone after ordering Sterling Falls a set of August Horn bed linens. A lavish gift for the lavish Visconti referral. She knew the gesture reflected the slight insider's joke that Gabri lived vicariously through Sterling's stories of sexual indiscretions.

Carly Posh bolted past Gabri's receptionist and burst into the private office. Gabri didn't know Carly very well. She did remember the property she had sold her in Bel Air, rumored to be haunted. Haunted house legends meant big sales in L.A. and Gabri knew she could sell it again with a couple of fast phone calls. Oh yes, Gabri remembered, the woman had an interior design business, Posh Possessions. That was her name, she thought. Etiquette equals sales.

"Ms. Posh, what brings you by?" Gabri asked, ignoring the brazen interruption in hopes it would pay off. She was not to be disappointed.

"I've found a house I want to buy. I need you to handle the paperwork for me," Carly said.

Gabri felt her toes tingle. This little piggy wasn't having roast beef. It squirmed with delight for a juicy and rare filet mignon. Still, she was surprised. She'd attended a Fourth of July party at Carly's home that summer. The designer had just furnished it with custom-made pieces and antiques from all over the world.

34

"I can sell your home, given some time and working my connections," Gabri fudged, not wanting her job to sound too easy. "When do you want to close on the new house?"

"We can close next week. It doesn't really matter. And I'm keeping the Bel Air house."

"Oh, I see. Buying a second home? Maybe Big Bear?"

"Nothing like that. I've found a place near the Hollywood Hills."

"But you're staying in Bel Air?"

"Using it as more of a rental. It's taken care of."

Gabri gasped, but before she could say anything Carly said, "I think you'll find all the information you need here." She tossed a thick manila folder onto Gabri's mahogany desk. "I just need you to look the title work over. Stuff like that."

"Who's the listing agent?"

"It's between me and the seller. I just thought it prudent of me to involve you. Right? I'll pay you, of course."

And Gabri agreed. For a fee. She reached her chubby hand over her desk and shook hands with Carly.

I'm going to owe Sterling Falls more than bed linens, Gabri thought, if her rich friends keep buying all this real estate.

Gabri decided it was time to host one of her legendary dinner parties for Sterling and her circle of affluent friends. She penciled in some names on a legal pad.

The list amused her. Sterling proved to be something of a *Jekyll and Hyde*. A daddy's girl, for sure, and daddy thought she was a virgin.

"In truth, angelic Sterling is a virgin, nine hundred times removed," Gabri said aloud to herself while wondering who might be her newest escort.

35

Lauren Visconti had big bucks. More than she figured her for. Old money, Gabri thought.

Then there was Carly Posh to add to the guest list. Odd name. Choppy sounding. But who cares? Sterling Falls' referrals, and Gabri's ability to keep them loyal were making Gabriella Criscione a very rich woman.

Chapter Twelve
It's Just a Glass of Wine

TWO WEEKS PASSED. It was a stroke of luck that the fifth floor of the office building I bought sat empty. The executive offices of *CoverBoy* were available for me to lease until the close of escrow.

Likewise, Sukie Fields managed to move her photography studio and lab into the basement. The existing tenants didn't seem to mind at all as they watched the endless stream of gorgeous male models riding the elevators up and down between our two departments.

Sukie entered into contracts with seven young male models. My own computer geek, Geoff Hayes, would make the debut cover, but only after setting up our online presence. "Geek above gorgeous," I told him.

I stepped inside Sukie's photo lab to see her lift off the last of the 8x10 glossies.

"Damn, these are good," I said as I helped her hang the drippy papers. They were the usual shoots. Hunks in jeans, studs in tuxedos, and lots of almost nudes. Sukie had a way with the camera. Every ab glistened, every curve on the thighs fell rich with texture. And then there were the eyes. In truth, Sukie captured far more depth to the eyes than the models exhibited in real life.

"By the way," Sukie said, "I grabbed the mail at the PO Box and accidentally opened something personal of yours." She grinned. "You'll like it."

We both knew nothing was too personal in my life that Sukie couldn't see it. I succumbed to my own curiosity when I saw the feeble, shaky looking handwriting on the small pale blue envelope. I could barely make out the words in the short note.

Thank you for returning my wallet. I was beaten up pretty bad by those boys.

Broke my hip. The receipt ain't mine.

Don't want anything that don't belong to me. The money is your reward.

I looked back inside the envelope and pulled out a receipt and the cash. The receipt was actually a claim check from the Tom Bradley International Bag Service at LAX. I slipped the ticket into my purse, along with all the cash. My reward was three worn one-dollar bills.

I scoured the junk mail. Opened up a few bills. How did they find me so quickly? Another envelope caught my eyes. White. Typed with my old address and forwarded. No return address.

One piece of paper. Three little words. Sometimes that's all it takes. The typed message read:

It wasn't suicide.

A LATE LUNCH AT Catrozzi's was already a single hedonistic ritual that engulfed my soul. I sat there, unaccompanied, after ordering the chef's daily special.

The Chardonnay smelled of a buttery liquid with a good hint of oak, just the way I liked it. The wine clung to the crystal glass, dribbling down the sides with the thickened leggy brush strokes of a Van Gogh. It reminded me of Pasquale's, in Chicago, where my family took me for my twenty-first birthday. We had my graduation party in a back banquet room. We held a small wake for my mother in that same room. I flashed my new engagement ring to my father at the bar.

Catrozzi's head waiter brought me the delicate abalone and disappeared before I could thank him. Or was the movement even him? I had the distinct feeling someone was watching me. I'd taken my table. A big table with six chairs. Maybe a large party was waiting for it as I sat there alone? Maybe someone was casting pitiful looks my way? Poor little-rich-girl looks.

I glanced around. The narrow room bustled with power business lunches, a few young mothers enjoying an hour or so away from dirty diapers and drools, and flirtatious conversations. Another loner like me, a man of about sixty-five—maybe seventy, sat sipping an iced tea and reading a newspaper.

The waiter patiently allowed me my slow degustation, then reappeared with a second glass of wine.

"From the gentleman over there," he nodded in the direction of the old man. "It's from another vineyard, but he insisted you would like it."

The chair sat empty with the newspaper catching a wimpy occasional draft from the air-conditioning.

The waiter followed my gaze. "Strange. He was just there. Let me tell you, he chose a special wine for you. An excellent Chardonnay from a small winery. We mostly just serve the California wines here."

The small talk was a nice diversion. "Is it French?" The shimmering golden fluid had a strong bouquet of buttery oak.

"You'd never guess. It comes from Southern Arizona."

I had another plane to catch. I would be returning to Tucson. Carly and Sterling were coming with me.

Chapter Thirteen
An Empty Memory

FRIDAY MORNING I GRABBED my bags to pack for the short weekend trip to Tucson. The final chore was to switch out purses from a tiny black leather Chanel to a large Hobo. Exchanging contents, the airport claim check fell out from the smaller purse.

Tom Bradley Terminal. The receipt the old man with the stolen wallet had mistakenly returned to me.

I would check it out on my return.

I didn't give Carly or Sterling a choice. Neither of them held down jobs where they couldn't take a quick weekend excursion to Tucson.

Sterling had called it a *'Big Chill'* thing, sans any sexy male companions and long after any funeral. I had a different itinerary in mind. We wouldn't be lounging around the pool immersing ourselves in idle chat about the good old days.

Carly loved a bargain. She was in charge of lodging. We took potluck in finding a good hotel in Tucson, in late August, and she managed to snag a five-star suite at half the price of their winter rates.

While Carly wore a grin gained from her success at haggling over the cost of the room, it quickly faded when she, Sterling, and I folded our exhausted bodies against the silky Stroheim and Romann fabric of the suite's living room loveseats.

"It doesn't feel right, does it?" Carly asked.

"Christ," Sterling said, "maybe because last time we were here it was to say goodbye to Payton."

"No, it's not that," Carly said. She was fondling a bottle of cold water, pursing her lips to it without sipping, and then rolling it against her forehead. "You don't think she did it, do you, Lauren?"

"Payton did a lot of dumb-ass things, but not this. She wouldn't take her own life."

Sterling looked up from the room service menu. "Yeah. The cat, Teddy. She wouldn't leave her cat. Not ever."

THE NEXT DAY CARLY and I returned from a continental breakfast and jarred Sterling awake. As she finished applying makeup with the use of the car visor mirror, we approached the Pima County Sheriff's Office at ten o'clock.

The detective greeted us with a quick glance at his watch. The prepared speech was succinct. "Our department did a thorough investigation, just like we do with any suicide. Any death of a young person requires an autopsy. The coroner confirmed our findings. I'm sorry. The case is closed."

"Did Payton have a will?" Carly asked.

He looked at her with an almost humorous sneer. "That's the family's business. Again, it's not unusual for a young person not to have a suicide note, or a will."

Sterling considered the facts that weren't sitting well with her. "But her cat. She had her cat groomed right before she died. Her mother found it with a fresh bow around her neck."

I could see the grimace erupting from the otherwise reposed face of the detective. He answered, "Ma'am, maybe she wanted to make sure the cat had a good home. Made it presentable, you know? It's nothing else, I assure you."

"But she didn't sign her email to me," I said.

"Ma'am. I get that it troubles you. But give me some credit. I know a thing or two about these things. Your friend was about to commit suicide. She wasn't thinking about email etiquette. You need to *get* that."

His voice and a second glance at his watch signaled the end to our brief meeting.

"THE ONLY THING I KNOW is that we need to get inside Payton's house," I said, as we made the turn on Speedway heading west of town.

"Indulge me. Tell me why, again?" Sterling hiked up her skirt and placed her bare feet on the dashboard above the passenger seat.

"I don't know why, but I called both her parents. Her dad never returned my calls, but her mom said someone would meet us with a key."

Carly crouched forward from the back-seat. "Someone?"

"A friend, I guess. You have to remember their son disappeared a couple of years ago. This must be too much for her, losing her last child. She said she walked through Payton's house once, right after they removed her body. She took the cat and a few framed photographs and said she doesn't plan on ever returning," Sterling said.

I slowed the car down, looking for the turn. Carly and Sterling sat in silence. A funereal aftermath seemed to consume the air in the rented SUV.

"Her mom told us to take anything that may be special to us. She said she didn't know what that may be but—"

"All very sad," Carly said. "I feel sick we don't know her mom better, after all these years."

I'd only been to Payton's house a few times, but I was still in awe as we entered Saguaro National Park, greeted by dense towering cacti standing like regal guards. My old idea of a forest populated by pine trees was challenged every time I saw the majesty of these armed and god-like living structures.

"This looks familiar," I said as we neared a pocket of homes that were somehow allowed to be built, years ago, in the middle of the national park.

The voice of the Garmin need not have announced that we had arrived at our destination. Payton's home was the most quaint and charming on the short dirt road. The rows of dead potted plants made it the saddest, too.

The driver's window of the car parked in the driveway seamlessly rolled down. The man asked us our names, then handed Carly the key and started to drive away. He stopped and backed the car up, jumped out and opened the back-seat door.

"I almost forgot," he shook his head. "Mrs. Doukas wanted you to have this. She's allergic."

The man handed me an animal carrier. Inside, Teddy sat huddled in the far corner.

"Just great," I said, as the man screeched all four wheels out of there, leaving behind a blanket of dust. I turned to Sterling.

"Don't look at me. I don't do animals except under the covers, and Carly is a dog person."

Carly unlocked the door and shuffled inside. I preferred to stand for a moment on the small flagstone patio. Taking it all in. Shoring up my spirit. I couldn't help but smile as I looked at the colorful Mexican Talavera pots that lined the entry, in spite of the small fact that all the plants and flowers and vines were scorched and dead.

When I stepped inside, Carly sat at the kitchen bar, her eyes swollen with wannabe tears she held on to with all her strength. She mumbled, "I don't know why we're here."

"I shouldn't have asked you to come along," I said.

"No, I'm glad. But why?" she urged me. "We have to believe the sheriff's department has already looked around."

"But they didn't know her like we do. Maybe we won't find anything, but I have to believe maybe we'll *feel* something here."

Carly cocked her head in disbelief. A last-minute lift of her chin told me of her willingness to help.

"Let's look around," I said, placing the animal carrier near the door. Maybe there's something they missed. It wasn't a big investigation, Carly. Cut-and-dried, for them. I think we need to look for signs. Maybe signs that can affirm she did commit suicide and at least we'll know why. Let's look for anything financial that might tell us she was in over her head. Look for stock market records or certificates. Maybe something from the Paris Bourse."

"Paris?" Sterling asked.

I explained the wild goose-chase to see if by chance Payton had certificates through the Parisian CAC-40.

"That girl barely got by financially. Can't imagine why she'd look to overseas market indexes."

"Just a thought, while we're here. Or maybe she was having an affair that went sour and we didn't know about it. I'll check the medicine cabinet. Maybe she was sick— really sick, and didn't want anyone to know."

Sterling was already riffling through Payton's jewelry. Payton's mother had clearly instructed us to take anything we wanted. It was Sterling's nature and her business, and I found nothing wrong with it.

"She still had a few good pieces," Sterling sighed, "in spite of her brother."

"He took her for a lot of money," Carly said.

"He borrowed a lot of money before he went missing," I said.

"But she still loved him. She loved everything about him. When he disappeared I thought we were going to lose Payton, then and there."

I walked into the study. Although scoured clean, I could see every drop of blood Payton might have lost. I smelled the distinct smell of blood—copper. I could almost hear the gunshot.

"Wait a minute. Her computer is gone," I said, disappointment and frustration lacing my throat."

"Oh. Her mom has that," Sterling called from the other room. "She thought maybe she could learn how to use it."

We scoured Payton's house for almost two hours. Nothing affirmed a suicide. Nothing screamed otherwise. Sterling made a list of the few items of jewelry with any value. She thought she could contact Payton's mother and offer to sell the pieces for her. The only object we walked away with, and yes, I took it, was a large inlaid mother-of-pearl box holding Payton's sadness. The box was stuffed with small objects and papers that evidenced Payton's relentless search to find her missing brother, Mike.

Oh, and the cat. Teddy was going home with me.

Chapter Fourteen
A Sticky Situation

THE ALARM ON MY CELL sounded at five. Sleeping in the double King suite, Sterling groaned in the bed next to me. I grabbed my phone to silence the shrill ringtone. An early start would be the only way we could make a Sonoran desert hike in August and survive.

"Let me get this straight, because it doesn't sound like the Lauren Visconti I've known since grade school," Sterling whined. "We're supposed to start hiking somewhere in all this desert and assume we can find something, but we don't have a clue where to start or what we're looking for?"

Payton's last email to anyone was to me, and the words still made no sense to me.

Saguaro National Forest. CAC Trail. 3 skeleton. Import

Carly scrutinized the trail map. "Look here," she said. "In her email to you Payton wrote *'CAC Trail'*. It might not be the same, but here's a trail named the Cactus Canyon Trail."

"It clearly wasn't a trail of paperwork from the Paris Bourse, so we have nothing. That's *something*. Let's go hiking!"

We'd picked up some cat food and made sure Teddy had plenty of water, then we hit the road.

We missed the trailhead three times. When finally we parked our rental car and laced up our boots, I had a single goal. If we were on to something, we were looking for the next part of Payton's email. *Three skeletons.*

"Do you actually think we're going to find three dead bodies up here?" Sterling moaned.

"Of course not. For one thing, it's been too long. Someone would have seen them. But maybe it's something like a skeleton. And maybe it's not human," I said.

"Still," Carly added, "I think we should look for lumps in the grounds."

"You mean like graves," Sterling whimpered.

"Hell, I don't know what I mean," Carly said. "But Lauren's right. Payton was smart. Damn smart. There are other definitions of the word skeleton."

"Yeah, right. Like what?" Sterling picked off cholla cacti that had already jumped onto her legs.

Carly stopped walking. "Supportive structures. Like frames. You know, bare bones means the essential parts are left. There might be some old out-buildings up here from early homesteaders."

Sterling resumed the hike, hollering back to us, "Now you're talking. I prefer to think we're not up here looking for cadavers."

We hiked up a section of loose rocks, all of us with our eyes on the ground in order to see unstable earth and rocks, icky desert critters, piercing stickers, and to prevent falling on any three mounds of human remains.

"Skeleton could me something very thin. Like, skeletal."

"Are you kidding me," Carly said. "There's a billion skinny looking cacti up here."

"So we look for a grouping of three," I said, trying to keep the faith. Trying to make sense of it all.

Carly did a quick, "Pffft," but lead the way. "Still, there's a billion *Three Musketeers* up here," she said.

Three and a half miles seemed manageable, but after the first mile the terrain grew steeper. Luckily, we prepared for the harsh climate with plenty of water.

We stuck to the trail, assuming Payton wouldn't have ventured off it. Having lived in the desert for so many years she knew about the dangers of reptiles and wild cats more than any of us dared imagine. I only mentioned watching out for rattlesnakes and Gila monsters once, when Sterling fell out from taking the lead.

"I didn't even know Payton liked to hike," Carly said.

Payton had never mentioned hiking to me, either.

Carly stopped to take a gulp of water and her vaporous eyes fixed on mine. "If we're even close to the *where*, just *what* are we looking for?"

"I don't know, but we all agree it must be important."

"Yeah. Maybe that's what she meant when she typed the word import. Nothing she's importing, but it's important," Carly said.

Sterling fiercely nodded her head in agreement, pulling out a clip to secure her long blond hair off her neck.

Every time we spotted an obvious cluster of three cacti or bushes, we hiked over to them for a closer inspection. We'd root around at the base of them, look across the horizon from where they stood in case something jumped out at us. Nothing jumped out at us but for the cholla cacti.

Carly cursed at the spines of the fuzzy cactus now piercing through her boot.

Using leather gloves we'd picked up at the hardware store, we took turns trying to reach inside some of the lower holes animals had carved into the giant saguaro. I quickly deduced no one would hide anything that way unless they didn't want it to be discovered for a hundred years, when maybe the cacti would finally topple over.

There was nothing. No outbuildings. No mounds. No aha moment. No epiphany. No catharsis to bring us hope. We left the national park grimy, sweaty, and emotionally stifled.

Exhausted, we headed back to the hotel.

"What do you make of the last word in Payton's email to you, Lauren?" Carly asked.

"Screw that. We don't even know what she meant by the three skeletons," Sterling bitched from the back seat.

I glanced in the rearview mirror at the glamorous Sterling, now reduced to sweat and stringy hair. "I think maybe she was writing the word important. Then again maybe imports, like we said. It just confirms to me that because we are trying to figure it out—because we know there is something to figure out, we all agree Payton didn't kill herself.

"Remember she always signed off on her emails with a big BFF. One click on her computer to include a signature. She ran out of time. And that wouldn't have happened if she was holding the gun to her own head."

Maybe we were wrong. Misguided friends unable to admit they weren't there for another in time of need. In time of life, or death.

On the way back toward Tucson Sterling cried out, "Stop!"

"What?" Carly asked as I already slowed the car.

"It's a tattoo parlor." Sterling reached both arms up toward the front seats and pressed them firmly on our shoulders. "Remember our plan with Payton?"

We did, and we stopped. An hour or so later, after enduring the pain of what felt like a knife attached to a jackhammer, all three of us walked back to our rental car with identical tattoos on our right ankles. The artist told us they were the Chinese symbol for friendship.

We had agreed, when there were four of us, that we would stain our skin in friendship under the needle of a tattoo artist. Without Payton, I suppose the entire idiotic act was of a permanent gesture. Like blood sisters. And for Payton.

We really had no idea if the symbol was authentic. It could mean walking slut, for all we knew.

With stained skin, we returned to L.A. Lala Land. With Teddy onboard.

Chapter Fifteen
Questionable Motives

THE MAN BEHIND THE counter at the Tom Bradley International Terminal at LAX looked at me, his face registered with surprise and maybe, suspicion. "This claim check's pretty old."

"Well, yes. My trip was extended. I forgot all about it."

He grumbled something and disappeared behind the doors. Moments later, which seemed like an eternity and long enough for me to feel like a thief and a fool, he returned with a long travel case.

"Golf isn't my game, but you'd think you would remember your clubs" he barked.

Golf wasn't my game, either.

CARLY RETURNED HOME to the mayhem of packed and stacked boxes. It was time for her to move. Her heart leaped with excitement, tempered with a strong dose of worry. But who didn't worry when making a big move?

STERLING LEFT THE AIRPORT in a white stretch Hummer limousine. Something about a football player.

HARLAN COAL SAVORED ONE more evaluating look at himself in the mirror, donning his sunglasses before walking out onto the grounds. His assistant, Armand, crossed the play area to meet him.

51

"That's it," Armand said. "I delivered the keys. That's the last one."

"Sold them all in three weeks. I guess we should celebrate."

"Baseball?"

"Absolutely."

The two men disappeared behind one of the only locked doors on the entire compound where four lines of cocaine had already been cut out on the table.

GABRI SENT OUT invitations to her dinner party. Following etiquette, the more formal the invitation and the earlier it went out, the more elaborate the event. She didn't want to compete with the *CoverBoy* opening coming up in two weeks. Most of her dinner guests would likely be on that guest list. She decided it would be a hoot to follow the *CoverBoy* event with an even more memorable evening. She knew real estate and she knew how to schmooze. Hand-in-hand.

Gabri got off the phone with Sterling Falls after thanking her for the new referral to handle Carly Posh's house closing. Sterling seemed surprised. *She didn't know Carly was moving?*

Stabbing at the Posh Possessions' envelope with her silver letter opener, Gabri pulled the papers out in front of her. She read the documents page-by-page.

"Sonuva bitch," she said aloud.

For the first time in her life, Gabri Criscione questioned grabbing a quick commission.

Chapter Sixteen
The Gala

GEOFF RECEIVED a call from his mother. It wasn't good news. His mother heard the voice of her dead Jamaican Obeah mother, and the living all better be listening. After ending the call, Geoff knew that Lauren was in danger. And Lauren's refusal to admit it would make it more evil. So he had been warned. And the number six. The number six was satanic, and all-around Lauren Visconti. When and how could he tell her?

IT WASN'T SUICIDE. It wasn't suicide. It wasn't suicide. This is what I knew. But what could I do? How was I to react but in numbness, blinded after my futile attempts to get at any truth. I had a life to live. I had to be and live amongst the living.

The *CoverBoy* gala was in good hands. With an applauded caterer at the helm, I knew all I had to do was dress and show up. And that might be asking a lot.

I remember feeling thankful to be there, although I still knew my footing was uncertain in Lala Land.

The nagging did not cease. It wasn't a suicide. The anonymous note? I didn't take it as a threat, or even a warning. It only confirmed what I knew in my heart. Suicide did not become my friend's nature. She was too damn feisty to not go down without a devil of a fight. Any fight.

I was in the middle of big changes in my life. What do they say causes the most stress? I'm pretty sure death, moving, and a new job all make the top of the list. Add that my new job was my own company, and I now had over thirty people relying on me for their livelihood.

Baby steps were huge for me. I was wearing the gown I had bought for my wedding rehearsal dinner. A few more steps and I'd walk out of my private office into the main lobby for the opening gala for *CoverBoy*. A party. No rehearsal needed. I glanced in the mirror to make sure my dress hadn't turned to paper.

"Lauren, you look scrumptious," Brock called out from the crowd ahead of me.

I hadn't seen Brock since the night of my arrival in L.A. He understood I was busy; I understood he was a dickhead for going to bed with my good friend within 24 hours of screwing me.

"Glad you could make it," I uttered.

"Are you kidding? I wouldn't miss it!"

"Excuse me," I said. "I need to greet some other guests."

Sterling found herself already surrounded by an entourage of men. I guess I was glad Brock wasn't one of them.

"You aren't ignoring me, are you?" Sterling asked.

"Of course not." I always grew a little jealous around Sterling. She was breathtaking, as usual. Her blond hair, thickly braided and pinned on top of her head, allowed my eyes to follow down her neckline to the diamond necklace dangling in chunks more dazzling than all the ice sculptures in the room.

"C'mon. You've been here for a couple months and we haven't had one drink together. You didn't even ask me to borrow a *bibelot* or two to wear tonight."

I reached up to touch the small necklace around my neck. A gold circle with my engagement diamond mounted in the center. "Look around. I've been a little busy," I defended myself.

Carly interrupted, making an appearance in a vamp Eddie Bauer look only she could pull off. After Hollywood kisses, she said, "I have to run, but just wanted to say hi."

"You just got here," Sterling protested.

I knew differently. Carly had been on-site since the early morning setting up the last-minute furnishings and handling a hammered woodworker who was getting a little too creative with his tools.

"Does Carly ever come with a date?" Sterling asked.

"Not her thing," I said as casually as I could. "You know that."

"You're telling me she's gay?"

"No. More like A."

"A?"

"Come on, Sterling. How long have we all been friends? Carly isn't interested. For now, at least, I think she's asexual."

Sterling choked back her drink. "Sounds like she needs serious therapy."

"She's in therapy. But I don't think it's about her preference for abstinence." I was surprised I knew more about Carly than Sterling. Although we were all supposed to be best friends I instantly regretted saying anything, afraid I'd betrayed a confidence.

Sterling's eyeballs rolled toward the ceiling. She burst out in a hearty roar of laughter that even took the nearby goggling men by surprise. Diamonds bounced and toppled as she hunched over the table. I could tell she was now immersed in a new subject as I watched her zero in on her night's prey. He was a tall, athletic looking blond and as yet unaware that Sterling would win him for the night.

Daddy's virgin little daughter would score with a stranger, again.

Yes. It caused me to glance back at Brock. He circled the *rumaki* bar. Good.

I moved across the room to check on Geoff and Sukie. Geoff had forgone his stardom as a model and was showing off his new website design to a round of potential advertisers.

Sukie peeked at me with a smile that dissipated into a grimace. "What's wrong, Laurs? You like you've seen a ghost."

"Who are those guys over there standing in the corner?" I pointed to two men with cameras slung around their shoulders. No question about it. They were the same two men I saw outside my hotel bungalow window. One had too much hair and the other, too little.

Sukie shrugged, "The press is supposed to just shoot cameos as guests arrive. Otherwise, I thought I was in charge of all the photography for tonight."

"Do me a favor. Go check them out," I asked as nonchalantly as possible.

Sukie came back a moment later. "Sure enough. Press," she said.

"From where?"

"I didn't ask. They both flashed me ID cards. I figured all press was good press. They said they wouldn't use their cameras inside the doors."

I turned to scan the corner of the room again. They were gone. Occupying the same space, a handsome man with impeccable dress and even more perfect dark hair cast a smile my way.

Sukie whispered, "Ah, and their eyes meet across the crowded room."

"There are no eyes to meet," I insisted. "He's wearing shades. Even in L.A., I find that indifferent."

"Maybe he's a rock star."

I looked back, and again the corner of the room stood empty.

Chapter Seventeen
The Beach & a Shrink

AFTER CLOSING ON MY BEACH house, Carly Posh had four weeks to decorate it top to bottom, while I stayed on at the bungalow. The day for me to move in came none too soon.

The Posh Possessions delivery van pulled out of the driveway as I walked through the transformed rooms. "I can't believe it," I told Carly. "You're unbelievable. I've never turned over the reins and let someone choose everything for me."

It was everything I wanted. Mostly, it was nothing like my apartment in Chicago. Carly offered me a seat in my brand new chair and hurried to the kitchen to retrieve the bottle of champagne she had chilling in the empty refrigerator.

"It wasn't as easy as I thought," Carly said. "I mean, I've done this kind of thing a dozen times, but you had me a little worried." Carly poured the champagne into two flutes I'd never seen before.

"What do you mean?"

"I think I know you. Back in school you were so whimsical and free and colorful. But the last time I saw you in Chicago your place was pretty austere, to be honest. I took a gamble and decided you needed something a little more cheerful. Beach-happy stuff."

I raised my glass to toast her. "A lot's happened to me."

"I wish I could have been nearer you," Carly said.

"Weird, huh, that I took comfort in that old apartment, when I thought I was so happy."

Carly looked at me with a bleak smile and the slightest shrug rising from one shoulder.

"I love what you've done. It's just what I need to bring me back amongst the living."

"You're still thinking about Payton, aren't you?"

"She always signed her emails to us, Carly. Always. In caps. BFF, YOUR BLOOD SISTER, PAYTON. She had an auto signature for us. One click. And I called her mom. Asked her about Payton's computer. She said she couldn't figure the thing out and donated it to charity. She couldn't even remember which one. The hope of finding anything on that is long gone."

Carly shifted, in obvious mental discomfort in the overly comfortable chair. "Remember, Lauren, when I told you I had started seeing a psychologist?"

"Sure." An uncertain panic laced my voice.

"Look, I'm just here to be your friend, no matter what." She reached into her handbag and pulled out a business card. "Furniture, champagne flutes, even a house on the beach—they aren't going to make you happy, Lauren. Here's the name of the guy I go to, and honestly, he's the best."

I accepted the card. The plain raised black ink read *Harlan Coal, Ph.D. Psychologist. Therapist.*

Carly must have read the blank expression on my face. "He's created some breakthrough therapy that produces measurable results. At least for me. God knows, you've been through enough. I've been going to him for several months. In fact, I just moved on to his compound."

"Compound? You're kidding me!"

Carly wasn't kidding. It had freaked out Gabri, too, I later learned, when Carly had asked her to draw up the sales contract for a house on a compound.

"Don't look at me that way," Carly said. "It's my own home and I'll make a killing on it anytime I want to sell. It works for me. It's near the Hollywood Hills, not too far from your office and on a chunk of property I didn't even know was there."

I tossed the card onto my new table. "Sounds creepy if you ask me."

Carly sighed. "I get more out of my therapy living there and hanging out with people like me, whenever I want." She shook out her choppy black hair. "Come on. Let me show you a couple more things I took liberty to pick up for you."

We walked into a second bedroom and there was Teddy, spread out like royalty on his new cushy be and next to an enormous cat tree. He looked perfectly at home.

I ran over to scratch his belly. "Perfect Carly. You really didn't need to do this."

"And there's more. Come look."

Carly knew I liked my tunes, and she was quite correct that my entire sound system was sorely outdated. She slid back the left side of the burl wood entertainment center to reveal the top-of-the-line components. "And I know you need your daily news fix," Carly said. She pushed a button on a remote and the large television screen lifted up from behind the cabinet.

The six o'clock news was on. "Perfect. You've thought of everything."

Carly walked over to the sofa to retrieve her handbag and a pile of loose manila folders. "Just think about it," she said. "I mean, getting an appointment with Dr. Coal. I'll set it up for you because he fills his calendar fast. I know he'll work you in if I ask him."

The television news flashed a series of what looked like yearbook portraits, one after another. The commentator announced, "Timothy Lyons did not fit the runaway child profile, and evidence of foul play was found at the scene of his home, including a substantial amount of blood and hair samples. DNA results will be in soon. This brings the year's total to twelve young boys that have disappeared from the Los Angeles and Southern California area under suspicious circumstances. The missing all seem to have vanished without a trace. Police need your help. Foul play is now being considered and their missing status is now listed as suspicious. Concerns are rising that there be more missing young boys, possibly expanding the course of many years. Please contact the police department if you have any information."

"This is too much," I said aloud. "Carly, did you hear that?"

"I don't listen to much news. Blank it out."

"Do you remember Payton's brother?"

"Of course I do. Mike. I think that's maybe why Payton might have committed suicide. I don't think she ever got over losing him."

"Right."

"What's right?"

"He was lost. No one ever said he died. They never found a body. He just disappeared and his parents didn't give a damn. But Carly knew he wouldn't have just skipped town without contacting her."

"So?"

"I don't know. Too many coincidences. Too many loose ends."

"Dr. Coal will help you sort it all out."

CARLY'S VAN BLOCKED my driveway. When she left I decided to pull the car into the garage. Only when I

61

walked back to the door did I remember the golf clubs in my trunk. Unloading the travel bag, I unzipped it, just in case there was something more to see inside the case. All I saw were the heads of a dozen or so clubs. I threw the unwelcome bag against the far side of the garage. At least they'd make it look like I had a life.

Chapter Eighteen
Voodoo

A WASTED TRIP TO TUCSON, more time wasted at the luggage claim at LAX, and now I had to come to terms with the big fake smile I had worn at my own opening gala while suspect that every guest predicted my great demise. It did little to lift my mood. Driving up the 405, I felt like I'd hit the wall both emotionally and physically. I reached for my phone and pushed the auto-dial. Without thought, I suppose.

"Brock Townsend," he answered.

"Hey. It's Lauren."

"This is a surprise. Last time I saw you I thought you were mad at me. Treated me like shit at your grand gala opening, if I recall."

"I'm sorry about that. I really am. It was a stressful night for me. I'm a far cry from being the hostess with the mostess."

"I'll second that emotion."

"It's just there were a lot of people there that had no right to celebrate with me, and on my dime. I'm pretty sure they're all of the opinion *CoverBoy* will be deep-sixed within a year."

Brock took his time responding. Too much time. Finally, "Since when does Lauren Visconti give a rat's ass what other people think?"

I remembered why I had called him in the first place. I didn't give a rat's ass. I cared that I had was checked out of the bungalow and on my way to a sexy bedroom in a beach house in Malibu. I remembered Brock's smell, and how I longed for that musty scent on my bed linens. I was a smart fool, and very human.

"Can I make you dinner tonight to make up for my bad behavior?"

"Sounds great, but I've got a game tonight. It was a fluke I could make your grand opening."

Instant embarrassment. Mortification. I tried to redeem myself. "At least you know I extended the olive branch. I know I was an ass."

"Do me a favor. Pull the thorns off that olive branch next time you offer it my way and we'll be cool."

I WAS CORRECT. My party was over. Too many people were telling me my magazine was destined to fail before I even ran the first local issue. At best, I was called the newest L.A. cheesy cougar, which I detested because I didn't deem myself old enough to be a cougar and I didn't think I was particularly cheesy, either.

"Don't listen to them," Geoff consoled me.

"Yeah, well, easy for you to say. They're knighting you as the next Rock Hudson. Read this." I handed him the morning paper.

"Honey, it ain't all that bad to be known as a femme fatale Hugh Hefner. Let me show you our advertising dollars." He clicked on the spreadsheet and turned his monitor to face me, full well-knowing he'd see my wide grin as I read the numbers.

Geoff was not only a brilliant computer techie; he also had business savvy gained from an MBA from Tulane, although he rarely touted it.

"Laurs, there's something I need to tell you."

"Your voice just dropped an octave. Talk to me."

"I talked to my mother the other day."

"Oh, Geoff. Not again."

"Hear me out." He removed a vial from his breast pocket and set it in front of me. "She overnighted this to me. Told me to get it to you right away."

I'd met Geoff's Jamaican mother once, and even his eccentric grandmother before she passed away. In her late eighties, the grandmother's mind functioned something on this side of scrambled but still gooey raw. I had listened in as she had a long and engaged conversation with her mother. As if she was on the phone and I could only hear her side of the dialogue. Except there was no telephone. And her mother had been dead for ten years.

Then there was the wee legend that the deceased grandmother held court as an alleged high priestess of Obeah Voodoo.

"What does your mother have for me this time? Something from your grandmother's grave, right?" I grinned. "Crushed alligator teeth? Grave dirt?"

"Don't make fun of this. The last time she had something for you it cured you of the flu in twenty-four hours, didn't it?"

I wanted to come back and tell him maybe I had the twenty-four hour flu, but spared the attitude. I unscrewed the top of the vial and smelled it. "Rum-based. That works for me."

"She told me to warn you of a negative energy all around you. And she wants you to beware of the number six."

"Isn't six the sign of the devil?"

"Triple six," Geoff said. "The sign of the devil. But my grandmother said six. Only the number six."

"Well, I would thank her but she's dead. You can tell your mother thank you, but I don't have a date with the devil and the only thing on my calendar for six o'clock is a haircut. I think I'm safe."

"Don't shoot the messenger, Laurs. Listen to me. How's a little rum-based potion gonna hurt you?"

I laughed.

Geoff grew more serious.

"There's something else."

"Please spare me," I said.

"My grandmother had one more message. You will sing and have no memory of it, and that will be a good thing."

"What the hell is that supposed to mean?"

"Like I said, Laurs, don't shoot the messenger. But let's face it. A good thing is a damn good thing these days!"

THE SICKENING NEWS didn't smack me in the face, but it did raise the hairs on the back of my neck. A reporter called on my private line. I found his questions obnoxious and the situation a travesty. But mostly, I admit, I found the whole thing to be rotten timing.

The call concerned our first official issue. Gone was the skirmish over the steroids and bribes our preview issue presented. This time we ran a powerful story on the tragedies of eating disorders. We interviewed several top runway models who agreed to reveal the secrets to their beauty. Those dark secrets hidden within the veils of the industry. Eileen Ford's insistence that her models strictly adhere to the fish-and-water diet had nothing on the newest up and coming talent agencies. They touted the cocaine diet to properly manage their weight. For one young woman who became our feature article, the cocaine use led to heroin. She told us this. We printed it.

Today's news? Police had found our most outspoken young model's body in east L.A., splayed out in front of a

Laundromat at four in the morning, stabbed six times. Her ring finger had been severed off for the bauble that had adorned it. The bauble, a ten carat emerald flanked by diamonds, was a gift from her agent, of course.

The authorities came to a quick resolution. The model was trying to make a quick score in the wrong part of town at the wrong time of night. Whacked out and stupid would be the only reason she would wear a ring like that in that part of town.

I'd met the model. I'd been present at the interview. The familiar pain of curling flames of fire surged through my spine. I'd met up with yet another death.

I looked at the vial of an Obeah Voodoo concoction. I unscrewed the cap and lifted a few small drops to my mouth.

Chapter Nineteen
The Bad Seed

IT WASN'T GEOFF AND HIS heebie-jeebie voodoo that bothered me, nor did I expect it to rescue me. It was my life. Never mind that I gave thought to my watch at six o'clock that night. Stuck in traffic and already running a half-hour late for my haircut, I finally called to cancel the appointment. I barely had time to get home and prepare my first real meal at the new house.

The steaming sauce of garlicky oil, tomato, carrot, and basil came to a gentle boil as I slid in the *Osso Bucco*, then placed the heavy lid on the casserole dish and shoved it into my virginal oven.

Sterling strode in juggling a bag of fresh bread and a bottle of Silver Oak Cabernet. We uncorked the wine and took our plates out to the deck.

The temperate evening air held just a hint of salty breeze coming across the Pacific waters. The beach was quiet but for the token Frisbee-chasing Golden Retriever in the distance, accompanied by a chattering of white gulls.

"This place is perfect for you, Lauren." Sterling refilled her wine glass. "But how are you, really?"

"Cut right to the chase, huh?"

"I'm not over Payton. I know you aren't. It seems like there's a hole in the whole."

Tears wanted to rise to the occasion but I denied them. "It's the Visconti curse. You know my background."

"That you've lost loved ones? Big deal."

"It's more than that. My DNA matches a spineless woman who managed to survive a violent rape. That means half of me is the seed of a rapist. I can't get that fact out of my head."

Sterling gulped down the red liquid and set the balloon glass back down on the table. "So we're back to the fact that you're adopted. And you were loved. What is your self arguing about now?"

She surprised me sometimes. Inside the body of a bimbo was an intuitive soul. Smart as hell, too.

I curled the edges of my napkin, purposely avoiding eye-contact. "Look at my life."

Sterling, my friend but an outsider. She would think I had everything going for me, but the truth was I had nothing. I had no family. I had no love, and if I loved it, it would die. And that's because I'm the heir to the devil. Yes, the devil and his sixes had crossed my mind, although I had no idea what it might mean for me.

I continued what felt like a soliloquy, "I'm the bad seed. Sometimes I feel him. I feel the evil soul of Nathan Judd residing inside me."

Sterling hadn't heard his name in years. Nathan Judd had died when his victim, my mother, fought back with a blow poke. The authorities had ruled the death self-defense with the agreement to cover up the adoption of the child conceived in violence.

Unsure of where the conversation had left to go, I removed myself and grabbed the *Couvossieur* from the newly stocked bar. The sun had set, and the cool air began to engulf us. I lit the small gas fire-pit. Shifting back into my chair, I was aware of the strain I'd brought to the evening. It seemed lately I managed to ruin most good moments.

Sterling hesitated, then reached into her pocket. "I'm sorry. I just don't know what to do with these."

Payton's keys to her house. We'd never been instructed how to return them.

"I'll hold on to them. Maybe call her mom," I said. I walked inside, pulled out the box we had taken from Payton's home and placed them inside.

"I shouldn't have dumped them on you."

"Why not?"

"The new surroundings are great, Lauren, but they won't heal what's inside of you. You've had a lot of loss in your life; this much I know is true. Maybe you should consider some professional counseling."

I heaved back onto the chair. "Seems like a popular notion these days."

"I'm the worst one to offer advice, but I think you need to get hold of your priorities, and it doesn't seem like it should be business. And just so you know, we're your family. Me and Carly.

"You're all I have left in the world."

And I'd fear for my life if only I were them.

Chapter Twenty
Celebrations

DR. HARLAN COAL COULD always shake off the flu-like symptoms his body endured after a night at a good baseball game. It was worth it, he thought. A cocaine celebration well-deserved. All of his community homes had sold for full asking price. None of his clients, or buyers, or patients, or whatever he decided to call them, had the good sense to haggle over his inflated sales price. Exorbitantly ridiculous, even by Hollywood Hills standards.

There wasn't a space unsold for his therapy sessions, either—all booked out months in advance. And he'd be juggling his next book tour after he finalized the deal with his new publisher. Of course the publisher didn't know that he wasn't going to sign books in some damned storefront. And in certain states where the threat of his being exposed loomed too large to risk. He'd be holding seminars where attendees would get a free book, for the steep price of admission, of course.

An appointment he anticipated with alacrity dragged on for forty minutes before his patient finally got around to asking him what he wanted to hear. He cleared his throat and excused himself for a moment. In his private bathroom he took a cold washcloth to his face, then breathed. He took a tissue to his nose. A little blood. No big deal. Just a little too much baseball. He studied himself in the mirror, then returned.

"I'll squeeze her in, Carly, but only as a favor to you. You know I'd do anything for you. You said her name is Visconti? How do you spell it? And her first name?"

I ENTERED MY BUILDING through the lobby's brass and glass doors and crossed to the bank of elevators. The center cab opened and three little elderly ladies decked out in Rodeo Drive hats and matching handbags stopped short their chattiness. All three raised their eyebrows to me as I waited for them to exit the elevator, as if I should have apologized for my intrusion.

I'd closed on the sale of my building and had bought out all the tenant leases except for one. The cranky geriatric psychiatrist on the tenth floor refused to be bought out of his lease, no matter my offering price for any inconvenience. It made me wonder what the difference was between a geriatric shrink and every other Hollywood mind-guru. I guess I really didn't want to know the answer. Mostly the doctor kept to himself, and mostly his clients did the same. Still, I felt like I was the outsider.

Closing my private office door now on the top floor, I willed myself into a capricious state of mind. I'd self-prescribe that for my over analytical mind.

CoverBoy sales looked promising, given the inclement market. Subscriptions were up seventeen percent over our predictions and, just as Queen Geoff had speculated, we discontinued our discounted launch prices on advertising. There were no complaints from our growing list of advertisers, unless we were out of units to accommodate them.

I wasn't going to let Geoff's constant warnings ruin my day. We had run a story about the model. And we were going to run many more, if the fates would allow. Our articles were provocative. We had the glistening abs thing going, but we did the real stuff in investigative journalistic reporting. Sometimes we got flack. Sometimes we even got hate mail. I was aware this would not change. And I stood firm. We documented every word we printed.

Even our critics seemed to back off. We had a good format. We conducted concrete interviews. We didn't sensationalize. We told the truth. Sadly, the truth was often sensationally sickening.

CoverBoy ran these stories next to pictorials depicting what women wanted to see. Real men in real situations. Some male models wore extravagantly expensive suits, a few were almost naked and with visible arousals. Our top models were in their twenties, but we filled bountiful pages with men far older, including a seventy-three-year old swimmer who wanted us to show all of him. Sukie did a *Women of Rylstone* thing at the last moment, strategically placing a life preserver in front of his family jewels.

We had plenty of female portraitures, too. Real women. We had one rule that shocked the women's media world. Sukie did touch-ups and used filters, but no photograph received digital enhancement. No body-shop parts, either.

Our formula worked.

The hate mail kept coming in. No surprise, this month it came from the top model agencies, their owners, and their talent agents. They didn't like our inference that cocaine diets were a prescribed means to fame on the runway. We didn't infer, anyway. We reported the facts.

Chapter Twenty-One
The Centre

CARLY'S NEW HOME looked nothing like her mansion in Bel Air. One-fourth of the square footage. Far less opulence. Nothing more than a Mexican kitchen and I knew she loved to cook. I choked back the shock, relieved to see she still surrounded herself with a few personal treasures, including a worn leather chair and a few framed photos. Other than that, the place was a Shaker-style of barren.

I asked Carly to show me her house before my introductory meeting with Dr. Coal. I hoped it would calm me down but, in spite of the lovely grounds, the warm reception, and Carly's rapturous state of mind in her new home, something didn't feel right.

Me. And a shrink. That wasn't right. It wasn't a Visconti thing to do.

"Some of the homes are co-ed. Some are more like bunkhouses," Carly said. "There are a few families on the south side where the play equipment is. Stuff like that. If there's any pressure around here it's in not sharing your home, because they're all sold and so many people want to live here. I need my privacy. I paid for it."

"Privacy? With no locked doors?"

"You noticed. Ultimately it's about respect," Carly added.

"Respect?"

"Spatial respect and respect of property. The people want to live here. There's even a waiting list. It's hard for me to put into words, Lauren, but they're like family to me. The family I never had. I have all the privacy I need, but I also take comfort in knowing so many wonderful people live and hang out around here."

Carly explained that there were only a couple of locked doors on the entire compound—none in the privately owned homes. Most of the public areas had no doors. Screens here and there stood as the only sentry to protect interiors from critters or inclement weather. As I crossed the grounds toward the building where I would be meeting Dr. Coal, the structure unfolded with open archway after archway. Gateways, Carly called them.

ARRIVING ON TIME, I wasn't sure what to do. Knock on the wall? Give out a 'yoo—hoo?' The inner passages seemed inviting enough. I walked in.

I'd already endured a series of involved oral interviews from staffers at The Centre. A written questionnaire seemed to be the length of a novella by the time I completed it. Apparently, I was applying for therapy. Apparently, I had passed the test.

From what I knew of him the barren room personified his platform for both his community and the successful practice he'd created. Polished Santos wood floors gave way to his small wooden desk and chair—quality pieces but in a plain minimalistic style. In lieu of the traditional therapist's sofa, a variety of aged Dhurrie rugs dominated the floor space and pillows scattered recklessly across the floor. The lighting was natural, enhanced with a few full-spectrum bulbs. A faint and unobtrusive scent of chamomile and cypress lingered. The few notable extravagances were a pair of woodcarvings—lions standing guard over the open space, a large altar framed by white candles, and a most unusual statue on the desk.

"Go ahead. You can touch it. Almost everyone does. It seems to attract people like a Buddha's belly," Dr. Coal said as he entered the room from behind me.

"It's one of a kind. The ivory elephant is the symbol of good luck when his trunk is lifted that way. He's setting sail in the small wooden rowboat, the lowliest form of transportation on the high seas, and he knows he's a hefty load. That symbolizes faith."

I didn't touch the sacred ivory, but my fingers glossed over the rich detail of the carved stone base. "And the marble?"

"Lapis lazuli, actually. The gemstone of powers and hidden energies. And either the artist knew that, or he was just happy to find a blue rock that resembled the ocean waters."

He extended his hand. "You must be Lauren."

I expected L.A. opulence, and I definitely expected the good doctor to be dressed in no less that a silk suit and alligator shoes. Tie—optional. Instead he greeted me himself, without a receptionist. Not even a receptionist's desk. As Carly had told me, there were few doors, not even to mark the entrance. He was dressed in a casual Ralph Lauren beach look, with a white gauze shirt flowing over white cotton drawstring pants; leather sandals on his feet.

Aware I might have been staring, I darted my eyes back to the statue. "Very informal."

"Does that concern you?"

"No. Not really." *A breath of fresh air.*

MOON BLADE SLATHERED the counter with a coat of fresh blood. It didn't matter for now where the blood came from. Insatiable, the copper tang of the blackened pool of liquid would make do to make the evening right.

The Macarta black-handled Damascus skinner, along with a Springsteel and an assortment of fine daggers, remained tucked away in their sanctuary. Rebuilding energy. Strengthening their pulse.

Soon. Very soon.

Chapter Twenty-Two
Let's Begin

"WE TRY TO MAINTAIN a family atmosphere around here and that goes for both the community homes and our therapy rooms here at The Centre. For those that insist, I have my wall of certificates and pedigrees, somewhere around one of these halls." He offered an easy laugh. "Do you have your questionnaire completed for me?"

I understood what he was really asking. If I was going to see him, even one time, I was agreeing to a true commitment. Most specific, the questionnaire made it quite clear that I would be asked to make regular appointments—or sessions, as they called it. When I thought about it, no matter what I claimed or fussed about, time was on my side. I was young, my company was launched and with an excellent and loyal staff, and so what if I had some major personal issues to resolve before I fucked anything else up. One issue. Why did everyone I ever love have to die? To expect that Dr. Coal could help me would be like me expecting a white picket fence with two cats in the yard, and breakfast and bed served by— well, someone handsome.

I wrestled and cast out any regrets or concerns. I caved into the serenity of Harlan Coal's office. And by caving, I had won. Twenty minutes hadn't passed by and to me it was as if Cinderella was there to greet me after I took a spin on the teacup ride at Disneyland. I felt warm, comfortable, and safe. Maybe I wasn't a lost cause and maybe I wasn't going to need years of therapy.

Maybe someone would love me, and live.

"Let's take a walk," Coal said, and grabbed his dark sunglasses. He reminded me of someone. A star, perhaps. Only a short time in L.A., and I was already inflicted by the dreaded celebrity-watch disease.

Coal guided me on a quick tour of his office and compound. The halls boasted slightly rounded angles. To the street-side, the walls were solid and lined with modern art. He corrected me. The paintings were the creations of his younger patients, although he never once used the word *patient*. He referred to the artists as clients, community members, and even friends.

On the interior sides, solid banks of windows and glass doors overlooked a triangular shaped courtyard. The mere size of the garden setting surprised me, especially for a plot of land in Hollywood Hills.

The core of the triangular grounds contained several stone tables with circular seating, a massive barbecue pit, three Jacuzzis, and a sprinkling of colorful children's play equipment at one end. The play area Carly had already mentioned.

I stood in the main building that formed the office side of the triangle. Small hacienda-style homes flanked the other two sides of the lawns and gardens. Structured from both stone and stucco and quite similar in design, Dr. Coal explained individuality was for the heart. All were privately owned. One lucky and proud new owner was Carly Posh.

At the far point of the triangle, directly across from the therapy complex, another structure loomed. Erected of the same stone and stucco, it was the only two-story building and much larger than the surrounding homes.

79

"That's my private residence," he said, as if reading my mind. "Truth is I occupy small living quarters in the front of the building."

"And the rest?" Immediately my face flushed, ashamed I'd been too nosey.

"The remainder of the building is my private library. It's our central nervous system. Without it, The Centre wouldn't exist."

He left it at that, and I didn't dare ask him anymore about it, but I did ask him about the lack of doors and locks.

"There are doors on the homes, mainly to keep out the elements, but we don't have locks."

"Why?"

"Privacy and respect go hand-in-hand. We don't need locked doors. Not unless you go and give some of your burglar friends this information."

"Sorry. I just have a curious nature. And I like to know how things work, and why."

We circled our way back to the offices. Coal jumped in front of me and said, "Let me get that for you." He then pretended to open an imaginary door for me.

"All of us are here to become better persons, myself included. If that's the intended personal goal, then it translates to a group goal. We don't have fear. We don't have secrets."

My mind raced, maybe with my own old fears. "What about doctor-patient confidentiality?"

"I can't say that I've ever treated anyone that's committed a heinous ax-murder, Ms. Visconti."

He'd called me Lauren earlier. Had I insulted him?

He continued, "It goes back to our idea of family and community, even if you don't live here on the grounds, and as you can see only a couple dozen or so people are lucky enough to do so. We all trust one another. And the path."

"The path?" I'd asked to quickly. The pitch of my voice rose too high. *Vulnerable, and he knows it.*

"The reason you're here." His voice remained calm. Paced. Secure.

I didn't know that much about his therapy or his path, only that everybody else seemed to think I needed it. He didn't look like the Beverly Hills shrink I'd envisioned, but he didn't look like a wild Charlie Manson-type, either. Then again, Manson wasn't too weird for the California sixties. And Ted Bundy was a hunk in the eighties. My mind froze while my stomach became a butterfly on speed.

"I don't mean to be rude, Ms. Visconti, but I have many people that need and want my time. They respect it. If you're uncomfortable with The Centre, then perhaps we should say our goodbyes now and not waste each other's remains of the day."

Damn my mouth! Damn my mind and my stomach! "It's nothing like that," I blurted out. "I want to be here. I need you to help me sort some things out."

"Then let's begin. Let's schedule a time to meet for our first session."

Chapter Twenty-Three
Two Moons

THE SKINNY GIRL DESERVED to die. It was her destiny. For the good of all humanity. Someone had to pay attention.

Moon Blade held no regrets about slashing the perfectly sculpted lanky body. For one, the model didn't even put up a fight. She was hopped up on dope, and even if she had thrown a defensive punch, Moon Blade would have easily countered it.

America's idol. The beautiful. But physically fit? Hell, no. She was a string bean steaming in a cauldron of her chosen poison.

Moon Blade liked the weapon of choice. No skull cracking. No chicken-shit bullets or too-impersonal of poisons. No awkward strangulation.

The sword suited Moon Blade. And the emerald ring carved from the victim's finger? What to do with that but something divisively delicious.

FIVE DAYS LATER Brock Townsend showed up on my doorstep, armed with brilliant coral roses, a supermarket rotisserie chicken, and an exuberant smile that transcended all our past failures at relationship snags, or rips, or broken bones. In fact, he should have been the poster boy for world peace. If there was any indiscretion tainting our past, I forgot.

After touring him through my new home and introducing him to Teddy, the cat, we ended up in the kitchen. I gathered up the bag of chicken and grabbed a bottle of Chardonnay to take out on the deck. Brock rambled around in my kitchen in search of glasses and napkins. His casual gentle-giant presence reminded me I had a friend I could always depend on. A friend who happened to be a major-league hunk who slept with my friends, but that was beside the point. At least for the night.

We attacked the whole chicken like savages on a wild boar. I wiped my greasy fingers so I could pick up my glass of wine without it looking like a two-year old's sticky fingers had been handling it.

Brock lifted his glass in a belated toast. No words. The glasses clinked. The Greeks used to say we could see the wine, smell it, taste it, and even touch it, but to toast was to hear it. Finally, he spoke.

"What's gonna be in your next issue, Ms. Magazine?" he asked.

"Besides nearly naked men?"

"Just waiting for you to ask me to pose for you. But yeah, I'm talking who you gonna nail next?"

"Afghanistan. A brilliant female doctor named Dhurra Sulayman. She's been chastised and abused. Even tortured. And she's given us an exclusive."

Brock contemplated his wine, twirling it for its rich legs trickling down the inside of the glass. "I'm guessing that took some guts. I'm proud of you."

"Not me. The doctor! She's the one with the courage. I'm just the medium for her to get her message out."

"I heard about that runway model. Ugly."

"Ugly, but I guess she shouldn't have been hanging around a Laundromat in the wee hours with a fucking

83

emerald on her finger that rivaled the Hope Diamond." I immediately wished I hadn't said that.

Brock nodded with a gentle smile that told me he was proud of me, no matter what. We sat in our old familiar comfortable silence, the only voice—that of the waves crashing below us.

"Have you broken in this new deck of yours?" He tilted his brow and studied me as if analyzing my batting stats in some pre-game coaching conference.

"I don't follow you."

"Have you made wild and mad and passionate love in the arms of a capable man, right here with this full moon and the ocean waves crashing behind you, in rhythm with your own movements?"

A muscle quivered somewhere down my spine and through to my inner thighs. Flesh quivered, too, of that I was certain. I thought about my bedroom and getting that sexy man smell layered between my new sheets and my skin. I was open to alternative suggestions.

"Let's see. Carly was here to introduce me to my new posh possessions, Sterling came by for dinner, and I've interviewed a housekeeper. None of them are my type for breaking in a deck."

"Too bad."

The beach was deserted. The moonlight—intoxicating. I knew Brock would spend the night with me afterward, like he always did after we made love, or had sex, or whatever it was we did so well.

Without words, I went inside and retrieved my old plaid stadium blanket. Within minutes, per our usual M.O., we were naked in a tangled heap of flesh on top of the scratchy wool.

He had no idea how long it had been for me, I thought, but for the last time we were together. In the bungalow.

84

When I wanted him to spend eternity with me but was too stupid to ask him to stay even for another day.

We thrust forward and rolled back like a ride on Space Mountain with all the dangerous curves, twists and hard bumps, with more to follow, and then we silenced our bodies, perfectly still. He pulled up from me and instinctively nibbled and tantalized me into ecstasy. Sensing I'd brought him to his own urgent needs, I pulled back. And then I pushed. I gave him all of what was me, and he responded. The ocean waves were no match compared to the undulations of our synchronized bodies.

Brock reached for something from his jeans pocket next to chest. He raised it to my nose.

"Take a whiff, Laurs. You'll like it."

I recognized it instantly. "What the fuck?"

Jumping up from our tussled blanket, I covered myself with what was left of my crumbled clothes.

"What's the matter with you, woman?" Brock looked shocked more than angry, as if I were the problem.

"Get out!"

"It's just a little amyl nitrate. What the hell's the big deal?"

"Get out, Brock. Now," I shrieked, tossing his clothes at him.

"You crazy bitch. Laurs. What's the matter with you?"

I didn't wait for him. I grabbed what I could to further shield my body and stormed into my bedroom, locking the door behind me.

He'd get my picture, baseball legend that he was. Only my rules were *two* strikes and you're out.

A vial of amyl nitrate? I'd never seen it before, but I knew what it was and I absolutely knew how Brock got it. It was a classic. It was Sterling Fall's trademark post-coital indulgence.

Chapter Twenty-Four
A Session for Sanity

COAL SMILED, REVEALING perfect white teeth and dimples. "Thank you for escorting Ms. Visconti in to see me and holding her accountable for getting here," he teased.

He took Carly's hand, giving it a gentle squeeze as he watched her from behind John Lennon-type wire-rimmed glasses, only much darker than Lennon's preferred rose tint. It proved to be a simple but effective way of signaling it was time for her to go. I'd noticed that technique before.

As Carly walked out onto the grounds she turned back, "Dr. Coal. You're helping so many people. I'm grateful to have you in my life."

Coal flipped on a tape recorder. He saw the instant hesitation register across my face. "I keep the recordings under lock and key. They are confidential. Everything that occurs between us is confidential. But when I talk to you I want to listen. I don't want to be taking down cryptic notes. I find it's far more effective this way. Okay?"

"Sure." I guess so.

"This is just an introductory session, Lauren. Nothing heavy, I promise."

He pointed to the pillows on the floor, and seeing again there were no seating options outside of the simple Scandinavian desk, I propped myself up in a corner of pillows, mortified with my too-short skirt, my too-high

Manolo Blahnik heels, and the captivating if not commanding charisma of my newly appointed therapist.

He asked me core questions about my background, reviewed the notes on the oral interview I'd provided, and scoured my completed questionnaire. My novella. If he knew what he was doing, there was no out for me. The conversation would quickly turn to the subject of love and death.

"For starters," he said, "maybe you need to realize how lucky you are. I know it might sound trite, but you've heard the old saying, 'It's better to have loved and lost.' "

I found it very trite but I said nothing. And he was good. There we were on the subject of death. Opening line.

"It seems to me as if you've had a life rich in wonderful relationships. Loving relationships. Do you know how many people I see going through life with no love at all? Not the love of a good parent, a sibling, a companion? Not even a good friend."

"So you're saying I'm spoiled rotten and should count my blessings."

He chuckled, "Well, that's being a bit hard on you, Lauren, but it does bring up a second point. You're more than just a bit hard on yourself, aren't you?"

I noted that I was no longer Ms. Visconti, but surely that's not what broke the ice that sealed my soul. I really don't have an explanation. In less than thirty minutes this man penetrated my very being and began dissecting the vessels of my pain. Somehow he made me feel stronger, without all the psychiatric 'you-talk, I listen' bullshit. He engaged in conversation with me. And I talked. I still wore the veil of the newest poor little rich girl, but I wasn't hiding behind it. I talked about my family. I even fumbled through my handbag and produced photographs of all of them. I talked about my engagement. And the plane crash. With each story, an ounce of weight lifted from my heart.

Until I got to Payton. Payton was fresh death. Unacceptable death.

Dr. Coal ended our session. I'd only been at The Centre for an hour.

"We have a gathering, third Saturday of every month. Food, a little wine if you like, and a nice talk. If it fits for you, join us. Meanwhile, let's get together again sometime next week. You can sign up for an hour on our website calendar. And you'll always know I'll give you a full hour."

Only then did I realize he didn't wear any jewelry, including a watch. I hadn't even seen a wall clock, as during our session I myself had to sneak glances down at my Rolex several times.

Lauren Visconti would have found this too much. Too soon. Too much vulnerability. Instead, I found hope. I was hurting, and I'd finally found a road to kill the pain. Or at least, ease it.

Two young boys gathered outside his office. They peered in, since there was no door, but immediately backed away when they saw me with the doctor.

He reached his hand over to mine in one swift motion. He gently squeezed my fingers and pulled his glasses down from his face with his other hand. His eyes confirmed it was time for me to go. It was the end of my session.

"Hey, Lauren," he called after me. "Next time, wear sweats and sneakers!" he teased.

Chapter Twenty-Five
For Better or Worse

MY WEDDING DRESS. AGAIN. Cut low in the back. Braided silk pulled tight across my waist. The gown cascades to the floor in layers of scalloped edging.

I can't make out who is walking me down the aisle. My father's dead. It can't be him.

The music is too loud.

My wedding dress is made of paper.

Please! Please! Who is walking me down the aisle? His face is blurred. His body—abstract.

The tang of smoke fills my lungs. The funneled wind fuels the flames of fire. My escort drops my arm and falls away from me, engulfed in a bonfire of human flesh.

Why am I the only one not burning?

The phone rang and I reached for it, grateful for the interruption from the nightmare, even though receiving a call at three in the morning is most always unwelcome news.

"You're in danger. If you keep at it you're the only one to blame."

The line went dead. I checked the caller I.D. and it read Pay Phone. It also showed a number. I called it back only to have it ring and ring. The area code smacked with familiarity. Chicago.

Chapter Twenty-Six
Prime Rib and Cacti

GABRIELLA CRISCIONE HELD her legendary dinner parties four times a year, always avoiding any major holiday. She wanted no competition. Nothing to detract from her imprint as the fairest real estate agent of all. And four times a year even some well-known celebrities found themselves rifling through their mail and making last minute pleas or bribes if they didn't make the guest list. She knew if such a thing existed she would own the Oscar for dinner parties.

For those that might arrive without a chauffeur, the valets lined up in front of Gabri's digs, hustling keys and cars in a stream of headlights.

I never flourished in a flowing gown the way a woman should. Or better put, I languished without a man at my side. Don't ask me why. Ego. Loneliness. Abandoned by an always elusive love. Or a dead one. I took a deep breath and told myself I wasn't just a sketch of a figure in an artist's pad of forgotten drawings. I was real. Full-color. Three-dimensional.

Reaching to accept the hand of the valet as I stepped from my car, a second hand appeared.

"What a nice surprise, Dr. Coal," I responded to his touch. Uncomfortable in my choice of dress in front of him—a clingy red off-the-shoulder number, with the CFM shoes to match. Thank god I had left the boa at home.

Coal didn't stray from his casual whites, although again I noticed his sunglasses. It reminded me of something. Someone. His sandals were replaced with white loafers. No socks.

"Don't you think you should call me Harlan tonight? It would be less awkward for both of us."

Harlan. For the night. "I didn't realize you were a friend of Gabri's," I said.

"I'm not. Not really. She helped your friend Carly close escrow on her home with us at The Centre. To tell you the truth, I think our hostess *du jour* is doing a little background investigation as far as I'm concerned."

He must have seen the probing question in my eyes.

"No problem," he added. "I understand she's just concerned, and I think I'll pass her test just fine.

"You look beautiful tonight, Lauren."

The flattery caught me off guard. I must have blushed to a shade more crimson than my dress, but he didn't seem to notice. He took my arm, escorting me through Gabriella's massive double-door entry.

I didn't care much for Gabri's taste in decorating. She seemed to be stuck in some Gothic romance novel, starting with the moat that surrounded her home, and then there was the full-suit of armor that greeted guests in the darkened gray entrance. Not exactly a warm welcome. Cold slate floors and dark walnut walls completed the sense of austerity. Dark, low ceilings with cavernous hallways added to the gloom. The severe ambience never seemed to fit with the feisty Italian woman that was worth a laugh a minute. Instead, I saw haunted halls.

"You've come together!" Gabri squealed upon seeing us.

I shot a glance at Dr. Coal—*Harlan*, who quickly informed our hostess that we'd only met outside.

"Call it intuition, but I must have known something, darling," Gabri said to me with a wink, "as I've seated Dr. Coal between you and me at the dining table."

In all, thirty-two of us gathered around Gabri's dinner table. It could have seated more, and had on many occasions. The aroma of prime rib, divine *polenta* bathed in garlic, and the faint but deliciously sweet scent of sinful desserts greeted us as we took our appointed chairs.

I tried not to look at Sterling and Brock, sitting next to one another. Had Gabri known this would be like a knife to my back? Of course not. That was my choice. I dismissed the idea.

A full slab of prime rib arrived by servants. Gabri eagerly stood to receive the carving knife.

"My father was a surgeon," she laughed. "Only I carve the meat at my table." She finessed the beef in such a way the rest of us sat in full appreciation of her skills.

"Dr. Coal, tell us about yourself," Gabri engaged everyone's attention from the head of the table as the meat was portioned out to the guests by the staff. Indeed Harlan Coal would be put under the microscope for the evening.

"I'm afraid I'm a little boring, Ms. Criscione, considering this magnanimous audience. What about you? How is it you came to be one of the top real estate agents in the country?"

Gabri didn't miss a beat to talk about herself. "That's easy. I'm old and I'm fat, so my looks aren't threatening to the Hollywood wives, even though I have a pair of the only real boobs in California."

"Not exactly true," flat-chested Sterling piped in.

Gabri continued to probe Coal but received little back. He skillfully turned the conversation around every time she asked a question of him. I delighted in his ability to frustrate the hell out of our nosey hostess. I guessed it to be in the nature of his work that made him the superior inquisitor.

He turned the attention toward me. "Tell us about your magazine. What's new?"

"The current month's issue is out. All produced here in Los Angeles and from our new headquarters. But for most, it will seem old news," I said. "My photographer, Sukie Fields, offered to take one more traveling gig. A big one. She went on-location to Afghanistan. Plenty of women's issues there. We arranged for an interview with a woman of blighted power."

"Pretty easy thing to do," Brock said, as if he hadn't heard about the story before.

I ignored the comment. "A doctor. She put herself in great danger by even seeing us, and we all knew it. We have photos. We have storylines. We have names.

"The response has been huge. I think she'll be coming here to L.A. soon for a lecture tour at some of the major universities."

Suddenly embarrassment flushed and marred my face. I was sitting across the table from the famous documentary movie producer, Jack Helms. Doubt began turning my color to gray as my words turned to mush. Here I was, a lowly publisher, pitching my magazine in front of one of the most respected producers in Hollywood. "But surely some of you have more fascinating stories to share." I deferred my gaze over to Helms.

Helms jumped at the chance to seize and dominate the conversation. I might have regretted letting go the spotlight if I'd only known how far he would run with it.

He sat next to Carly. It appeared to me that pure instinct told him getting lucky with Carly would not be in the cards. He turned his shoulder away from her and more toward the other females at the table, me included.

93

"My new film project is up and running. Anyone care to hear?"

Applause. Applause. Hollywood style. From our chairs we all blew kisses to his cheeks. I had no doubt he imagined those kisses landing on other more prominent body parts.

He waited with great pause for the quiet of anticipation, then whispered in a husky voice, "Missing Children."

"Not exactly a new subject, Jacko," another guest jeered.

"This will rock and shock," the producer barked back. "Documented death. A blind eye to the worst secrets you can imagine. Even those of us without children—we fear it but we never face it unless it faces us and takes up residence in our souls. Hell, each and every one of us sitting here even helps cause it. I'm telling you, there's a rhythm to it I will set to music."

"You can be a prick, Helms," Gabri said.

"Yes. A fucking cactus in the middle of the desert," Helms replied to our hostess, "but I'm one of those rare giants, you know. The saguaro, with looming arms full of those pricks."

Cactus. Saguaro. Tucson. Payton.

Nausea engulfed me. Gabri's succulent prime rib suddenly looked like human flesh and body parts.

"Excuse me," I said, and departed the table.

When finally I emerged from the powder room, Harlan Coal was sitting on the slate floor in front of me. He looked up with an engaging smile. He held up two glasses of warmed brandy and swung his head to one side, indicating a spot next to him.

I kicked off my pumps, hiked up my red gown, and sat on the cold surface of the floor next to him.

"Tragedy is a fact of life, my dear Lauren," he whispered.

"I'd rather pay more taxes."

He smiled again, then put his arm loosely around me. We sat propped up against Gabri's cold wall.

"But Helms is right about something," I added.

I could barely make out his eyes from behind the shaded glasses but I felt his piercing stare.

"I've been turning a blind eye."

He winced, I think. Did he feel my pain? He said nothing.

Was it really about my blinded eyes? Was it the subject of missing kids and my memories of Mike, Payton's brother?

Chapter Twenty-Seven
This Gift Will Keep on Giving

"I'M SORRY, SWEETHEART," Coal said. "I have obligations at The Centre. I need to get back. Would you like me to see you to the valet?"

He let go of my hand. I hadn't even realized his fingers had laced through mine.

I shook my head, watching as Brock and Sterling made their way out the front door. "No. I'm a sucker for desserts. I think I'll stick around and gorge myself."

I gave him a peck on the cheek and Dr. Coal stood to leave. The suit of armor no doubt monitored his exit, if not the innocent kiss.

Engaged in conversation and perhaps given the mostly narcissistic company, not one guest seemed to notice my absence. Staff presented domed silver trays around the table of guests. My coffee had been replenished, another warmed brandy I did not request nor want, beside it. The moment I sat down, I was served, not offered, the flaming Baked Alaska. I wouldn't have said no, anyway.

One of the servants confronted Gabri as she returned from somewhere down the long hall. "Ma'am," I heard him say, "The package is in the way of the butler's pantry. Do you mind if we move it?"

"What package?" Gabri shrieked with delight. She commanded everyone's attention.

The staff member pointed to a large wrapped gift propped near the entrance to the butler's galley.

Gabri feigned surprise. "No card. Now, which one of you brought the hostess a gift? You know I said no presents allowed."

No one confessed to their abuse of the house rule.

The package proved too enticing to refuse. Thin, and about four-feet wide by three-feet high, and wrapped in yards of plush burgundy velvet, it blended into the shadowy background of Gabri's room. Still, it was hard to imagine no one had witnessed its appearance. Then again there was that narcissism reigning thick in the air like banks of neon-backlit slot machines in Atlantic City screaming, "Choose me. I'm a winner."

Gabri asked Jack Helms to help her with it, and he lifted the package to a high sideboard. With one swift tug, she untied the braided cord wrapped around the gift.

"Holy shit," Helms muttered. Others gasped and cried out, horrified, as the sheath of velvet slid to the floor to expose the painting for all to see.

I would have imagined that Gabriella Criscione held a dark side, or at least a tough side. She had to be tough on the business ladder as she climbed to the top. But I never guessed her for the offensive goblin that appeared before us.

She ranted and flared. She tossed her arms out as if the maestro of the "Be cursed and be damned" to all that bore witness. She rattled off what might pass as grade-school Italian. And then, in a blink of finite time, she transformed into a weeping child.

97

Chapter Twenty-Eight
Art is Subjective

HELMS STAYED BEHIND with me as the valets scrambled to bring all the cars up for the urgent exodus of guests.

I went to the kitchen and scooted staff out of my way in order to put on a pot of water for chamomile tea, then I took a serving tray into the drawing room where Gabri sat curled up into the corner of a garish red sofa.

"Who hates me this much?" Gabri moaned, hugging her chubby knees close up against her body from beneath her satin gown.

Helms pulled the velvet back over the painting and moved with alacrity toward the kitchen. He ordered to Gabri's chef, "Get it out of here. Stash it in the garage for now."

Underneath the shroud of covering, none soon would forget the clear depiction of Gabri, one of L.A.'s top ten Realtors, captured in timeless oil as a grotesque nude. A compilation of an ancient Miss Piggy and an equally aged and vulgar Elvira. Pimpled flesh spilled in fatty folds across the canvas. A swollen hairy arm held firm around a gleaming medieval suit of armor.

I proffered Gabri the cup of tea. "Take this."

She cowered.

"Gabri, at worst it was just someone's idea of a harmless joke," Helms said. "You're a tough woman. It's not necessarily a bad depiction. Maybe it was meant to be funny. Come on. Political humorists do it all the time."

"Evil," Gabri choked.

We all knew the painting was malicious by intent. That's why the other guests scurried out to their fancy cars and off to their fancy houses. Imagined or real sanctuary, they were off to find it far away from Gabri's moat-protected castle.

"I've made a lot of enemies over the years," Gabri groaned, "but I would never have imagined someone would stoop to this. Real estate is a cut-throat business and here I am, an old *dago* from Chicago. Honestly, the only way I could make a living in this town was by being a pain in the ass rather than the typical royal bitch that floats through life. I never thought this—" her voice trailed off.

I didn't know her that well, but my heart ached for Gabri. I didn't know she hailed from Chicago. I wondered why I didn't recognize her name, but maybe she wasn't doing real estate back then and there.

"People adore you. They respect you. There's a reason for that besides just being tough. If it isn't an ill-appointed attempt at critical humor and homage to your success, then just one person is jealous of you. That's all," I said.

I stumbled for more words. Gabri's aggressive personality now wilted in my presence. She was a spirit, broken.

Gabri asked Jack Helms to fetch her some amaretto. On ice. With a strange veil of timidity, he obeyed.

"Maybe we should notify the police," I blurted out. Oh my god, why did I even think that?

Gabri retorted, "So, you do believe it's a little more than sick humor we have going on here?"

"Wait a minute," Helms said. "The police will find nothing criminal here. They'll walk away never to return

99

and you'll wind up in some cheap tabloid. But Lauren has a point. You need to notify your security company. And for shit's sake, ask them who came by here tonight that wasn't on your guest list. It's just being prudent."

My mind still functioned, even after the second brandy. Jack Helms had a profitable history with Gabri. He'd bought and sold many a home with her and in return she'd provided top L.A. digs as hot locations for his film projects.

Helms interrupted my thoughts. "Leave it to me. I'll take care of it. Let me make some phone calls."

A voice inside me kept guard. Everyone has a dark side. What did I just witness? And why?

Gabri grabbed my arm with grizzly force. "Did I tell you I fucked up one of Brock Townsend's deals?" Her voice quaked.

"It doesn't matter. None of it matters right now. Brock wasn't behind this. He's an asshole, but he wouldn't do this."

I knew the territory. Gabri probably did have enemies. Brock was not one. He flew and flittered in and out of huge business deals like a bee might sip at moldy sugar water at a hummingbird feeder. It didn't matter. He was in. He was out.

"I probably cost the man a few million, Lauren," Gabri said. "Not that he doesn't have plenty of money, but money has a way of pissing people off."

"Brock was here. He enjoyed himself."

"But he left before this fucking unveiling. He must have known."

"Not Brock," I said.

"Whatever. Like I told you, I have a lot of enemies."

I LEFT GABRI WITH her dutiful staff. No matter how rude she was to them, ultimately she reeked of something pitiful and they were there for her.

Jack Helm's followed me out the door. The valets had dropped our keys onto the foyer's marble table. I guessed we had overstayed our welcome. Gabri needed time to sort things out, on her own, and in her own space I called a dungeon but she called a home.

"I think you're right," he said.

"About what?"

"I didn't want to alarm our hostess, and for sure the L.A.P.D. has better things to do than chase down some phantom pervert whose only weapon is a paintbrush. But I know a couple of guys that can help."

"With what?"

"One guy is in forensics. Another, stalking is his claim to fame. I mean, he *was* a stalker. Reformed, maybe. Something's not right here. I don't think it would hurt to run this evening's events past both of them."

Our cars had been pulled up near the entrance. Helm's helped me into my car.

"About your missing children program," I said.

"What about it?"

"Can we talk?"

"I'm flying tomorrow. Call me in a couple."

101

Chapter Twenty-Nine
Fresh Cherries

FOR A SECOND TIME I cancelled my plans to meet Carly and Sterling for lunch. Too much to do. Too much to avoid. The dream was forever on my mind. I tried to abandon all consciousness of it but it permeated my life. The best way I could protect my best friends was to stay away from them.

I REMEMBER THE STAFF meeting well. We had gathered around our small but functional conference room table. Up for debate, the entire expose on plastic surgeons. And the naysayers spoke up with the same old objections that I was running old stories past their prime.

"You're right. Everyone has heard of Cat Woman and the Barbie Doll. So what else do we have?" I asked.

One of my new staff writers spoke up. He probably had figured out his position was tenuous and I was the boss. It was no guts, no glory for him. "We all know that there's a lot of genital mutilation. Last month's story on Dr. Dhurra only scratched the surface. Does the general public know about the plastic surgeons out there making zillions of dollars doing clitoris cosmetic surgery?"

His knees shook, only visible because I preferred glass tables. This new guy dared to speak up and claim his turf. He was there to write, and writers brought facts to the table that turned into stories if they were any good.

102

"Tell us," I said.

"They're most often called vulva beautification procedures. Labia minora reconstruction. If the need dictated—and it was always purported as a need, thin labials were fattened up with injections, while if patients come in with too thick of pubic fat pads, they'll be happy to reduce them with liposuction."

"That can't feel too good," a female writer added as she squirmed her own butt deeper into the chair.

"And then there's clitoral dehooding."

I smiled at my young protégé.

"And there's a helluva lot subscribers that have never heard of revirgination," the new writer added.

My token naysayer and favorite critic shut up. I wondered where the hell the writer came up with this stuff and what he did on the weekends.

"Women are going in for elective surgery to get plastic hymens implanted."

"I've heard of it," another writer said. "Like, with blood bombs and all."

"That's right. Gel sacks full of fake blood. So the guys can get the cherries they cherish."

My small audience spoke nothing. "I want to know why. Is it a woman with one big fat lie because she's no virgin? Is it a woman, submissive to her man's pleasures, or is it something else? A couple seeking something new and different?"

My senior writer was the first to speak. "It sounds like major surgery to me. Not your ordinary sex toy. And for the record, I've never heard of it."

I said, "Get their stories. I want to hear from the patients, anonymously, of course. But as for the doctors—"

"I know the drill," said my junior writer. "Print the names of these fine plastic surgeons. But first, get their 'no comment' comments."

103

TWO WEEKS LATER I was still debating what 'a couple' meant, for that's when Jack Helms had told me to call him back. I'd picked up the phone a good ten times, but never dialed his number.

My insecurities insisted that maybe he wouldn't even talk to me. I phoned him only after preparing myself to hear his voicemail. Or some call screener. That might be better than listening to his morbid thoughts about missing children, because maybe he *would* take my call.

He responded via webcam. Away in Italy, he thought I might be interested in another story idea.

"There are certain provinces here where wives are still regarded as property," he said. "The women sit on front porches with their husbands, forced to face the walls of their home. They can't look out on the street.

"They can only listen as their husbands choose to describe to them what they see. Or conversely, choose what to censor. Anything and everything. Passersby, activity—anything, Lauren. This prevents the women from making forbidden contact with other men."

"It sounds good. I mean bad, but good," I said.

Helms was researching yet another documentary idea.

"I have that last issue of yours," he said. "I think you should show the full cheese."

"What?" He caught me off guard.

"The entertainment biz is about dichotomy. You have your exposés going for you, all juxtaposed next to dirt-ass male models. I'm just saying do more with the skin thing and the male models. It sells. Women keep getting all the glory these days."

I didn't exactly want to be known as the next Bob Guccione and his *Penthouse*.

"Can I ask you about your project? The missing children?"

"Fire away."

"I've been looking for a missing child. My friend's brother. It's been years. She hired a private investigator and all that stuff."

"And you got zippo, right?"

"Right. He just disappeared. They somehow determined he was a runaway of his own accord."

"It's kind of like the missing prostitutes. They make for an easy mark because no one reports them missing."

A man called out from the background, "It's show time, Mr. Helms."

"Gotta run, but send me what you have on this kid," he said. "I have sources. Oh, and as far as Gabriella Criscione and any stalker goes, it's nothing."

"The painting was nothing?'

"Nothing that my guys could come up with and I'll take their word over the L.A. cops any day of the week. Let's just say she has enemies, but no one wants her dead. At least not yet."

DR. COAL LEFT ME three messages. I ached to return them. I needed to schedule another appointment with him. It was time to figure out my life and why the Lauren Visconti Curse made love a certain death threat. I just didn't have the time.

And I was afraid.

Chapter Thirty
Let's Ride a Pony

GEOFF RELISHED THE limelight and the new backdrop of the city of angels agreed with him. Some critics had called Sukie's artful portrayal of the male body as something akin to Rodin's masterpieces. Geoff chimed in that he would go down in history as the conclusive reason behind Mona Lisa's mystifying smile.

We'd been friends too long for me to turn down his offer to meet me at the Santa Monica Pier. True to his word, he was easy to spot in front of the arcade and dropping handfuls of quarters into pinball machines for eager children.

"Not how I usually spend my workday," I hollered in between whirling bells and the cling-clang of metal balls slamming against rubber bumpers.

"Hey, Babe, you ain't lived until you played hooky at the pier. I figured that out the first week we started operations down here."

"If you're setting me up for a raise your plan is seriously flawed," I laughed.

Geoff turned away from the children, willing to forgo the anxious looks on their faces already pitting skills against one another at the arcade.

My beautiful puerile friend announced, "Let's go ride a pony," he said. He led me over toward the historic carousel.

I began to suspect I was in for more than a pony ride, but if it wasn't a raise he was looking for I was duped.

We stopped long enough for me to purchase a bag of caramel corn.

"Breakfast of champions," I explained as we gave the ticket taker our red coupons. "Now tell me, is this a pony ride or a phony ride. Just why are we playing hooky?"

"It's bad, honey," Geoff whispered in a hoarse voice. We had just taken our seats in a golden chariot for two; two magnificent white wooden Clydesdales prancing us through the woods, or at least up and down through a fading forest mural scenery.

"Our reviews?" I gasped. "No way! We're on top!"

He ignored my mock horror and looked away. "Remember your doctor from Afghanistan?"

"Of course I do. Brave female doctor. She's coming to L.A. to do some more photo work with Sukie. She's a guest speaker at some huge women's conference this weekend."

"She's already here. She was here."

"What do you mean?"

"There's no easy way to say this, Laurs. She's dead. She was killed."

"What?"

"Rumors are already flying. Not sure if it was crazy L.A. locals or her own government. Word got out quick about our article. Maybe to the wrong people."

Geoff reached into his linen shirt pocket and pulled out a package of mini-tissues, prepared for my emotions to gush the tears that would stream down my cheeks in two rivers.

I shook my head. "We don't know that. It's L.A. Anybody could have done it. A robber. A doper. Anybody."

"It looks personal. That's all I've learned. She was knifed eighteen times. The detective I spoke with said that ranks it up there as a likely crime of passion."

"Why am I just hearing of this now?"

"Because I stepped in. I wanted to be the one to tell you."

My throat felt lined with something the thickness of creosote. "But she doesn't know anybody in this city." I pulled at another tissue only to blacken it with streaming mascara. "Geoff. Oh, no, Geoff. Are you saying our story killed her?" I finally managed.

The chiming music from the carousel became distorted. The display of bright lights became dizzying.

"A crime of passion means someone probably knew her, Laurs. And if not, it was a bad society that killed Dhurra. She knew what she was doing. Taking risks. In the long run, by her talking to us, maybe she knew she could save more lives than she could have, ever, in any medical practice.

"Listen to me, Laurs. A man can kill a woman there for dishonoring him. Any time. Any place. Any reason he wants."

"But she was on American soil. We should have protected her."

Death's putrid orifice once again came to stare me in the face. But this time I'd bargained with it. And I'd lost.

"She had no family. Her husband is dead. No children," I offered Geoff.

Our wooden chariot glided up and down the slick brass poles. Relentlessly our Clydesdales pushed on, in circles, trying to reach to our unattainable destination.

"God, Geoff. I thought we were helping her. I thought our article would—"

"Would what?" Geoff broke in. "Change the world? C'mon, Babe. Hang in here with me."

"The thing is Dhurra loved her life. She was allowed to practice some medicine and medicine was her life."

"Operative words there. *Allowed.* And *some.* Dhurra couldn't travel without a male escort. She couldn't vote. She had no rights. Hell, she couldn't even show off her beautiful face in public!

"All we did was let her tell her story, the way she wanted it to be told."

Tears continued to stream down my face as our dear Clydesdales came to a rest. Geoff took over in an unexpected display of manhood, signaling the ticket boy to leave us alone for another ride on my chariot of gold.

The music cranked up again as our horses lifted their muscular bodies into mid-air. A spray of salty ocean water comforted my dry throat. A pesky gull honed in on my caramel corn but I was in no mood to share it.

I worried that I would have to postpone any plans to go to Tucson.

Geoff worried for me, for my friends, and for the future of *CoverBoy.* With an ashen face defying his black skin he told me now was the time to use the Voodoo potion.

Chapter Thirty-One
Friends & Foes

I ANTICIPATED A CALL from Brock. I didn't expect his phone etiquette.

"You need your friends right now, Lauren, and what the hell do you do? You blow us off!"

"You're compounding my morning headache and interfering with my ritual of experiencing pain."

"Damn it. Damn you. Turn it over. Turn it over to God, or Buddha, or Mother Earth. Hell, I don't care if you turn it over to Casper the Ghost. Just don't turn anything over to that creep of a so called doctor."

I shuffled in the seat of my Porsche, searching for comfort while at a complete stop on the 405 freeway. "Let me do it my way, Brock."

"Wheres that sweet little innocent girl I met in grade school?"

"I thought you only remembered the bad girls."

He continued pounding me with words. "What was her name? A cute kid with flaming red hair, green sparkling eyes, and even some freckles. "I'll tell you. Her name was Lauren Grace Visconti. She trusted everyone, including herself. She had no fears."

"She also had yet to learn about the Lauren Visconti Curse," I said.

"You're making choices here."

"I didn't choose to be the product of rape."

"Listen to me. You are a child of the universe. Innocent. Growing. Living and loving. People die. Death is a reality in life. But what you've gone and done is given your heart and soul to it. Just think if you could cast out all that hurt and fear and turn it back over to the universe. I guarantee you there'd be more room in your heart. Your mom's spirit never left you. She's right there along with your dad and your fiancé, but you have your soul so cluttered up with angst they can't reach you. They can't reside inside you."

"A woman is dead, Brock. Yet another woman I loved."

"It's your decision, Laurs. There are a whole lot of us walking and living and breathing, and we want to love you but there's no room inside."

FEAR IS NOT MY FRIEND. It can feel shaky or it can immobilize. It can be butterflies in your stomach or jagged slabs of concrete.

I knew a man waited for me inside my office. I knew why he waited. My first clue was his name was Wray. Detective Tom Wray.

The press hovered all over it like blowflies on fresh kill. Pretty much *CoverBoy* and Lauren Visconti were that kill. Only I could handle my own state of vengeful autolysis without their help, thank you very much.

Runway model slaughtered. Stabbed to death. Was it self-destruction? She allowed herself to be doped-up on cocaine and various other pleasures and was a target for the taking. *CoverBoy* ran the story.

Dr. A. D. 'Dhurra' Sulayman. From Afghanistan. A promising female physician. Murdered. Stabbed eighteen times.

An atrocious coincidence. A nightmare, but a coincidence.

Or maybe the detective was here about Payton. Of course!

I took one last deep breath, exhaled both butterflies and concrete, and moved my stiffened body toward the closed door.

Detective Wray introduced himself. For every way the joints in my body felt like they were made of shattered crab shells, Wray exuded Jello. Pudding, maybe. Chocolate pudding. African American. Nice looking. Dressed well. He could have been one of my star models except for the keloid scar running thick across his face from his left ear to his lip.

He caught my stare.

"I could have the scar removed, you know. Chances are it would come back. And plastic surgery is not my thing. Going under the knife scares me to death."

No longer butterflies in my stomach, the blowflies were gaining weight as they ate away at me. Had Detective Tom Wray heard about my latest issue? It was at the presses. He couldn't have seen the article on plastic surgeons. Exposed. I didn't withhold a single shot at the doctors. Sukie's camera lenses captured the likes of the Cat Woman. The Barbie Doll. And then she turned to the surgeons, themselves. Some of the more narcissistic ones even posed for her camera, *almost* as Helm's had suggested. Almost naked. It was a killer issue.

So much for introductions. I didn't need to say a word. I couldn't say a word. I motioned to the deep-seating sofas opposite my desk.

I could relax. Or at least fake it real good.

I brought two glasses of water over to the table that would serve as crystal armor between us. A Feng Shui thing. He watched.

"How can I help you?" Did he hear the nervousness in my voice as I did?

"I won't take up much time, Ms. Visconti. Get right to the point. That's what we both need to do. But I'm trying to be the peacemaker here, if it matters to you."

He was not irenic. Peace did not exude from the man. In fact, it was exactly as I knew our meeting would play out as he challenged every word I said with an arrogant half-smile. What I didn't expect was for him to splay across my beautiful table the photographs of my runway model and Dhurra, both sliced into pieces and lying in pools of blood, with only the bones to still held them together.

My naïve runway model. My brave Dhurra. So many gashes across their magnificent bodies. I looked away, one moment from nearly barfing down my blouse or voiding on my skirt.

Wray didn't wince. The barrage of questions commenced without pause.

"Do you have any idea why these two women would be murdered? You see, as far as I can tell they share only one thing in common and that would be you. You know I have to ask."

I didn't know. I didn't say a word.

"Do you have any enemies, Ms. Visconti?"

Nothing. I had nothing.

"Come on. Give me something. You aren't a tabloid. I know that. Me, myself? I respect your work. I like it. You're doing good things. But your magazine may not settle in right with some folks.

"Ma'am?"

"Please call me Lauren. And yes. My magazine has and does evoke emotion. Mostly it's positive. But, yes, we have our share of those who grow agitated with our stories. We stand by them. Every word. Every photograph. *CoverBoy* is no tabloid and far from it. And we sure as hell are no *WikiLeaks*. What we print is common knowledge if anyone would take the time to look and read and learn."

His curled graying eyebrows arched. "If you don't mind me saying, you sound like that's a statement you've prepared for the press."

"Maybe it's a little canned, Detective, but it's the truth. It's not like this news isn't preying on me. I'm deeply saddened."

"Have you received any hate mail?"

"Even bloggers receive hate mail."

"I take that as a yes."

"I repeat, we get far more support."

"But, what? What aren't you telling me, Ms. Lauren?"

I closed my eyes. They sealed up with Super Glue. I didn't want to talk. Damn me. And damn him!

Detective Wray waited in silence. Did he feel my guilty conscience? You see, I felt my guilt. I, via an instrument I called *CoverBoy*, exposed real facts. Bad facts.

How I wished I could make this visit about Payton. How I wished he would have said he somehow got involved and was there to tell me I was right. No suicide. They had found the monstrous thing that had gunned down my beloved friend in her own home.

I returned to silence. Dead silence.

Chapter Thirty-Two
Under the Knife

DETECTIVE WRAY HAD my full attention. The thing about his keloid scar. The plastic surgeon. The stabbings. I got it. Maybe more so than I wanted.

The next issue was at the presses. I loved it. And maybe I would come to hate it.

We took the stories in-depth.

One of Beverly Hill's finest surgeons had seventeen patients who had all endured at least eleven surgeries. And we did our research. They all walked through his door, first time, as the most near perfection of beautiful womanhood. It's not as if they were going through a series of surgeries to correct a birth defect or a trauma to the physical body.

Maybe they weren't made for the cover of *Vogue*, or *Cosmo*, or the likes, but they refused to believe they were nothing less than imperfection at God's wicked wrath. They didn't understand that Photoshop and the body-parts stores were used for all the pretty movies, glossies, and advertisements.

I had already shed more light on the plight of anorexia, bulimia, and cocaine as part of the runway model story. This was different. This was surgery. I included my personal recount of a friend whose mother had taken her to New York as a getaway-shopping excursion. The daughter took an early flight home, disgusted that she couldn't fit into the clothes she so desperately wanted, while her mother stood at her side begging that a larger size would be fine. The daughter scheduled a tummy tuck for the following week. She died on the operating table.

And then there was that little ugly story about re-virgination.

Chapter Thirty-Three
A Simple Sanctuary

THE BRASS KEY TURNED the inner chamber and the cylinder clicked open. Harlan Coal took a quick look over his shoulder and, seeing no one, slipped through the door that would automatically close and relock. He crossed the first narrow chamber lined with files and shelves stuffed with DVDs and books. With a second key he unlocked another door.

"Ah, Armand!" Coal said. "You've found your way into my soul."

"Not a place I really want to reside," Armand answered.

The steaks sizzled on the Viking grille. A state-of-the-art exhaust system purified the air, removing any tale-tell aroma of a carnivore's delight. It eliminated tobacco smoke, too. Or any other odd scents that might occasionally permeate the air.

"The girl. Visconti. I think you've got the wrong mark this time," Armand said. He lit a cigarette and passed it over to Coal's generous lips.

"She's a fucking gold mine. I've been planning this one for years."

"She doesn't fit your profile. The profile you've crammed down my throat for ten years. She's smarter than you, and as independent as you. She isn't going to fall for your polarized mentality shit. And lonely? She knows way too many people."

"Her friends are all our marks. And Visconti fits my profile just fine. She's going through a difficult time. Her entire life has been a nightmare, at least so she thinks. She's beautiful, sexy, and she's fucking A-Bubba loaded. That makes her perfect. I have great plans for her."

"She's trouble."

"Don't insult me, Armand. Just cook me my goddamned steak."

Coal sucked on his cigarette, putting it out just as the rare steak arrived at his table. He devoured the beef between sips of the Krug cabernet.

Armand cleared the plates, then followed Coal to the living area. He cut out four perfect lines of white powder across the shiny stainless steel cocktail table.

"We've got a problem with the Carly Posh home," Armand said. "Her bug's not working. That's one more bad omen in this whole Visconti deal."

"I'll be the only omen around here. Send someone in when she's not there. How hard can that be?"

"That's the problem. She doesn't leave the house."

"Bullshit. She goes to work. She attends our sessions. And you make goddamn sure she never sees you! In fact, you and all the boys. You need to stay the hell away from here."

"You're not paying attention. She's not working, or if she does, she's in and out with no schedule and we can't rely on the time we'll need. And she hasn't been at the last several rallies."

Coal laughed from somewhere deep within his looming skeleton. "I get it. I think we have a case of good old female jealousy. That's all. She introduces me to Visconti and now she regrets the attention I'm giving her. I planned on this. I'll take care of it in the morning."

Coal left the living room, crossing to another open section of the capacious floor plan. Two locked doors afforded him all the privacy he needed. Here, within the confines of his sanctuary, walls were limited. He entered the master bedroom space. With a single remote control, the first button operated the tin ceiling tiles which would slide to reveal a bank of mirrors above the bed. The second button opened up the Velux skylights that flanked each side of the mirroring. There were no windows on any of the outside walls so the skylights provided a welcome relief of fresh air against a starry night, but only after the exhaust system had expunged any trace of the grilled steak and cigarette smoke.

A series of buttons cranked up the sound system. Limp Bizkit screamed their songs of obscenity. With a couple more buttons, the lights dimmed and the bath began to fill with a flat gush of water that swished into the huge black marble basin like a mountainous Alps waterfall. The final button confirmed all doors were secure; the monitor would alert them if anyone was within ten feet of the first door. After all, Dr. Coal had an open door policy.

Coal rolled the nightstand drawer open and tossed the remote control into it. Next to where it tumbled lay the almost empty bottle of Rohypnol. His favorite drug of choice. The roofies would remove any trace of memory or flashbacks that might linger in the fog of his young boys doped-up brains.

Coal spoke with the low pitch of a finely tuned base guitar on steroid amplifiers, "Lauren Visconti will succumb to my mystical pipeline. I am the one that speaks a truth that will resonate with her and turn her into my favorite little ant. Not on the farm, of course. I'll be buying her soul, but she's the one paying."

Armand heard and answered. "I like that Carly cunt. I bet she's a real bed thrasher."

119

Chapter Thirty-Four
Inconvenient Lives

MY PHONE RANG AT daybreak. With my shutters open, the sun cast a faint glow through the dismal bank of fog along the shoreline. I switched on my nightstand lamp in order to help wake my conscious mind. I read, *Caller ID. Italy.*

"Mr. Helms, how kind of you to phone me back."

"I've been called far worse than that, but call me Jack. I'm getting back to you about the kid. The missing kid," he said.

"Payton's younger brother. Mike Doukas."

I rubbed my eyes, but rather than the relief that comes with eight hours of sleep, they scratched as if I'd been on the beach in a windstorm.

"The last viable information on him, according to my guys, is a street address in New York. A flop-house of the worst kind."

"The thing is this address is old." Helms apologized. "About 800,000 children go missing each year, Lauren. You have runaways and parents that don't give a damn. It's a bad mix. You've got kids that don't want to be found and in some cases don't deserve to be. And you've got family secrets."

"What kind of family secrets?"

"One in five girls and one in ten boys are sexually molested, most often by a family member. And of those, you're lucky to get one in three to talk about it. It's sorry statistics."

That didn't fit Payton's family. No way. Not that I could imagine. But then again, the words were *family secrets*.

"Anything else I should know, Jack?"

"One more problem. If you do come up with hard evidence that indicates a death, that's a whole different ballgame. The kids wind up in pauper's graves, squeezed together and stacked on top of each other. It's a real mess trying to unearth them."

"Exhumation?"

"Tough to get a court order, probably because it costs so much. They're jammed in so tight and so deep there's no telling who the lucky sonuva bitch is that's on the top. And I doubt they know who's on the bottom since they didn't know who they were in the first place."

Payton always had faith that Mike was still alive. Maybe she learned some piece of truth and the acceptance that he was gone was what did her in. New York? My god. None of us thought to look east of the Mississippi. "You said New York was the last official address on him. What else is unofficial?"

"Tucson."

Did that make sense? Maybe he didn't contact Payton but he wanted to be near her?

"I'm not done. One of my guys found a street kid hyped up on meth so don't take it as gospel, but he saw the picture of your kid and said he left Tucson to head to the west coast. Something about working the land."

I wrote down the old New York address Helms provided and thanked him for the information.

"You're still in Italy?"

"For a few more weeks. Why don't you come over and report on that story I'm scooping out for my documentary.

The way some men still treat their women like shit over here."

"Think I'll have to pass for now."

"How about the cheese. Showing more cheese?"

"Gouda or smoked havarti?"

"You know exactly what I mean. Skin."

I hung up, wondering who would prove to be the real villain, if we were ever to investigate the Italy story. In describing discrimination in Italy, Jack Helm's had just used the words *their women.*

Chapter Thirty-Five
A Simple Meal

MY STEPS SLOWED as I entered the lobby of The Centre. I felt bathed in an inexplicable abundance of love. Protection. Hope.

While true I hadn't returned Dr. Coal's phone calls for weeks, I had read a few of his many published works. I'd gone to sleep with his books for as many nights.

Dr. Coal sat on the floor of his office with two young boys in front of him. He motioned me in as the boys scrambled up and disappeared behind me.

"I'm sorry. I didn't mean to interrupt," I said.

"No way. Those kiddos were just getting ready to give up on me. They wanted movie money and they realized they weren't getting it from me."

I remembered the play equipment on the grounds. I'd never seen a single child there. But I guess these boys were too old to play on swings and slides.

He laughed and at once I felt at home, but just as I began to sit on the floor next to him, a seating style I thought I might enjoy in my more comfortable attire, Coal stood up.

"Have you had lunch?"

"No. I hadn't really thought about it."

"Come, then."

For a swift moment I regretted the offer because as his protocol had suggested, I wore sweats. Designer sweats, mind you, but sweats nonetheless. Nothing suitable for a lunch date.

Oh god, I thought. *A date?* That wasn't it at all. I had to get that idea out of my mind.

"My assistant has prepared lunch and he always makes enough to feed the entire Pacific Rim."

"Assistant?" I wondered if the offer of lunch signaled there would be no private session with me. I *worried* that it might.

"You've not met him? Sorry, I thought everyone around here knew Armand. Sent to me straight from the heavens. He's my right-hand man. He takes care of me and he takes care of the business part of The Centre. The financial stuff that drags me down, to be honest. He takes the load off me so I am not polluted with the physical world and that helps me stay in the spiritual world I much prefer."

We hadn't discussed this spiritual side of him although I sensed it was deeply rooted. His philosophies revealed themselves slowly in the context of his numerous published discourses. His teachings evoked the aura of the 'good journey,' whatever that meant.

I realized we had crossed another path. A physical one that led directly to his private home. Butterflies again emerged in my stomach, but these were born out of ancient cocoons that hadn't been disturbed in years. A man of mystery always got the best of me.

A screen door served as the only barrier to the large building.

"A minimalist?" I teased.

Harlan roared with laughter, "Well, I do have a real table and real chairs to take meals upon."

The space was quite similar to his office. Dhurrie rugs, pillows, and a single futon in the corner. The only luxuries appeared to be a wall of leather-bound books and dozens of lit white candles atop patina-aged brass that formed an altar of sorts.

In an obscure corner, a man stood behind a kitchenette, slicing avocados and tomatoes still on the vine. I could see the garden of edibles more clearly than the man, and I could smell a simmering soup. Rosemary and lemon. As for the man, all I could see was a long and braided black ponytail.

Dr. Coal set the table for two, along with a soup tureen and platter of avocado-topped bread slices. He excused Armand for his immediate absence. "He had another engagement. You'll meet him another time."

We dined in silence for an excruciating time. For me. Dr. Coal seemed as if he was oblivious to me and more focused on inhaling the distinct aromas. I liked that. He appreciated excellence in simplicity.

"All fresh ingredients," he finally said.

I kept glancing at the wall next to us. It was solid rock and an odd interior material for California, I thought. A large teak door in the middle of the wall closed off what had to be the bulk of the massive building.

"It's our Hall of Records," Coal said, as if reading my curious mind.

"What do you mean? A library?"

He laughed. "Yes. A massive library. Our central nervous system, remember?"

"May I see it?"

"No. No one sees it."

My eyes swept to the floor in embarrassment. "I'm sorry. That was presumptuous of me. I guess it's my journalistic nature."

"I find your inquisitiveness to be adorable. Now, then, do you mind if I do some of my doctoring, even over lunch?" he continued. "It's hard for me to disengage from my patient relationship with you."

I felt relief shimmy down my shoulders to my spine and maybe somewhere below that. "Sure."

"Our brief discussions have already shown progress. They're open. I like that. You know you are on a path and I hope you agree it's a healthy path. We've certainly managed to analyze your life's crisis points. You've made some new decisions which include not wanting to continue doing the same things which result in the same outcomes. Now it's time to move on. It's time to fill up the void we've created."

"Void?" I felt great. Coal made me feel great. I didn't suffer a void for the first time in years.

"You've rejected old values. Old dogmas. You're giving up a past belief system that everything you love is taken away in death. This is huge. But you've created a void. You're starting to take away all that bad and you need to fill it up with goodness."

"I don't understand," I admitted while remembering something similar Brock had told me.

"Take this home with you," Coal said as he handed me a thick booklet from the side of his dining chair. "It's a paper I wrote last week and you are the inspiration."

He must have seen me cower.

"Don't worry. It has nothing to do with Lauren Visconti. But somehow after our first meeting you made me realize it's relevant now, more than ever, and it was time for me to put my thoughts into writing."

"It isn't exactly light reading, is it?" I laughed as I accepted the huge document.

He did not return a smile. "It explains our therapy practice in detail. I only wish you could live here at The Centre, but of course that won't work. This will give you a booster shot into a new world."

"I'll read it this week. I promise."

"Yes. You will.

"And come to our gathering dinner this month. We're having a special celebration. You'll enjoy yourself. One of my patients works at a nature preserve where they treat injured gulls. We have the honor of releasing the healed ones. And it's the fall harvest. You won't walk away hungry. Not in your stomach and not in your soul."

Dr. Coal made me smile.

"That's new. I haven't seen that before," he said.

"What?"

"A full smile. Natural and unforced. You wear it well."

I admit I think I felt some sexual tension. Maybe I was just getting my act together. Finally. Dr. Coal was helping me. I thanked him for the impromptu lunch.

Coal called out after me as I left. "Hey, Lauren, I like the sweats!"

Chapter Thirty-Six
The Farm

SIXTY-FIVE ACRES, and the blaring horn sounded throughout all corners. It signaled roundup time.

Workers dropped their tools, along with all conversation. They collected what bushels they had already gathered and placed them into the giant bins located on every four rows of crop. They then proceeded to flood toward the farmhouse and the platform in front of it. All of them.

Dr. Coal stood before his people in the grandeur of pure white linen. The long sleeves, the hem of his tunic, and the flowing pants all swayed in the gentle breeze. The image projected a mortal man engulfed in gliding white doves. His dark sunglasses protected him from their sins, as he often reminded them.

A mere hand direction by Dr. Coal and his audience praised the gathering with a resounding and unanimous, "Yes!"

Coal sat down. His followers immediately bowed their heads. No murmurs could be heard. No shuffling of shoes. Only silence. Even the birds and the winds seemed to respect the need for a calm quiet.

"I am happy today. Our fellowmen, Abraham and Juan fell ill. It was God's will. They cheated God. They cheated all of us. They did not provide their tithing. They stole our food and we were hungry. They rested even as we worked. They were weak. They had fallen, but they came to recognize their sins and they paid their penance. They are healed.

"I have promised you healing. All the medical care you need you can find right here with me.

"There shall be no thievery amongst you. No sins of the human flesh, the mind, or the spirit.

"Some of you may think to defy my laws. Think again, for these are not my laws. They are the laws of your soul and your very being. Therefore they are God's laws. Think how we could heal the aching world if only they knew our secrets. You are blessed. I am blessed and I bless you."

Designated helpers began the ritual of chanting.

"Bring forth your tithing and your weary bodies from an honest day of work and you shall save yourself from the destruction of this earth."

Coal rose from his chair. The chanting subsided and heads were bowed once again.

Coal disappeared behind the veil of white stage draping.

Chapter Thirty-Seven
The Centre Gathering

AFTER NAGGING, BROCK finally agreed to go to The Centre for their Saturday night feast.

We toured the grounds, now decorated with white tablecloths and chairs and tables laden down with colorful edibles. Blooms from plentiful scalloped gardens competed with the scents of baked goods to enchant the evening air.

Dr. Coal appeared from behind a draped-off cabana, the kind you might find at the beach resorts. Our eyes immediately met, except for his sunglasses that shielded his. He pulled the curtains closed again and headed toward me with an elegant gait, like a Triple Crown champion horse might prance to enter the gate for yet another victory.

Again, I thought he reminded me of someone.

After a long embrace he said, "I hoped you would join us tonight."

A mass of people had congregated on the lawns at The Centre. Instantly I noticed they all wore jeans and a similar type of denim shirt. While I was smart enough not to wear heels knowing I would be traversing the lawns, everything else about my attire screamed inappropriateness. My white dress was short and cut to fit every curve.

"I guess I overdressed," I said.

"Don't be ridiculous. You are a breath of fresh air. Besides, we look like a couple," he laughed, raising his arms so the breeze could catch the sleeves of his white tunic.

Brock stepped forward, ensuring his presence didn't go unnoticed.

"Dr. Coal, this is my friend, Brock Townsend. Brock, this is Dr. Coal," I said.

"Oh, yes, the baseball giant," Coal said. "Good to have you here, Slugger."

Only I could detect the hairs rising on the back of his neck, but Brock made nice. Sort of.

"The name Slugger is usually reserved for batters, but I guess you don't know much about professional sports."

"You'll excuse me," Coal said, and slipped away.

"Tell me again why you dragged me to this thing," Brock mumbled as he sifted through the crudités.

"Because all my good friends are busy," I answered.

"Thanks. Two insults in less than three minutes. Doesn't Carly live here?"

"She has a place here, yes."

"A place?"

"She still has her home in Bel Air. She just prefers to live here for now."

"I thought you told me this was a family picnic thing," Brock said.

"Sure."

"Well, excuse me for noticing, but where exactly are all the kids?"

Without wasting any time, Brock signaled me to follow him to the main food line, ever the athlete with the hearty appetite to match. Colorful bowls lined the first table with assorted fruits—plantains, blackberries, and papayas. Another table offered corn, snap peas, broccoli and cauliflower. The third displayed baskets of cracked wheat and pumpernickel bread, pitas, and tortillas, and a huge wooden bowl of pecans. Brock looked on to the last table, offering large apple pies and cakes.

"I hoped maybe we could get caught up with one another over a decent meal," Brock said.

"What's wrong with this meal?" I asked.

"It's weird, Laurs. If anything, high-protein diets are still hot, but there is barely a trace of protein laid out here. Not exactly a health cult," he roared.

"Is there a problem here?" a woman cutting pies overheard Brock's complaint. The six-footer backed away from the table.

"No problem," he said. Brock took my arm with his free hand and escorted me away.

I looked at the trays of drinks being served. Carrot and orange juices. No wine.

"See what I mean?" Brock whispered. "Something's definitely weird around here."

"You're just used to being around athletes and their stinky cafeterias and swanky groupie-filled bars. And you need more protein in your diet than most people."

"People need protein to *think*," Brock grumbled. He picked at the food on his paper plate before tossing it into a nearby trashcan.

We walked around the grounds a bit more while waiting for the release of twelve injured birds that The Centre community had rehabilitated. I kept trying to spy Carly in the crowd, but no luck.

We passed Coal's house. The screen door was closed but we could see a man dressed in black standing erect just inside and looking back at us. I smiled at the man, but what he returned to me was something more like what you'd expect from the Royal Guards at Buckingham Palace. Not exactly congeniality. I thought I caught a glimpse of a long black ponytail. I wasn't certain.

"What's in there?" Brock asked.

"The director's residence is in the front. A records room of some sort is behind it."

"You mean it's Dr. Coal's house?"

"Yes."

Brock smirked.

From our position, both of us could see the small space dedicated to the living quarters and the stone wall that sealed off the rest of the building. The man with the ponytail was gone.

"Must be some kind of hall of records," Brock said. "I don't want to spoil things, Lauren, but this place gives me the creeps. I can handle being called 'Slugger,' but not from a slug. He appears to be some shepherd of mental health but it looks more like mind control to me. Let me take you back to Malibu.

"Idiot," he continued to mumble. "Batters are sluggers."

The flap of strong wings and short screeches of freedom sang out from behind us as the birdcages opened. The once-injured gulls swept across the grounds, each one guided by instincts to fly west toward their beloved ocean.

It was hotter than hell in the city. The beach would be much cooler. I was annoyed at Brock's ignorance about The Centre, but I was also tired of squabbling with him. And Dr. Coal had disappeared, anyway.

Brock clutched my arm again to take me back to Malibu.

I kept thinking about the odd familiarity I felt when seeing Dr. Coal. Something. And the man with the braided ponytail.

And then I decided I liked a good mystery.

Chapter Thirty-Eight
A Brother, Bullshit, & Braids

BROCK MADE HIMSELF at home, opening my refrigerator in search of protein. Not thrilled to find it almost empty, he finally settled on a slightly aged package of sliced roast beef and my specialty—moldy cheese. I filled the wine glasses, knowing he'd like some of his protein from alcohol.

Brock had been enjoying his best season ever. I didn't know much about baseball but I loved to hear him talk about his passion. His true and only passion. Brock's eyes lit up like a seventeen-arm candelabra when he got any chance to jabber about his favorite subject.

I didn't have to say much about *CoverBoy*. He subscribed. He bought extra copies before he boarded the team plane. I hadn't told him much about any hint of trouble. He knew the deal. Hate mail arm-and-arm with accolades from readers. Surely he received the same type of reactions from his fans when he was playing a game.

After he devoured the meat and the glass of wine, we headed down to the beach. Immediately, a sociable Golden Retriever indicated he was up for a game of fetch and my baseball hero sure knew how to pitch. Brock spied a suitable stick and the game began.

We moved down the beach with each throw of the stick. Sometimes Brock complained about his shoulder, but only when he wasn't throwing something. He proved to be a worthy companion to the dog who wanted to run and retrieve relentlessly.

We walked along the shoreline, four houses beyond mine. Brock paid scant notice, but an Italian aria was playing from somewhere inside the home. I knew the piece, *Tre Giorni.* My father had played it often. The tune intrigued me, probably because of my father's love of it. While Brock and the retriever continued their mission to outlast one another, I moved closer to the home and the music.

The man sitting on the patio was speaking on the phone. Yelling on the phone. He looked up, saw me, then rushed inside his house. The door was slammed shut and the curtains drawn.

"What is it?" Brock asked. "You've stopped dead in your tracks and now you're shaking."

I hadn't realized it. I took a deep breath of the cool and damp night air. "I just thought I recognized a man that was sitting out on that deck." *Or maybe it was I thought he recognized me.*

"Some movie star?"

"Just some guy that looked like the man we saw at Dr. Coal's house. Dressed in black and same demeanor. That's all." *With a ponytail.*

"Let's get you back to the house. You need a wrap. I'll make a fire."

There's never any real privacy on the beach. In spite of the laws that dictate the beaches are public, Malibu real estate-owners with beachfront properties fight for privacy. There *is* an unspoken tenet in beach etiquette that calls for spatial distancing. Maybe I was the one breaking the rules and this man I had seen felt his space had been invaded.

The dog seemed to comprehend the game was over. He tossed his head back and forth and ran off in the opposite direction. I hoped it was toward his home.

"You know I'm the poster boy for good behavior when I'm playing, but I'm a born rule-breaker," Brock said. "Let's finish that bottle of wine of yours."

As we walked toward my house Brock said, "How's Sterling doing?"

"I was going to ask you the same question. I haven't seen her since the infamous dinner party at Gabri's. I believe she was your date."

I controlled the pout in my voice but it did little to abate the humiliation and hurt emanating from my body language.

"That is weird!"

"Brock, if you say *weird* one more time, I'll—"

"You'll what?" He put his gentle and firm arm around my waist and cinched me toward him.

I shrugged, almost caving into the stealth shield of his body, but I kept on walking with a straight gait.

"I mean it, Laurs. I thought the two of you had conspired against me because she hasn't returned my calls."

The hurt intensified. So, he'd been calling her. I stepped outside of his reach. "I guess you're not quite the catch you think you are."

He changed the subject. Too easily. "How's Gabri?"

"I haven't heard much. She's keeping a low profile after news of her dinner party made the rounds. She still thinks you're mad at her for blowing some real estate deals."

"She'd be damn right. It was a few flips. Quick flips. I'd buy distressed properties, have some guys fix them up, and sell them. She wasn't paying attention. The woman lost me some big money."

I watched his pulse grow faster with flinched indentions at his temples. His gait stiffened and he walked with urgency.

"She thinks you might have been mad enough to commission that painting of her, then have the gall to be her guest when it was presented to her."

He turned to me, "For the record, I wasn't there when she opened up that damn thing."

"So? Did you do it?"

"Is that what you think?"

"I can tell you're mad."

"Mad as hell. But it's only money. Now I might have commissioned that painting if I'd had the time to dream up such a scheme, but I'm a gentleman. I'd never be her guest, eat her food, and drink her wine, only to let her open that piece of atrocious shit."

"I know," I said as we neared the stairs that led to my deck. "I know you better than that. I've seen you rescue a chinch bug from your kitchen floor and deposit it outside rather than just step on it."

"That's not to say Gabri's any better than a chinch bug."

He made it sound like a joke. A sick joke. Brock was mad. Mad as hell.

He pecked me on the cheek and called it a night. A big brother thing. No friendly benefits.

As he pulled out of my driveway I noticed a black convertible Corvette pull down the street. The driver had a long black braid.

Chapter Thirty-Nine
Skeletons

CARLY CALLED TO SUGGEST a cocktail hour. I finally concurred. Per usual, Sterling ran late.

We sat at a window table at the crowded restaurant, Insolence, where sandwiches were pricey and the caviar—the priciest in town. A show-me-the-money kind of pick-up place. The waiter summed us up. He might as well have said what was on his mind. Show me your bank account register before you order.

I guess we passed his scrutiny although it crossed my mind Sterling would have helped if she had arrived on time and oozing in her *bibelots du jour*. We ordered two Stolis.

"I'm still in awe of your design work at my beach house," I told Carly.

"I'm glad." Her words—laconic.

"No, really! You're an incredible talent."

She scowled and pretended to look at the menu.

"What's wrong?" I asked.

"For starters, I'm bored to tears."

"How can you be bored? You're booked out six months in advance."

"I truly enjoyed doing your house, Lauren, but most of my projects suck."

"Not fun anymore?"

"Anymore? My entire career has been about prying painters off the ceiling because they show up to work high on god knows what. I have to deal with damaged or late shipments. Do you know last month I finally had time to sit down and read the morning newspaper with a cup of coffee? The words popped off the front page of the business section. A barge sunk in the middle of the fucking Atlantic. And guess whose furniture was on it? My biggest and most loud-mouthed client. And take one guess as to whose fault it was? *Mine.*"

"Not as glamorous a business world as it sounds, huh?"

She rolled her eyes and said, "If I have to place one more Barcelona chair on a slab of white travertine in a house that looks like an abandoned igloo I'm going to puke."

Her eyes diverted to some place far away. I knew the look.

"You already have a plan, don't you?"

Carly giggled. She never giggles but with a mischievous and feisty guttural resonance from deep within her larynx. "It's going to take some time, Laurs, but I want to open an antique store. A big antique store. I'm going to have the best of the best in furniture, art and collectibles, even architectural obscurities. Hell, I may even throw in some old cars."

"Wow. You've thought this through. So what's stopping you?"

"Capital. And before you ask, I'm not looking for investors or loans. It's going to be all mine or nothing."

I didn't have to ask. Carly was the most stoic and proud woman I knew. She would never accept monetary help. Never.

"What about the equity in the Bel Air home?"

139

"Not available." Her answer was curt. Off limits to further discussion.

A glistening light walked toward our table. *Sterling.* We hadn't been together, the three of us, since our failed and dismal trip to Tucson.

"Sorry I'm late," Sterling's voice roared above the noisy gathering spot. "I had a massage at Calm and got stuck with some Russian masseuse. She was belching up more vodka than they have lined up on the shelves in this place."

Sterling got the attention of the waiter along with every patron in the place, and ordered a drink.

"First time we've been together since we did it!" Sterling said. She lifted her lanky but curved leg up to the table and showed off the friendship tattoo. We all succumbed to the impulse of staining on our ankles.

"And I can't stay long. I have a date with a hunk."

"A name we should know?" Carly asked.

"Yeah. Hunk!"

"A professional athlete?" I asked.

"I have no idea. It's a blind date. Why?"

"They seem to be your type," I said, probably laced with sarcasm.

"If they have money, an Adonis body, and a penis, they're my type." She quickly added, "Hair is a bonus. I like hair."

"But in the right places," Carly added.

Sterling scowled at us mockingly. "Don't be snippy. I have some information you'll want to hear."

"You're engaged to the Prince of Sheba," Carly said.

"I'm not even sure there is a place called Sheba, but in a tin of cat food. But I am sure about something more important. Skeletons."

"Skeletons?" Carly asked.

I didn't need to ask. I knew immediately it was news about Payton's email to me. Three skeletons.

"Turns out they call the innards of a dead saguaro skeletons. They're ribs. Big thick rib-like wood."

Carly sat speechless.

I fumbled with the words, "You fake a dumb blonde real good, Sterling. How did you find out?"

"Crazy. Something called Google," she smirked. "Believe it or not, I even know how to turn on a computer."

"When we were there, we looked for three tall and very much alive saguaro. Or anything else we saw in threes. But we weren't really looking at the ground. Not for any fallen cacti. So who's on board to go back to Tucson?" I asked.

"Sure," Carly said. "I have nothing better to do than go looking around for three dead cacti in acres of desert."

Lala Corriere

Chapter Forty
Like Duct Tape

I RETURNED TO MY BEACH house. Exhausted but fulfilled. Winning. What I was winning, I hadn't a clue.

Something about the beach always made me feel centered no matter how much frustration I felt toward the world. I guess that's the way most people feel. And why beachfront property is about a million dollars for every lineal foot of ocean frontage.

Mostly when I was feeling too confident, when I thought I was on top of this world, I would return to the beach to have it temper my ego with its omnipotence. The sun had been replaced by a brilliant glow of moonlight and this night it offered me a boost. I felt significant and alive. And very humble.

A wrapped gift package sat by my front door. Usually I would have pulled into the garage but instead I parked on the driveway, grabbed my mail, the iridescent package, and my keys, shoving the gold one into the lock that would permit me into the sanctuary I so badly needed.

The package screamed of Queen Geoff. Rainbow-colored ribbons smothered the neon wrapping paper. I laughed. Out loud. What could Geoff have possibly dropped off as a house warming gift, I wondered. Whatever it was, it would fit into the category of the outrageous.

142

I struggled with my key to fit it into the lock. It wasn't working. I jammed. I twisted. I stuffed it in further, then pulled it out just barely to try and turn the chambers in the lock.

Nothing.

I'd have to pull my car into the garage and enter my house through that door. I heard nothing, my focus so intent on the lock that would not turn.

The black glove slammed across my mouth. Leather. I could smell the leather. My attacker reined me in taut against his body. As my legs buckled with the limpness of a jellyfish, he pulled me up tighter by grabbing onto my hair and yanking my head back closer into his chest. He held me flush against his body. More black leather. That is all I could see, or smell, or feel. My vision spun in circles like a kaleidoscope with broken stained glass. No focus. Just the colors of the rainbow streaming from the pretty gift-wrapped package amid all the blackness.

The monster's other hand barely allowed for my breath. Apparently the only true sense I had left was that of hearing.

"You have no business in Tucson, Bitch. That ship has sailed. You need to disappear off the radar map or let us make that happen for you. You understand?"

I nodded my face up and down under the steel leather-cloaked hands that still bound my mouth like duct tape.

"I'll be leaving a friend to watch out after you. You do as I say and you'll have no problems with any jugular bites."

Chapter Forty-One
Wolf Dog

THE MONSTER DREW BACK in one swift movement. The weight of my body fell free from his massive arms, which caused my knees to buckle and drop to the hard flooring of my front porch. My keys clanked as they scattered across the terrazzo tiles. Out of reach and I didn't care.

His car sped away, so dark and in so much fog I couldn't make out anything but blackness.

His sentry showed up in the same thicket of mist. My intruder had promised me bites to my jugular if I were not to behave myself. The wolf-like creature, black and with demonic red glowing eyes, snarled at me from my porch steps.

Too weak to stand or try and square off with the animal, I managed to pretzel myself into a ball against the door, hiding my face between trembling legs. I had no false sense of security. This was a real threat. This was when I had to face my demons. Unfortunately, my head was lodged between my knees and I didn't think it would come out any time too soon.

Then I saw it. Lodged between my legs was my cell phone. Slowly I reached for it and dialed 911.

Help was on the way. How long? It would be too long, I was certain. I lifted my head and focused on the glint of light. The sliver of the waxing moon's light streamed from the brass umbrella stand Carly had appointed to my front door. I dared to reach out for the object. Being only seven or eight inches away it might as well have been a fathom and the seas between us ran red with blood. I managed to grab the stand by its rim and pull it slowly toward me.

The wolf-dog, for I still cannot believe it was a mere dog, howled with the rage of evil chromosomes. Its fangs, too, glowed in the slight moonlight.

Weighty, I struggled to pull the brass stand near me. I clutched it between my legs, secured my grip on it and heaved it toward the creature, smacking it on its nose. I swear I heard some of those fangs crack. It whimpered and retreated, but I could feel its eyes still fixated on me.

Backing up, I neared the side of my garage and the key pad. Fingers shaking, I pushed in the five digit code to raise the garage door. The creaking noise did little to disarm the creature. His stare grew fiercer. Glistening bloody drool fell from the sides of his mouth to the ground.

There was nothing between us except a garden hose, and his fierce stare told me even a fire hose wouldn't deter his desire for a fresh kill. Instincts told me that I couldn't outrun him. Still, I lifted my feet out of the high heels. I'd stand a better chance barefoot and the spikes on those shoes just became my only weapons of self-defense. I threw one at him. It bounced off his front leg and caused the broad body to flinch.

I glanced around in the garage and spied the bag of golf clubs. I hoped if only I had time to unzip the travel bag I could possibly defend myself with the steel rods.

The animal strode forward. Taking his time. Making me squirm with fear. Stalking me.

I backed up further into the garage and, with two more short steps, I managed to drag the golf bag in front of me as if it would be a buffer from harm. The animal moved five more steps closer. He sounded a predatory call, half-bark and half-howl, and he was now no more than five feet from me. I had another twelve feet behind me to reach the safety of the door.

Thank god I was sloppy when it came to security. I knew that door would be unlocked.

I pulled from memory anything and everything Brock had taught me about pitching baseballs, then hurled the second shoe at the wolf-dog with perfect aim. It smacked him square in the eyes. I knew I had only seconds to unzip the golf bag and pull out the steely weapons.

I had only a split second. The wolf-dog whimpered, shook off the pain like a sheet of warm water, and lunged at me.

Having freed the clubs, I grabbed all that my hands could hold and slung the rods at the animal, then I ran for the door and my very life.

The door slammed shut as the wolf-dog's nose poked through. I thrust my weight against it and recovered my phone. I called Carly. No answer. I called Sterling. Then I called Detective Wray.

It was Sterling that arrived first, even before the police and with twice the miles to travel. And the wolf-dog was nowhere in sight.

While waiting for any authorities Sterling opened the package as I watched. The box fell apart with absolutely nothing inside it except for black tissue paper.

Sirens neared. Sterling rocked me in her arms and we spoke no words.

Chapter Forty-Two
Oh, and By the Way

MY VOICE MUST HAVE sounded like mud to Detective Wray. The Malibu police had all but shouted out their joy when the detective showed up and told them he'd take care of the situation, meaning me. There was no fight over jurisdictions like you see on TV. They sped away.

"I guess there were a few things I didn't tell you the other night, Detective. I just didn't think they mattered at the time."

"I guess there are a few things I didn't tell you the other night, either, Ms. Visconti. Because they hadn't happened."

"You have something to tell me?"

"And always a pleasure to let the lady go first. Maybe you can start with what occurred here tonight."

I recounted what little I knew. The shiny package. The black glove snatching at my face. The hushed, gravelly voice that delivered the warning. The wolf-dog.

"What was in the package?" he asked.

"Nothing. I knew it was lightweight. I remember thinking maybe it was a scarf or something. Sterling opened it. Nothing."

"Figures. A distraction."

"What?"

"You were focused on the gift. Gave the perp opportunity to catch you off-guard."

147

The detective asked me to describe the scene. Any sights. Sounds. Smells. I didn't see anything but the wrapped gift and the black glove. I'd already told him the voice was but a graveled whisper. And the only smell was from the leather glove.

He asked me to relay the man's words. The meat of the threat. The warning to stay away from Tucson. I told him about Payton and her suicide that wasn't a suicide. It *couldn't* be a suicide. "That's what you need to know! That's what I should have told you!" I screamed.

The dismissal that registered in his eyes scared me even more.

"Did he have a weapon?"

"His hands were his weapon. That was good enough for me."

"And the dog. Did you see where it headed off?"

"It was no dog, Detective. It was a wolf. Or something," my voiced trailed and even to me sounded like an old LP on too slow a speed.

"But your attacker threatened you with this animal, right?"

"The creature arrived after the man left. Maybe moments. Maybe minutes. I don't know. It scared the shit out of me, but not for long. I have a way with animals. We'll be sipping champagne from our water bowls together next week."

"Yeah. I can tell that by the dent in that umbrella stand and the spilt blood. You'll be good friends.

"Your situation at the house tonight is grave, Ms. Visconti. Your ability to make light of it is actually a clever skill, as long as you keep your wits about you.

"I suppose most of my superiors would expect me to tell you that right at this moment you're in big trouble. Some of the guys back at the precinct are probably taking pools to see if I bring you in."

The detective paused. Closed his notebook. Stared back into my eyes. "How long have you been in L.A.?"

"You can count my months here by the *CoverBoy* issues we've run, subtracting two months of test and preview issues. From there you can do all the adding and subtracting you want. The truth is I've been here long enough to call it home. And long enough to want to leave."

"Okay. Two issues prior to your arrival in California. Those issues originated in Illinois. Is that correct?"

"Yes. I owned a publishing company there. A travel magazine. It made sense to use my resources in Chicago to launch *CoverBoy*. A test period, if you will. Given the economic times, I found this to be a prudent means of exploration. And one that proved successful." I couldn't believe I could actually speak with so matter-of-factly.

"And did you have any negative ramifications from those two issues?"

I bit my tongue and saw my world twirling. Then I unleashed that tongue. "You mean, was anybody I profiled in those early articles slaughtered?"

Wray didn't play his hand. "More or less."

"No."

"And what were those early articles?"

"I'm certain you've already pulled them up in our archives. One on drug lords. Stale, but we had some new information and a new angle. And my timing was off on the second issue because everyone had already ripped apart certain corrupt Chicago government officials."

"You get a lot of hate mail. You've already told me that. Anything else? Any lawsuits?"

"We keep our legal department plenty busy. But I've been assured it isn't libel if it's the truth. For the record we win our cases, Detective."

"Clever girl. I wonder about that," he said.

Chapter Forty-Three
Tit for Tat

I DIDN'T NEED a roaring fire. I didn't need a glass of wine. I didn't need an Eiderdown pillow to float my worries away.

I'd offered Detective Wray to follow me out to my back deck. Sterling fell behind, pretending to clean my kitchen while assuring me she was within earshot. My kitchen wasn't dirty and Sterling was no maid.

"You said you had something to tell me, Detective Wray. Please. What is it? *Quid pro quo.*"

"That prominent plastic surgeon you wrote about, The Dr. Scars-Away? Dr. Wrinkles away—and the one that left your lady friend dead on his table after a tummy tuck."

"His name is— "

"Hell, I know his name. You might as well have given out his social security number."

"He's a jerk."

"He's a dead jerk. Slashed to death. Thirty-six times."

"So you jump to the conclusion because, again, this upstanding man in our community—his death is somehow related to me?"

"Numbers are games. Games are numbers. You may not even know you're playing this game, Ms. Visconti, but you are, indeed. And the numbers out there are starting to add up.

"You have my attention. But you did tell me that you were no good at math."

"First, you promise not to repeat this. If I hear it on the streets or see it anywhere in print I'll know it came from you. You got that?" he demanded.

I nodded.

"There's a chain of evidence that directly ties these murders together. You are the common denominator."

The nebbish man crossed the threshold and yet I was the insulted one. I also realized I was at the top of his list of suspects. I was a strong link in some horrific chain.

"Lauren, go back with me to one of your first feature articles. The models. In particular, the lovely model that got herself involved in cocaine and god knows what else. We found her passed out and dying in front of a Laundromat. We know she was near a known drug dealer and she liked to chase the dragon. You hearing me?"

"Yes. One of my first articles. Correct."

"She wore some fancy bauble on her finger. I'm told it was a five-carat emerald."

"I know about the ring. Closer to ten carats."

"And we found the ring finger severed. The emerald, gone."

"Actually, it was her index finger. The stone was that big."

The detective managed an uneasy grin. "I'm going to tell you something, and not because I particularly like you or your magazine."

I met his stare. "I thought you liked *CoverBoy*. And I don't think I particularly like you either, Detective," I said.

"The model's ring and her finger were gone long before we got to the crime scene. Eyewitnesses placed it on her finger that night. Not hard to imagine someone chopped off her finger to get at it. That stone would have pretty much paid my mortgage for a year. I would have noticed it.

"Then we have your woman from Afghanistan." He opened up his notepad again, rifling through the first pages.

"Her name is—was, Dhurra. Dhurra Sulayman."

"That's it. Good girl. Well, the first real evidence was that one-of-a-kind emerald ring—the one someone so eagerly carved off your model. It turned up in Dr. Sulayman's throat. Inserted after she was stabbed to death."

I gasped. I felt dizzy in my stomach. The thoughts of the model and of my dear Dhurra. The thought of the wolf-dog. It would have gone after my throat. His mouth hung open with rabid-looking foam drooling down both sides. All he had to do was pounce and snap his powerful jaw closed on my throat.

I only then noticed that I'd kicked off my Pradas and was curled up in a tiny ball again. This time I was on the back deck. With an armed detective. The fear felt the same.

"I'm afraid it gets worse," Wray said. "Do you want to hear it?"

Immediately I regained my posture. My legs went to the floor. For support? My back straightened and again I looked directly into his coal eyes.

"Dhurra Soyl—"

"Sulayman," I said.

"Right. Well, she sustained more injuries than the external slashes."

I fidgeted. He watched me as I tried to be invincible. I hoped he couldn't hear my hammering heart. I sat on my hands to steady the shaking. "Go on," I said.

"Her attacker carved off her, uh, her labia."

I sat up so that my hands could go now go to my forehead. My head sank back between my legs, which were already poised back under my body where my hands had been.

"We found the doctor's privates in your notorious plastic surgeon's throat."

A violent shudder seized me from my hair to my toenails. Shockwaves pulsed through my bones as if they were dense and powerful electrodes.

The detective's relentless words continued, "You see, now. The murders are directly related to one another. And we've known for some time that they are directly related to you."

Chapter Forty-Four
Next Victim, Please

STERLING BROUGHT ME a Bailey's on the rocks. I asked her to stay. Detective Wray's scowl insisted that he speak with me alone.

He told me the time had come for me to discuss Tucson and Payton Doukas, but first he warned me again not to repeat the information he had shared with me on the chain of evidence that linked several murders together. He knotted that chain around both my mouth and my heart.

I told him all that I knew, which wasn't much, but I found it alarmingly easy to be candid. I had nothing to lose this late in the game.

I explained my frustration, more certain than ever that something was very wrong and it started in Tucson. After Payton's death, grief came swiftly. Then the anger. The whys of it all with no reasonable answers. Anger is a much more painless emotion than grief, but when it reaches the precipice of rage the toll is far worse. I was reaching that edge.

And no one was going to threaten me. I wouldn't scare away.

"So this threat tonight, and others before. You think they are about your friend in Tucson?"

"Yes."

"Did you feature her in your magazine?"

"Of course not."

"Was she stabbed?"

"Gunshot."

Detective Wray listened to me with care, making a few notes and more than a few scowls. Finally, when I had nothing more to say, he dropped his notebook into his pocket.

He asked me to show him to the door. His eyes told Sterling not to follow and she behaved.

"I understand you are upset. But from what you've told me, there is no connection between your friend in Tucson and what I have here on my hands."

He thinks they're on his hands?

"You have someone in another state dead by gunshot. You happen to be questioning an entire authority that has ruled the incident—the death, a suicide.

"Now here I am dealing with a slew of stabbings. Multiple stabbings and those, Ms. Visconti, are murders. They're acts of rage. We call them overkill. And those are connected to you."

My hands began to tremble. Nothing made sense to me but that the Lauren Visconti Curse continued.

"Are you saying I'm a suspect, detective?"

"I am saying you're involved, whether you like it or not. And that makes you a person of interest. Why don't you give me a heads-up? What's your next great story to hit the stands and when?"

I laced my hands behind my back to hide my nerves. Why was I so nervous? I couldn't think straight, let alone speak. My dry mouth felt coated in volcanic ash.

"Ms. Visconti?"

"It's about Catholic priests. And it will start hitting mailboxes tomorrow morning."

"Oh, great," he said. "I'm gonna need the names of your next victims."

Chapter Forty-Five
Cat Fight

DETECTIVE WRAY DIDN'T leave until I printed out the entire article.

He scanned it, shook his head, stood, shook my hand, and left saying only, "I'll be seeing you."

"It is pretty explicit," Sterling said, after perusing the contents of the new *CoverBoy* issue on my computer monitor.

Sterling stayed with me through the wee hours of the night. She wanted to know more about why a man had attacked me at my door. I told her the truth, for even Detective Wray said it had nothing to do with the stabbings. A warning to stay away from Tucson. That's all.

Sterling gasped, "What do you mean, that's all? We only just decided to go back there. Who the hell would know about that?"

"I don't know, Sterling. Why don't we start with who you told?"

Sterling's steel gray eyes flashed with anger. "No one!"

"You're lying! This is serious."

She shifted in her too tight dress, "Well—my dad. I mean, you think I'm some bimbo princess that will be heir to the entire company, but he still makes me put in my hours. I had to tell him I was planning on taking a few days off. He knew we were going to Tucson, but I didn't even tell him why."

"Anyone else?"

"No, Lauren. No!"

"What about Brock Townsend?"

"What about him?" She shuffled her feet and ruffled her strands of long blond tresses. Diamonds on her fingers reflected the glow of moonlight, reminding me of the brass umbrella stand I'd just slammed into my visitor wolf-dog's face.

"Did you tell him?"

"Lauren, it's not like that between Brock and me. You have the wrong idea. We hang out sometimes, but we don't talk."

Yeah. I bet they don't talk. I said nothing.

"For god's sake, Lauren, Brock never unplugged my pipes. Get it? We never did it! I don't even know why you would care, the way you treat him. He's only got eyes for you but you treat him like shit. And besides, what would it matter? Are you suggesting Brock would try and stop you from going to Tucson? Stop us from learning what really happened down there?"

The wind, bellowing off the ocean surf, caught my red hair. Strands splayed across my face and molded against my glossy lipstick. I pulled the gooey strands away and shook my head. "I don't know what to think. I can't think. I'm sorry."

Sterling told me Brock only had eyes for me. She was trying to spare my desperate feelings while attacking my own behavior. And I couldn't think.

"With all this shit coming down, I don't think we should go to Tucson now," I muttered.

"Good. I don't ever want to go back."

"No. You misunderstand. I can't go now. I have to deal with *CoverBoy* and any fallout to come. But I am going

157

back, Sterling, with or without you. I'm not wimping out. In fact, the asshole that greeted me at my door tonight has just dug my feet down deeper than a pauper's grave." And I'd only just learned how deep ant stacked that could be, thanks to Jack Helms.

Chapter Forty-Six
Veins of Gold

MOON BLADE HAD SOME serious thinking to do. What the hell better should be done with a cut-off clit but to cram it into the surgeon's throat? That came pretty easily. Now, what to do with a cut out heart? Could it be preserved? And for how long? There was no clear plan for another slaying. The act would be mandatory, inevitable, and deliciously fun.

COAL PLANNED ON ENJOYING a sizable income from his books and speaking engagements and the multitude of retainer fees that promised his hand-holding of patients once a month or so. He'd milk them until they were well enough. Of course, they were never well enough.

The farm turned out to be a bigger problem. Too much maintenance, yet full of boys. Wonderful young boys.

He had to admit he didn't plan on the extended financial gains that fell into his lap, for some of his patients would gladly pay him next Tuesday for their hamburger today. Who would have believed in L.A. so many successful social climbers were suffering hard times?

The solution was simple. And brilliant. Coal began selling his time for a portion of their businesses, no matter what those businesses might be. He'd already collected significant shares of everything from retail to service to industrial, and those stocks became the bottom level of his earnings matrix. After the savings accounts were emptied, stocks and company shares were turned over along with any trust accounts and the ample Social Security checks.

In little time, he found lost souls that had no home, even if they owned mansions in the city of angels. He seized those souls and carefully evaluated each one. He farmed most of the younger ones out to his acreage. As for the others, only after turning over the deeds to those awful mansions that haunted them with the binding of such earthly trappings, he kept them on a retainer. Of sorts.

He stood on the forty-second floor of another 'inherited' office suite. Stiff black leather covered the sofas, chairs, and ottomans. Structurally worthless architectural beams, harsh lighting, and polished stainless steel tables overwhelmed the space with glare, ostentatiously reflected in a multitude of mirrored walls. The abstract nude paintings cost the owner a tidy sum of three million. For Coal, their price was about twenty hours of therapy. Well-invested, Coal thought, but only because of the inherent value. He'd have to research how to divest of them at top dollar. To him, the art looked like the endeavors of a defiant five-year old that had just seen his mommy naked for the first time.

The stainless steel and black slate reception area was empty. No receptionist. No phones to ring. No business.

The air conditioning sat at precisely sixty-six degrees.

Coal lit up a Cuban cigar and poured himself a Glenlivet, neat, in celebration. He scored another big one today. Not as big as when he hooked up the Carly Posh woman. Just like any horny teenage girl lined up at a Justin Bieber concert without knowing what *horny* meant, so it was with Carly Posh and her friends lined up like prey in Harlan Coal's hands.

Coal flashed back to the two cock-sucking boy hookers he picked up the night before. He reveled that he could buy them, and a dozen more like them, every night. But it wasn't every night he was focused on. It was all their years he wanted.

He loved little boys. He loved their high voices and their itsy soft pubic hairs, and their easily excited but beyond-control penises that had never gone deep within uncharted territories.

He fancied himself in the mirror juxtaposed to his unused executive desk, admiring his own bulging erection, when he saw Armand in the reflection.

"Damn it, Armand, what the hell are you doing here?"

"You changed the locks, remember? You refused to let the building janitors have access. You gave me the fucking keys so that I can come by and clean up after you."

Coal stormed out to the balcony, calling behind, "Bring me my drink."

Armand followed Coal outside with the drink in hand. "I've been to the farm, like you said. We need to talk."

"I'm not in the mood for any of your problems, Armand."

"You're never in the mood for my problems. I think these rank up there as your problems.

"The little boys you keep insisting upon. They're the ones causing all the trouble. Now that you won't allow them at The Centre, they're rebelling. Our cells are full."

"I can't afford to have them around The Centre anymore. Not now. It's too risky."

"And I'm telling you it's too risky to have them at all. You discard them like used popsicles sticks when you're done with them, but let me tell you—those sticks are catching fire."

161

"Keep the troublemakers in the cells. Double them up, if you must. Just keep them healthy and hydrated. Keep them off the proteins. Doctor's orders."

"You're a fucking predator," Armand yelled.

"And you, my dear friend—you are my partner. You just have a need for a different form of bonus plan than me. You fuck your women, young and old, but the only way you really get off is by smacking the shit out of them. My savage pal, I've had to clean up after you, too. That's why we make the most excellent of partners."

Armand's voice throttled, "My messes bring in more hard money than yours."

"Child! You child! Quit counting and let's call a truce for the evening."

Coal called for the fifty-year old scotch and another glass for Armand.

"Now what, partner? What's next? I'm on board, whatever it is," Armand acquiesced after only a few ounces of the fiery brew.

"We have Carly Posh. She's the offspring of a troglodyte but in a little pretty shell of a body. She's an unenlightened dweeb longing for a home. Maybe that's why she's so good at interior design. She's always trying to make a home out of four walls of bricks and mortar."

"Fantastic houses," Armand murmured.

"I'm working on Visconti. She's a challenge."

"And god knows you love a challenge. But if she catches you with one of your boy toys it's all over."

"That's why I told you to keep them away from The Centre, damn it. And for the record, I need you away from there, too!"

"What about Sterling Falls?"

Coal brought out the coke. Time for some baseball. "She's worth more than Visconti, but nothing until her old man is dead. Trust me. I'm working on that. I'm having dinner with her and Daddy."

"Who are you this time?"

"I'm still good old Dr. Harlan Coal. Isn't it grand?"

"With this circle of girls, don't you think they talk? They have cell phones. One mention of you and you're screwed. It's all grand until someone discovers who Nathan Judd really is."

"Nathan Judd, the evil one, was my father. He also has another reputation, if anyone does bother to do any digging. He was the king of gold. And that's how I connect with Sterling Falls and Daddy. With the price of metals today no one will dig any deeper than the dirt that houses the veins of gold."

Chapter Forty-Seven
Quaking Threats

THE PRIEST ARTICLE HIT the stands with a big splash. And as a very bad idea. I didn't know L.A. housed so many Catholics and their high-powered Catholic attorneys.

Core staff had gathered in our small conference room. They were indifferent to the pending lawsuits. I had a reliable team, although I admit I was not indifferent to the names of attorneys splayed across my desk and flooding my email.

I read across my team's faces like a lawyer might try to read a jury: Averted eye contact. Pursed lips. Nervousness.

No one would speak.

"We were all on-board with this issue and I'm not going to apologize for it. We weren't the ones to break the story of the priestly child molestations back in Germany. We didn't break the story on the two-hundred children in Milwaukee at the St. John's School for the Deaf. We just kept the story out there for public view because it shouldn't be flushed away with the dirty dishwater.

"Do you know what the church did to Father Murphy? They sent him in for therapy! No other punishment."

Geoff, an integral part of *CoverBoy's* every foundation, was first to respond with a flat statement. "We broke the story about the therapist's involvement. They'll crucify us."

"He's a big boy in a major county mental health center. He's paid by our government. Our money," I argued on ground that seemed more firm then I'd ever stepped on before.

"Yes, but Lauren, he has patient-client privilege. And you're right. He's a big boy in the big church. What were we thinking?" Geoff's voice quaked.

"The man came to me. He called it some sort of trumped-up psycho babble for having a guilty conscience. He's getting up there in age and suddenly realizing he won't get past the Pearly Gates if he doesn't come clean with what he knows."

My junior editor responded, "Sounds like he's screwed either way. Might as well go and buy a pitch fork."

"We didn't use his name," I added.

"Doesn't take a genius," Geoff said. "We've identified that he's a guru in the mental health system and a deacon in the Catholic church."

"Again. We didn't use his name and he came to us with the story. It's all on tape and emails and evidential correspondence. No lawsuits."

"Let's hope he lives," Geoff murmured.

Chapter Forty-Eight
Gabriella Criscione

I HAPPENED TO BE IN the neighborhood. Dumb line, but I didn't have anything better. I wanted to see Gabriella Criscione. It could have been a mission of good-will, except I wanted to know more about what she knew of Carly renting her Bel Air home to The Centre more than I wanted to know about Gabri's welfare.

She must have thought it strange, my dropping in on her. I found it strange to find her at home on a Sunday, only because of her vocation.

Her black and vacuous eyes led me through the foyer; her sentry of the suit of armor allowed me the crossing.

"I'm not exactly booking any dinner parties these days, if that's what you want," Gabri said. She quickly added, "But I'm fine. Just fine."

"I'm glad to hear that. You have no reason to be—"

"Embarrassed? Mortified?"

"Gabri, you are an institution in L.A., and we're all here for you."

"You don't mean your boyfriend, Brock Townsend?" her eyes glared.

He's not my boyfriend, and no, Brock didn't exactly convey his concern for Gabri.

"I mean Sterling. Carly. Me," I offered.

Gabri snipped her scissors, attacking a bouquet of fresh basil. The kitchen already smelled of caramelizing

166

onions and garlic. One-inch cubes of meat sat on a nearby butcher's block.

"Making calf liver," Gabri said. "Damn shame. It used to be good for children to eat the damn stuff. Now it's considered a bad organ meat. All you need is onion and garlic. And don't tell anyone, but I add tongue. Its flavoring is divine."

I watched as she added cube after cube of *something* to the bottom of the copper skillet.

"Come," she said. "It's time for the feeding."

We walked outside—Gabri carrying a big bucket. She poured scoops of food into the murky waters of the moat that encircled her home.

The mottled Shubunkin fish gathered to dine on the tasty recipe of frozen plankton, beef heart, and bloodworms. They soon jumped out at the outstretched arm and gobbled every morsel within seconds.

"We all care about you," I said as we journeyed back inside.

"Sterling is a good girl. That Carly is a whacko. Living in that wacky compound."

I didn't even have to use my interviewing skills. Gabri did all the talking.

"That girl must be on steroids, or meth, or something. She's a nut-case."

"She can always go back to her home in Bel Air," I said. "If and when things may not work out for her, she could resell her home at The Centre."

Gabri huffed and puffed. But she'd never blow her house down. Not the concrete cave she lived in. She shook her head at me.

"What is it?" I said. Genuine concern. No interrogation.

"She isn't even pulling rent on that place. It appears she's *lending* it out. But not now. That foolish woman

went and gave it away. Not that it's any of my business."
She shook her head again, as if shaking off the water after
a dunk in a city sewer.

"You know this for a fact?"

"I ran an O and E on it. Ownership and encumbrances.
It shows mortgages, liens, and deeds."

"Ownership? Now?" I asked.

"Dr. Harlan Coal."

I heaved in a deep breath, finding some grounding in
the comforting aromas now coming from Gabri's skillets.
"I don't think we should jump to any conclusions," I said.
"Maybe there's some sort of explanation we don't know
about. Maybe a trade or something."

"You know, I manage to piss off a lot of folks," she
said, "just because I don't kiss the feet of those I disfavor.
In my business there's this cardinal rule that I'm suppose
to love everyone, and I say screw that! I make my money
the hard way and I do a damn good job. But, I've made my
share of enemies along the way. I just haven't fingered all
of them yet."

"All of us have burned some bridges," I said.

She murmured, "Yes, so I've heard. You push the
envelope, my dear. But so far you haven't received a
painted portrait of yourself. You're ahead of the game, at
least by L.A. standards."

"Animosity runs its course," I said.

"My course is encapsulated by one single wimp. He's
hiding," she tapped her stubby fingers on the counter next
to the trimmed fat and in rhythm to an unheard tune. "I'll
deal with the rat bastard."

Chapter Forty-Nine
Showtime

I PULLED UP TO The Centre and noticed Harlan—Dr. Coal, in the back seat of a red Jeep Wrangler, with two kids in front. All of them hopped out and started bundling up wooden crates of groceries.

"Need an extra hand?" I asked.

Dr. Coal jolted around with a grimace, but recovered with a toothy grin and a bouquet of yellow daises. "Indeed, if you can handle this load." He gave me the flowers.

"Looks like you have your hands full," I said, embarrassed that I had shown up without any regard to appointments. I'd already rehearsed my excuse that I was there only there to drop in on Carly. I seemed to need excuses to go anywhere.

"Provisions for our weekly meeting," Coal said.

I didn't know Coal or The Centre stuck to any schedule of meetings, but one of the boys affirmed, yes, every Tuesday night.

I helped them deliver the boxed vegetables into the compound cafeteria, probably best described as a community kitchen. To the best of my knowledge, anyone was free to use it for impromptu gatherings.

With a nod from Dr. Coal, I followed him toward the sizeable auditorium. I'd seen it before on my first tour of The Centre, but I would have never imagined the kind of energy now emanating from the eager participants.

The man with the ponytail, Armand? He appeared and disappeared, and I remembered the man on the beach. Coal had said Armand had no temperament beyond being finicky over the final touches of a floral arrangement at an evening gathering feast. The man I saw at the beach, so close to my home, was vituperative. Angry. Physical. I dismissed any circumstantial evidence. There were plenty of long braids in Los Angeles.

The audience dressed as if under a dress code of denim and white cotton only. With blue jeans, shirts, and denim dresses, my emerald St. John suit flagged me as an outsider. I took a seat in the back row of the large hall.

A small woman knelt on the raised platform, center stage. She led the group in an exercise of deep breathing, alternating between verbal affirmations.

Four persons lined up behind the woman. In pep-rally fashion, one by one they revealed their intimate histories with The Centre. Their emotive testimonials whipped the air. As I'd believed all along, Dr. Coal was causing significant change in peoples' lives.

Dr. Coal jumped out on the stage from behind heavy white draping.

"Time is running out!"

He swirled on the platform and the white linen gauze he wore swayed in curling drifts of movement, his eyes shaded from the lights with the dark-tinted glasses. "You have found a place of unconditional love. You are weak. I am weak. Yet here, together, we are whole and strong."

His audience numbered somewhere near sixty. They all fell into a whisper of chanting. I couldn't make out what they were saying. No matter how I tried to piece words together, they were more like syllables. Normally I would have shunned the spectacle, but for some odd reason I found it comforting.

"Let go of the past! Don't go back there! Never go back!"

Coal continued to sweep the stage. Left, right, center, back. His speech was patterned, but irregular. As his sheathed body faded and all but disappeared in front of the white curtains, I found myself swirling into a warm fantasy.

I imagined his tanned skin just beneath the surface of the gauze shirt. I imagined the texture of the skin and each muscular curve.

Too much *CoverBoy* in my blood, I thought.

The truth is I didn't hear much else of what Coal spoke that night. Each mesmerizing phrase seemed to pass over my head, but not before entering my heart and soul.

I felt warm. Loved. And part of me was realizing it was time to let go of Payton. Maybe it was true. Maybe I didn't need to return to Tucson.

Dr. Coal left the podium and the small woman who had led the chanting came back onto the stage, announcing the breakfast meeting would be at precisely 6:00 a.m. the following day. The strict schedule was something new to me. Carly never mentioned it.

Where was Carly? Impossible to find her in the crowd of denim. Surely she would see me in my unmistakable glow of green attire.

Three persons stood in front of me, as if I were but a green mist to be ignored. "He belongs to his people," said one.

"And we are lucky. We are his."

Now I felt creepy. I pulled the emerald jacket closer to my chest and was thankful that I had chosen a seat in the back. I dashed out to the courtyard. In the brisk air I found a welcome relief.

171

What was it? Sweet and salty, sweet and sour, or sweet and bitter? Something didn't set right with me.

Carly sat on a park bench along the winding path. Two squatty Pug puppies jumped around at her side. I was happy to see a familiar face and even happier she wasn't wearing denim.

"I looked for you inside," I said, scrunching next to her on the bench.

"Meet the new loves of my life," she said. "This is Elliot and this one is Antoinette."

"Wow. This is a surprise. I know you love dogs but I didn't think—"

"Why not?"

"Miss Perfect. Interior designer. As in, no dog hair or dog poop. For sure, no doggie breath and dog kisses," I said, letting the puppies lick my hands.

"Consider them my Foo Dogs with real fur, but less ferocious," she said. "Besides, I like to break the rules. You know that."

"Rules?"

"We're really not allowed to have pets here at The Centre."

"Allowed?"

"You know. Rules. Not unlike any H.O.A." She brought Antoinette up to the bench seat.

"They're adorable," I said.

"They're my replacement for you stealing Dr. Coal's attention away from me."

Carly knew how to drop bombs better than anyone I knew. Was she serious?

"Tell me," she continued, "does he like the work I did for you at your beach house?"

"Carly, Dr. Coal has never been to my home. Why would you ask such a thing?"

COVER BOYS AND CURSES

"Because I see the way he looks at you. It's like no therapist relationship I've ever known."

Carly switched gears before I could get my fighting gloves on. She slid off the bench, scooping one puppy in her arms and grabbing the leash for the second one.

"Don't go," I insisted.

"Come with me if you like. Dr. Coal has a book for me to pick up at his house."

"But isn't he still in the auditorium?"

"It's okay. He told me where to find it. Remember, we don't have locked doors around here."

Yeah. That privacy and respect thing they had going on.

The ground burst with summer delights. A second round of roses had begun to bloom and the lotus flowers cast their rich foliage against the glassy sheets of fountain water. Elliot and Antoinette were still trying to get the hang of their leashes, which meant Carly was having a hard time keeping them both out of the gardens and fountains.

Eventually Carly led the puppies, tangled leashes and all, up the short stairs of Coal's residence. Without thought, she threw open the unlocked door and nodded toward me to follow.

"Kind of weird being in here alone," I said.

"You're not alone. You're with me and two illegal puppies. And I told you, Dr. Coal told me it was okay."

I leaned against the massive stone wall as Carly picked up the hardcover from atop a large floor pillow.

"Carly, do you ever wonder what's behind this wall? It seems like it has the only locked door on the entire compound."

"Sometimes, I guess," she said, "But Dr. Coal says it's mostly records. I think of it like the Akashic Records, but better."

173

"It's a big space. There must be a helluva lot of records."

"You ask him if you're so interested. He'll probably give you a library pass."

"It's not like that, Carly," I said.

She tightened her grip on the two leashes. "I know what rules to break, and when to put on the *brakes*," she said.

And she walked away.

Chapter Fifty
Ding Dong

I HEARD IT ON THE morning news. Within the hour I would be inundated with phone calls and maybe even a few nosey reporters at my door. Maybe even a good old-fashioned barn burning.

One thing had already been set afire. The song in my brain matter refused to end my torment. Worse, I changed the lyrics without much effort.

Ding dong, the priest is dead.
That nasty priest is really dead.
Ding dong, that filthy priest is dead.
He had his ways with all the boys,
He used them as his own sex toys,
But ding dong, the nasty priest is dead.

I hated myself for what words I had streaming through my mind. Damn it!

My receptionist's buzzer would be my interruption. My reprieve. Or so I thought.

Not the media, lucky me. Detective Wray.

Unlucky me.

"You're not here to make me feel guilty this time around, Detective," I said. "That bastard might as well have tried to hide himself behind the thin veil of the *Shroud of Turin*." "You're aware the priest has been stabbed."

175

"Yes. And I'm sorry. I'm truly sorry for the whole entire world."

He shook his head. "I was never very good at math when I was a kid," Wray said. "Stunk at it, actually."

"And why is this relative to me?"

"Your priest was stabbed forty-two times. And his mental health worker—the one that was covering up for him? You forgot to mention him on my last visit."

"But you read the article. He's a deacon in the church and also happens to be high up there in the mental health system. He felt it was his duty and right to reveal the dealings of the dirty priest as the holy man continued to molest more boys. But I didn't *print* his name."

"Well, he's not showed up to work yet. My bet is he's not playing hooky. My bet is someone connected the dots, just like I did. "

I stumbled and fell back toward my desk chair. It was over. *CoverBoy* could no longer afford the price of human sacrifice, even in truth.

"But let's get back to my math issues."

"Sure." *Let's just get him out of my office.*

"You got your model lady. Stabbed six times. Then we got the good Dr. Solayman. Stabbed eighteen times. The plastic surgeon? Stabbed thirty-six times. Your priest? Forty-two times.

And that all leads me to you. All those stabbings lead me to you. And it doesn't take but fifth-grade math to start seeing the pattern."

"I assure you I passed the fifth grade, but I don't follow you."

"Damndest thing. Multiples of six. And they keep growing in violence. Intensity. Sheer number of stab wounds. Someone has quite an axe to grind. Or should I say—*dagger.*"

"The Obeah," I sputtered.

"Say what?"

The number six. Evil. Geoff's dead Obeah Voodoo grandmother had tried to warn me. Detective Wray didn't hear my words. It would have to be another thing gone unmentioned to him for I didn't speak of it again.

Chapter Fifty-One
No Cover for CoverBoy

"I'M GROWING MORE PARANOID," I told Sukie after Wray left the building.

"Most everyone around this place is these days," she replied through stiff lips.

I perused some of Sukie's new work. Shots she'd taken of male models up in San Francisco. No one would be looking at the background of the Golden Gate Bridge.

"I don't know how much longer we can continue, Sukie. I can't even think straight. I don't believe my good friend committed suicide when everyone else tells me she did. I get Detective Wray in here and he doesn't want to talk about Tucson. He thinks I need to worry about what's happening in my own backyard. And the other night I was in my therapist's house and I'm wondering what's behind some mysterious wall."

Sukie pulled the wire-rimmed glasses from the bridge of her nose. "Now that one sounds interesting."

"Not what you think. Carly and I were there and—never mind. It's a long story."

"If I'm unemployed, I'll have plenty of time on my hands."

"Now I think I just saw a ghost."

"Lauren, you've had a lot of shit happen to you in your short life. More death than most of us will ever see in our lifetimes. You have every right to be jumpy. Even paranoid.

Jesus, you just had a guy attack you at your doorstep while delivering you a warning."

"I saw an old man in the elevator as I came down to see you."

"You still have the space rented out to the geriatric psychologist. We have crazy old people in the elevators all the time."

Sukie's voice was calm. Motherly.

"Yes. But I recognized him. He bought me a glass of wine at Catrozzi's. I looked up. He was gone. And just now I swear he was in the elevator."

Sukie's eyebrows raised up like pitched tents. "Did you inform security?"

I'd already been spooked enough to broaden the scope of security in both our building and our parking lot.

"What do I tell them? Beware an old man with a shuffled gait, fake teeth, and has a habit of buying people expensive wines?"

DETECTIVE WRAY BECAME somewhat of a permanent fixture around *CoverBoy*. He showed up like Columbo, always uninvited and at the most inopportune times. It signified that my staff and I were still high up on the list of suspects.

I didn't really mind. I considered him a freebie in addition to the full-time security I hired. And my attorney advised me to fully cooperate with the man.

"Coffee, Detective Wray?" I offered, as I entered my waiting room and spied him sitting in the corner chair.

"Whoa! Too damn sweet. You gonna be nice to me today?"

"You do have an appointment this time?" I looked over to my receptionist and saw her wince. "Okay. Let's take a walk-about."

"A what?"

"A walk-about. I can show you our operations and you can ask your battery of silly questions. Do you have a problem with that?"

"Just the sudden change of heart," he groused.

"I'm worried about my people that work here. We're family. And I'll be honest," I said. "I'm worried about my own butt, too."

"Now there's my girl," he said.

With coffees in hand, the gruff detective followed my lead to the bank of elevators. We headed down to the dark and dank basement that promised an exciting tour of a small employee's cafeteria and Sukie's photo lab. Sukie gave us a two-dollar tour, tossing nasty glares my way every time she could without being caught.

"She's cute," Wray said. "Is she gay?"

"I can't believe you just asked me that," I said.

"Hey, I said she's cute."

Good lord, just wait until he started questioning Queen Geoff.

"Just between friends," Detective Wray added.

"We're not friends. I'm in toleration mode."

We toured the printing department, the writers' floor, the finance floor that housed both sales and accounting. With great interest Wray navigated his way through our research department.

"You skipped the tenth floor," Wray said.

"I'm with a real sharpie," I said. "Not my business, nor yours. I have a tenant that occupies the entire floor."

"I see."

He wore an obnoxious short-sleeved dress shirt with his tie in too tight of a knot and too short on the fall to his bulging waistline. I wanted to send him a courtesy subscription to *Gentleman's Quarterly* or something. Anything to help the man dress properly.

"You annoy me, you know?" A rhetorical question.

"I do most folks. Don't worry about it," he grinned.

"I'm not worried."

"What's his business?" Wray asked.

"Who?"

"The tenant on ten."

"Shrink. A geriatric psychiatrist."

"The entire floor?"

"Must be pretty hard, getting old in this city of beautiful angels," I said. "Makes a lot of people crazy, I guess."

Detective Wray scribbled something in his notebook.

"Don't worry. I may just need his professional help in a few years, that's all," he smirked.

"I believe that."

"I've put extra people on the case. As much as the department can spare and you can imagine these days that's not much. We're looking out for you, but you need to look after yourself. We have the guys over at VICAP involved."

"VICAP?"

"Violent Criminal Apprehension Program. I think these slaughters qualify, don't you?"

I bit my tongue.

"It's a division of the FBI. That's the Federal Bureau of—"

"Yes, Detective. I think I know what the FBI is, even in my shallow safe little world."

"That's what I'm telling you. Somebody's smashed the glass on your snow globe. It's not safe in that little world of yours anymore. Watch your back."

We picked up our pace as we walked back to my office. Geoff would be waiting for us.

Geoff didn't make it through the proper introductions. Neither of them required introductions. They knew of each other.

"You got any idea who is doing this? Who is responsible for all this killing?" Geoff demanded.

Detective Wray drilled back at him. "You got anything? Some little something you're holding back to test me, or something you're not thinking of?"

I rescued Geoff.

"If he's not thinking of it, how the hell can he tell you about it? And for the record, it's not correct to end a sentence with a preposition."

Detective Wray fired back, staring down Geoff, "Something you're not thinking of, Geoff Hayes?"

"That's it," I interrupted. "This interview is over. Geoff is a key man here, and I thought I would make nice and introduce the two of you. We're through here today, *Wray*."

I drew my finger to my lips to communicate silence from Geoff. Detective Wray said his goodbyes, looking back not once, but twice.

"Back to business," Geoff said. "I see we have the next two issues drafted. They're crawling worms of boring. Come on, June Grooms? Athletes and Steroids?"

"We're all trying to lay low. Way low. Be prudent for a couple of months."

"And lose all of our momentum? That's crap! So, what's the new issue idea of yours," Geoff flashed me the devilish grin I loved.

And he knew me. He knew I wouldn't back down for long.

"It's a bit of a journey back into the plastic surgery realm, but get this! This time it's podiatrists!"

"Feet fetish thing. Great," Geoff moaned.

"Geoff, you just whined that our planned features sucked. I have a new angle, and no one is going to kill a foot doctor. They might slice off his toes, but they won't kill him."

"Your humor in the morning is what sucks, Laurs. Blow me the highlights."

"How about a group of assholes taking advantage of more Barbie Doll wannabes by slicing off the tops of their imperfect second toes, or even completely amputating their little toes? They're perfectly healthy, beautiful woman that are led to believe the larger extension of their second toes is a deformity. Disfigurement. And the reason why they can't get into to the itsy-bitsy designer shoes is because their little toes are in the way. Women are going in for surgery to shorten their second toes, all to fit into the fancy designer shoes crafted of the oh-so-tight and sexy skins of exotic leathers. And for some, the shortening won't do the job. Those women are getting their little toes amputated.

"The surgery is painful. The podiatrist removes both tissue and bone, and thousands of bucks later, our patient walk away with the perfect eight toes."

"Or hobbles away," Geoff said. "But is it a comeback story?"

"Sukie already has a photo of a podiatrist dancing at the hospital fundraiser in two-thousand dollar croc shoes. And I bet he didn't hack off his toes to get his feet into them.

"The essence of *CoverBoy* is truth. A truth that bring to light the layers of fallacy in articles that find incongruence amid our centerfolds. We keep our stories real, fact-based. No trouble. And we keep the photos real. No digital crap. We use fat bellies, scars, and balding heads. And the occasional stud muffin."

"The story sounds like a sleeper, but it's your rag. Your run the articles you want to run. You are going to name names again, aren't you?"

"You bet I am."

"Then *CoverBoy* is back in business."

Detective Wray barged his way back into my office. Both Geoff and I knew he had heard Geoff's last comment. Geoff bolted.

Chapter Fifty-Two

Stashes of Stills

"THIS WILL JUST TAKE a minute, Ms. Visconti," the detective's voice boomed.

"Please be short and to the point. I've got a business to try and salvage."

"Entertain me, for just a minute. What do you know about Sukie Fields?"

"Sukie? She's a brilliant photographer. She rarely complains and she works overtime for free. She under promises and over delivers. And for the record, if you're still of an unjust curious mind, I don't know her sexual orientation. It's none of my business."

"What *do* you know about her personally?"

My fierce stare caught his congenial eyes and a soft smile. "She's a woman of myst—" I caught my speech. "She's a quite, private woman. She works behind the camera, Detective. She's shy."

"So you're telling me you know nothing about her beyond work ethics and acumen?

"You started to tell me she's a woman of mystery, right? What does she do when she leaves here? I mean, does she watch movies, go to gay clubs, play with—"

"Zip your mouth on your prejudices, Detective Wray. Are you trying to tell me that after all this time working your big slasher-investigation your prime suspect is a five-foot tall Asian senior citizen?"

185

"In a court of law you're innocent until proven guilty. In my court you're a suspect until cleared. That's the way it works."

"Sukie Fields wouldn't hurt someone's feelings, let alone their body."

"She has no alibis for the nights of any of these murders."

"Because I've told you she's a loner. Lots of artists are loners. Now I think you've over-stayed your one minute of intrusion."

"I'll be right back here until something makes sense with all these stabbings and this maddening numbers game."

"And I'll be lawyered-up along with every other employee that works here. You can call my receptionist for the lawyers' phone numbers."

"One more nicety from me before I leave. There are no leads on the man who showed up at your doorstep."

"And I should be surprised?" I snapped back.

I looked at my purse. Geoff's anti-number-six Voodoo potion was inside the zippered compartment. I could use a good dose of it.

"The thing is, mind you it's not official business, but I have a friend in Tucson."

He palmed a business card. Or rather, a number scribbled down on a torn index card.

"He's a former federal agent. Retired about a year ago. Good guy. Good friend, and believe it or not, guys like me have a good friend here or there."

"Tucson? This is about *my* good friend, Payton Doukas?"

"Still don't see any connection with what I have on my hands here, with you. But this guy knows his stuff. Beats you flying off to Tucson and getting yourself in more trouble. Give him a call and see what he can do for you."

I accepted the number for a Victor Romero.

"Just seems I'm always delivering you bad news. I thought maybe you could see me for the old softie that I am," he said.

"Thank you."

"Not saying he can do anything for you. Not saying there is anything to do."

I guess it was his way of saying, "You're welcome."

VICTOR ROMERO ARRANGED for the conference call. He'd give the Visconti woman exactly sixty minutes. He kept to a tight schedule, with nothing else to do. Retirement didn't suit him.

It took Romero forty minutes to deduce he wasn't wasting his time. Lauren Visconti rose up between the red lines and black dots as a little pistol. And as for her friend's pistol aimed at her own head? Not for a minute in his bones did Romero think Payton Doukas pulled the trigger.

The first thing on his new agenda was to find the missing brother, who may or may not want to be found. He cancelled the haircut and the golf lesson; they were the only two things on his calendar for the week and he loathed both appointments.

I AM THE PRODUCT of rape. My mother was dead. I'd not become a bride before the groom-to-be was dead. And the father of the bride, too. All facts.

A best friend was dead, too. Fact.

And in spite of all of this, or because of it, I turned all of my focus toward business, and the business took me to the west coast. My intention was to produce a magazine unlike any other. An emotive, intelligent, and sexy magazine well-received by women and some open-minded men, or at least the curious.

Now I sat in front of my fireplace with four file folders on my lap. The night cloaked the air with damp and cold. The roar of the fire comforted me for what I was about to do.

Spreading the contents of the first folder on the floor in front of me, I studied the colorful images of the stunning runway model. She reminded me of the famous model, Gia, who fell victim to heroin abuse and, then later, AIDS took her life, attributed to a dirty needle. And what we uncovered behind the glamorous world of models proved that chasing the dragon was normal, if not mandatory.

The second folder contained black and white photographs of a brave Afghanistan doctor who had become my personal hero. I would never forget Dhurra.

My disc player turned and Andrea Bocelli, my favorite tenor, bellowed. I turned the volume on high until the floor reverberated with its own drum.

The next file contained mostly collateral brochures from the plastic surgeons' clinics, plus a few candid shots my staff managed to snap, including one we ran in the article. It captured a zoomed-in photograph of a doctor leaving his clinic and stepping into his brand new Lotus.

The last file folder seemed to glare at me with a taunting stillness. I had requested it, yet I couldn't move myself to open it. It held all the notes, photos, research, and documents used in the article: *Priests, Power, & Pedophiles*.

My fingers ran across the top of the black string that laced the folder together. I knew what I would find inside. Everything would be in order. Our research department had documented and verified every printed detail. As is often the case, I had to open up the checkbook to get at some of the facts, but only because it was money and power that had put a lock on the truth in the first place.

The fire roared and spitted. The rain pounded in sheets against the sliding doors.

All of them were dead, I thought. My runway model, Dhurra , the plastic surgeon, and now a priest. And a mental health worker, the ultimate snitch, remained missing.

The pounding grew louder. Too loud. Lightning streaked across the dark sky and a roar of thunder boomed from somewhere over the ocean.

Pounding. Now knocking. Now pounding at my door.

Chapter Fifty-Three
An Open Invitation

THE POUNDING STOPPED. Now tick. Tick. Tick. I hadn't pulled the plantation shutters and could see it was Dr. Coal, clinking his keys against the window while bracing himself against the tumultuous winds with his other hand.

"What is this? Are you all right? I've been ringing the bell and beating on your door!"

Astonished at his presence, I signaled him one moment, and ran to the CD player to quiet Andrea's voice.

"Loud enough to fill the Bolshoi," he teased.

I grabbed his umbrella and helped release him from his raingear. "What are you doing here?" I tried to sound polite, but felt off-balance. Sweet and sour. That's all I could think.

"My aide is renting a home further down the beach. His power went off so I brought him some provisions. I thought I should check on you, too."

My mind raced in jagged circles. How did he know where I lived? Oh. Forms. I must have put it on the forms I filled out for The Centre. His aide? Near me? And my electricity was on, as evidenced by Andrea's music and plenty of lights. I fumbled for words. Why was he in my living room? Sweet and sour.

"Come in. Dry off," I said.

"If you'd rather be alone I understand completely. I shouldn't have just showed up here."

"No. Can I get you something to drink? Tea? Wine?"

"What are you drinking?"

"Something stiffer."

"I'll have something stiffer," he smiled.

I led Coal toward my kitchen where I handed him a towel and asked him to pour two scotches as I pulled out two glasses and the bottle. My eyes had already returned to the photos and files I had left sprawled out by the fireplace and I had no intention of sharing them with anyone beyond the lawyers.

Coal finished drying off, then joined me by the fire. I had scooted the file folders under the sofa.

"Allow me," Coal said, offering me my own scotch.

"Wow! The service is impeccable around here," I said.

Teddy, my incidental-adoptive cat, came lurking out from the dining room. He acted peculiar, but isn't that how all cats act? He hissed at Dr. Coal. I'd never heard him hiss before. He arched his back. I'd never seen that. And then he ran into his private bedroom Carly decorated just for him. I had seen that.

"How are you holding up, Lauren?" Coal asked, unbothered by Teddy.

My shoulders slumped. I could see it in his eyes. The pity party.

"You know?"

"Another tragic murder. Yes, I know."

"I'm holding up."

"Any more personal threats to you?"

"None at my doorstep. Just the usual rate of irate. We have some detective on our side, at least that's what I try and tell myself."

"A private detective?"

"Well, no. The one assigned to the cases. And me."

He sighed. "Oh. I see. One of L.A.'s finest?"

Sweet and sour. He was so handsome. So charismatic. He was sitting in my living room and filling the air with an energetic aura. Part of me wanted him to sweep me off my feet and take me to my bedroom. But he was also my shrink. And he was asking too many questions, too fast. I wasn't prepared and I didn't want to talk about it. I ignored his follow-up question.

"Luckily the next couple of issues are relatively tame. An article on steroids from users and peddlers already behind bars—a throwback from our test issue since we helped get them behind bars. And June Grooms."

"Your magazine will be just fine, Lauren. So will you."

I took comfort in the words. And in the way that they were spoken.

I must be crazy. Do not, under any circumstances, jump from the frying pan into the fire. Finish the drink with the man and show him to the door.

Harlan's cell rang. In disregard to what now had become a downpour, he removed himself and stepped outside to my deck to take the call while finding shelter under the small ramada.

Before I could second-guess myself I brought out some Gouda cheese and rye crackers, only after scraping off the sheet of green mold on the cheese and shoving it down the garbage disposal like any other perfect hostess would do. I also grabbed the bottle of scotch.

I glanced at my mantel clock. I patted down my hair. I ran my finger through my hair to lift it again. Hell, I don't know what I did. Coal was the one standing out in the pelting rain. I was the one that felt like a fool.

When he finally returned through my kitchen I ran to grab him another towel.

"I'm sorry. I'm so sorry," he said, mopping up his tracks.

192

"Don't worry about it. Is everything okay?"

"Now you sound like my therapist," he said. "Everything's fine."

But it wasn't fine. His tawny bronzed face was now a translucent gray, and not from the cold and rain.

"Bad news?" I asked.

He shrugged. "Sometimes it's easy to lose track of the fact that The Centre is a business, but economics dictate that issue," he said.

"Trouble?" He seemed to have acquired my trait of avoiding the questions.

His jaw tensed, betraying his frustration. "Seems I have good news and bad news. That was my banker. Our finance guy has been extorting money from The Centre. Big money. And now he's disappeared without a trace."

Coal was the steady rock everyone else turned to for help. I'd never seen him unnerved, not even slightly upset. I ached for the sudden change in mood and the serious expression that consumed his entire body.

"You'll go after him?"

"Sure, but it sounds like it might be a lost cause if no one can find him."

"I have the direct number for the detective—"

"No. Nothing I can't handle, sweetie."

"I'm so sorry."

"We have to trust, Lauren. I will never ever say that I trust too much. Sometimes, as you well know, humanity disappoints us."

"But you have good news," I urged, as we took our places back in the comfort of my living room and the roaring fire.

"Yes. The bad helps us see and feel and live the good."

"Tell me."

"I've already expressed that we don't have enough homes at The Centre. So many good people want to live with us. One of our homes has just become available."

His eyes were delicious with excitement, but I didn't understand. "Available?"

"Mrs. Conrad passed away today. A lovely woman. A devoted soul."

"How sad," I said.

"Believe it or not, if we think life is robbed from us in death it's because we don't understand it can be a journey to embrace when the time comes for us."

"But how did she die? Was she ill?"

"I don't know the details."

"But like Carly, this woman owned her own home, right? Won't you just buy it back from her estate? I'm sure Carly told me you have plenty of prospects in place with offers to buy any home on the grounds."

It was a question more than a statement.

"Not necessary. Mrs. Conrad was devoted to our path. And pure. She left the home to The Centre."

"Wow. That's a magnanimous gift!"

"I don't think she had any other heirs. We will respect her final wishes."

It was then that I noticed Coal had refilled my glass of scotch—did that make three?—and he had barely touched his own.

"Do you believe in synchronicity, Lauren?"

"Well, I guess I do."

"This is magical. Forget about the bad news and feel the good. The rain. The power going off. My checking in on you. And precisely when I am here with you I get the call about our having an availability of a home on our grounds.

"It's quite clear to me. I think you should buy our home!"

194

Chapter Fifty-Four
Secret Obsessions

HARLAN COAL STOOD at the gateway between his public residence and the huge stone wall that protected his inner sanctum. Armand was in the mood for an argument and Coal knew to get his aide inside the great chamber and out of earshot.

"Why would you have to tell the Visconti woman that I own a place on the beach near hers?" Armand roared.

"I didn't tell her that because you don't, do you? The Centre is borrowing it, and you're damned lucky to get to use it for your little emergencies. But don't be a fool. Visconti saw you there on the back deck. She doesn't know it yet, but if and when she puts it together, we're better off she knows now."

Coal opened the grand skylights to catch the rich scent of wisteria from the grounds below.

"You aren't paying any rent on that place, just like the Bel Air house. You're paying me to be quiet," Armand raged.

"My deal is between Gabriella Criscione and me. I don't let her tell me how to run my life, and I don't let her tell me how to run hers. The beach house isn't like our other properties. I don't see me getting my hands on the deed for some time, but it's my gift to you for as long as you want. Don't screw it up and you can use it any time you want."

"And what about the old man? Falls?" Armand paced the cork floors that afforded an extra cushioning of silence.

"He's going to meet his maker in a few weeks. Poor old geezer has a bad heart. He's on some battery-operated pump that needs a recharge every seven hours, poor guy. Falls will fall, and all that loot will become ours. Give it some time."

"Time is what worries me," Armand said.

"Then I guess it's time for some more baseball."

DETECTIVE WRAY called my cell. "Did you get a hold of that friend of mine in Tucson?"

"You have a friend?" I joked.

He actually laughed. A belly-bursting laugh I could almost see over the phone.

"I have spoken to him. He's working on it. He's trying to find my friend's brother, first. I gave him the name of a producer I know that seems to have connections with all these things."

"Missing children. That would be the infamous Jack Helms' new obsession."

"Right," I said.

Now how did he know that? Maybe I didn't give the detective enough credit, I thought.

IT WAS CARLY'S IDEA. Combat boot camp champion that she was, she wanted to play tennis and I agreed. Not my brightest moment, but neither of us had seen Brock in weeks and he was a member of the club. He got us passes and told us he'd buy drinks later. I wasn't sure that meant he would show up, or just pick up our tab via his golden association with the country club crowd.

"I haven't played in months," I said.

"It shows. It's thirty—love, girlfriend," Carly blared.

"I can't do a whole set," I whined, out of breath and ready to quit. "You must have some new vitamin regimen."

"Something like that," Carly said as she poured two glasses of water from the side court. "I guess it's my Purity Oath."

"What's that?"

"Abstinence," Carly said.

We finished the game in silence, except for my few gasps, screams, and 'oh shits.' After I'd finally expunged my last bit of energy I called a truce. We gathered at the net to collect our towels and gym bags, with Carly the clear victor.

We ended our exercise endeavor over gulps of water and then a glass of wine at a table, poolside.

"Abstinence, huh?" I asked Carly.

"You're one of my best friends. Surely you get this. I'm a virgin."

"Maybe. I sort of thought maybe. Do you have desires?"

"What the hell do you think I am?" Carly wore a mischievous smile behind her mock hurt frown. Friendship. We were on solid ground.

"I honestly don't know. It occurred to me maybe you just weren't interested in sex," I answered.

"Are you crazy? Have you never heard of a virgin? Good god, you don't think I'm a lesbian, do you?"

"It wouldn't matter to me if you were."

"As long as I don't come on to you," Carly laughed.

"Deal. You are a good friend but I have my limits."

"I'm the only virgin my age left in L.A., and when the right man, the *golden man*, comes along, I've got a precious little package for him. And it's not implanted by one of your plastic surgeon nuts."

197

Carly pulled at her *Pinot Grigio*, as if it were that golden man's lush lips. She was stunning, in every way. Choppy black hair, short and flirty. Curves. Real curves. And I felt saddened I didn't know her secret. After all these years I recognized my ignorance. She was a virgin by choice until her prince arrived. I made wrong assumptions. I didn't have a clue that she was on a chosen and widely respected path. I did hope she would find her prince.

Still, I wanted to suggest she loosen up. Experience her body before she committed to a monogamous relationship. As I studied her, she read me more deeply than I had ever read her.

"Anyway," Carly said, "a man would only get in the way until I have my antique store up in running. That's my first goal. I have a new big design job, Lauren. It may just be enough to do it my way."

"Where is it? One of our famous or infamous stars?"

"You know how that goes. No one wants to let on that they're dumping a ton of money into their property."

"You sound like it's patient-client privilege confidentiality. Or a lawyer thing."

"I've been in the business long enough. The more hush-hush they are, the bigger the deal. And I'm familiar with the house. It should be quick, easy, and prosperous.

"So let's flip the tables. What's your goal these days? You have this way about you when you're uptight. You crank your neck around in circles, and when it's real bad, you even pull on your ears," Carly said.

"Really?" I had heard it before.

"Yup. And you're doing it right now, even while you're drilling me about my sex life and business concerns."

"I didn't know I was that transparent."

"Like a day-old guppy," Carly said.

"I haven't had time to tell you, but I've hired a private detective in Tucson to look into Payton's death and maybe even help track down her brother."

"You're kidding? And you didn't have time to tell me?"

"It happened so quickly. I got his name from the detective hammering me here about—well, you know what about. I honestly didn't think it would go anywhere. Turns out this Tucson guy seems like he might take a peek at things for us."

"Who else knows?"

"Like I said, it happened fast. You're the first one I've had time to talk to, but here comes the devil, himself."

Chapter Fifty-Five
Mi Club es Su Club

I NODDED TOWARD THE six-foot-plus hunk that strolled through the country club's lounge in black shorts and a just-so-tight black tee shirt. Brock's season would soon be coming to a close, and I could sense his aching muscles screaming for a time out. They still looked divine, believe me.

"Who won the match?" Brock said as a waiter appeared from nowhere and delivered him a beer.

"Don't have to ask, do you?" I whined.

Carly patted on the seat next to her. "Sit. Lauren has big news about Payton."

Brock's penetrating eyes stole all three bases, as they always did with me. "What's going on?"

I explained what few details I had, which was nothing but a vague hint of someone willing to investigate two cases that weren't even really cases. But Payton's brother was still missing. And Payton didn't put a single bullet into her own head.

I looked up to a familiar voice and a swash of white fabric. "Hey, Slugger. How's your game going these days?"

Brock stood to attention. Firm and guarded attention. "What are you doing here, Mr. Coal?"

"It's *Doctor* Coal. And I'm early for a private appointment. Couldn't help but notice two of my favorite girls."

Coal sat next to me in the remaining chair. He didn't look at me. I found that odd, but in a way, a relief.

"So," Coal repeated, "how is your ballgame?"

"A very decent year, all and all," Brock said, stretching his muscular arms out in a full sweep then landing them around both Carly and me. Real smooth. If you're twelve years old.

"Your old college injury still getting to you? Rotator cuff?" Coal asked.

Brock dropped his chin. "Guess so. How did you know?"

"I read the papers," Coal said. "See the news now and then."

"I didn't take you for a sports guy," Brock said.

"You needn't take me for anything," Coal responded.

The waiter arrived with three flutes of champagne as Coal signed for them. "Hope you don't mind, girls, but the very sight of you is cause for celebration," he said.

"So now you're a member of my club?" Brock asked.

Carly broke up the exchange of squabbling before I even realized the tones of voice had become more callous than the words themselves.

After diverted fierce glares, Carly announced that her business plan was complete and she knew her vision of an antique store was nearing reality.

Brock seemed surprised. Coal seemed to know all about it. But then again, both Carly and I had seen little of Brock, and Carly surely saw Dr. Coal all the time.

I didn't mention the offer to move to The Centre. I can be an idiot but I'm not plain stupid.

Brock noticed the jewelry-pitching blonde I'd seen on what seemed like every other commercial on television. She arrived at a table next to us and it seemed to me she secured the best viewing advantage to take in Brock's abs-fitting black tee. Now I was the twelve year old.

Coal spoke up when he saw us all stare at the magnificent spokesperson.

"So-called stars read lines someone else wrote. They step where someone else has directed them to step, and then they rely on someone to splice and dice their films to take out all of the real stuff.

"Lauren has a first-class magazine that rocks. Carly has a successful design business and a dream. That's real world and world class."

Brock downed his beer.

Carly drooled under the pool of accolades that kept on coming from Coal's perfect mouth.

I pulled on Brock's arm and asked if he'd go to the bar with me. He jumped to his feet.

"Why don't you tell me why you and Dr. Coal have to keep going at each other all the time?"

"Because he's playing mind games with me. He's a psycho-nut playing mind games with all of us."

"He's just trying to be supportive of his patients," I said.

Brock grabbed the cold beer offered by the bartender.

"Why do you think he's here? You think he just showed up at the same time we happened to be here?"

"You heard him. He has a meeting here."

"Right. He signed for your drinks. That means he's a member. Mr. Doctor Good with no need for worldly possessions went and joined a country club. *My* country club."

Chapter Fifty-Six
A Change of Names

CARLY POSH SHOPPED the shops, and especially any with a *For Lease* or *For Sale* sign in front. Demographics didn't factor. She'd become the demographics. Her growing clientele grew along with her reputation, and she knew in her gut the business would come to her.

Although her mission was largely a secret, she gave Gabriella Criscione a heads-up. Look for maybe two-thousand-square-feet to begin with, and grow from there. Calculated and most wondrous baby steps.

VICTOR ROMERO SAT at his desk and drew in several deep breaths. Again. Again. Upon his retirement he took Vinyasa Flow Yoga classes. Too damned slow for him. But he had learned to breathe nice and slow. Breathing is a good thing, he thought.

Now he was back swimming with the sharks. And he had spotted one of them. And his breathing quickened. He liked that.

One more deep breath, if only to placate his wife, and she was spending the night in Sedona. But like all wives, she had eyes in the back of her head that could see over mountains and count the pixels in his mind.

Romero moved to the patio overlooking the Catalina Mountains and placed the call. "Hey, good old Wray! It's Vic. *Que Pasa?*"

"You're the good old fart and I'm just plain good. And what's up with you? Pretty early in the day for you to be calling me in your golden retirement years," Detective Tom Wray said.

"Cut the bullshit and listen up. I think I have a lead on that missing boy."

"What missing boy?"

"It sounds like it's your mind that's taken early retirement. I'm talking about the brother of the friend of your Lauren Visconti. Ring a bell?"

"Oh, yeah. She won't let me forget it. That's why I pawned her off on your fat ass!"

"The kid's last known address was some shantytown crack house in New York. But funny thing, the kid disappeared about the time a slew of kids went missing. Some psycho-guru doctor lost his license to practice up there. Something about money laundering, espionage, and toss in some pedophiliac complications for good measure. Makes for one helluva recipe. I'm convinced the missing Doukas kid is somehow involved with this guy. The guru fled New York and headed to Tucson. I still don't know much about that fling, right here in my own backyard, but rumor has it that the creep moved to your neck of the woods and took his favorite followers with him; whatever that means."

"So you're telling me that missing kid may be in my backyard and with some psychotic psychiatrist?"

"We always loved working together, didn't we, Champ?"

"Shit. Shit. Shit. We have a dynasty of cults and ashrams and guru wannabes. The missing kid might as well have fallen off that ship with Osama Bin Laden. Better chance of finding him."

"Except, I'm damn better at my job than you. I can give you the name of the place. Damn simple name. It's called The Center," Victor said.

"Center for what?"

"Hell if I know. It's your territory."

"Looks like we're a despicable team, again," Wray said.

"Wait. I have more for you. It seems this doctor's name changes with the seasons."

"What the hell does that mean?" Wray asked.

"Whoever this doctor was in New York may have changed his name. When they yanked his license from the state of New York, the guy and his records both vanished. Not sure why. It's probably under that secret veil of steel red tape called surreptitious payoffs, but rumors have it he then moved to Tucson and began scamming bleeding-heart victims for money. All their money."

"So that's your turf. What do you have to give me?"

"No name. Another vanished doctor. The same guy that came here from New York. This shrink came into town with a bunch of young boys. And the timeline fits with the guy that fled New York."

"The shrink with the disappearing name keeps heading west, and now you think he's here in L.A.?"

"Something like that. Hey, I'm not God. I turned in a lot of chips to get this information."

"I'll look into it. What about the dead girl down there? The sister of this kid. The suicide?"

"This is a small town, but no cow town. I'm going through the sheriff's files now. Clean files. I haven't run into a Barney Fife yet. Seems to be a clear-cut ruling for suicide, but something doesn't sit well with me."

"God, if I had a nickel for every time you said that."

205

"I'm serious. The ME found bruises around Payton Doukas's neck."

"Ligature marks?"

"The official finding is that she tried to somehow hang herself before resorting to the gun. Girls don't like guns, you know."

"I guess that makes sense. She wanted to get the job done, one way or the other."

"The blood pattern can pass for being consistent, but it's awkward. She would have had to shoot herself standing up and then fall back into her chair. And there's something else. I see here the gun fired a single 38-caliber bullet. That would decrease the recoil from a .357 Magnum, and the gun residue was a match for recoil. Something a girlie would do if she wasn't strong enough for the big bang. There's some tattooing to confirm the short-range. The ME also reported bruising on her hands and wrist."

"Only one shell casing found?" Detective Wray seemed to be getting the same bug up his ass. Things weren't adding up.

"That's affirmative."

"One bullet. One death. Close range or not, maybe she had a hard time handling that gun. A .357 Magnum, even with sissy bullets, is a pretty big toy for such a tiny little lady. Maybe she took it outside in the boonies for some practice rounds. Build up her courage. Go check the nearby fields."

Victor let out a guttural sigh. "Yo, boy! This ain't exactly like living in the amber waves of grain down here. We have miles and miles of cacti. You come down and have a look around with me."

"You can bet your ass that's not going to happen. Any other bullets in the chamber?"

"No."

"Where'd the gun come from?"

"I thought you'd never ask, buddy. The good old Chief in the Sky must want us working together again. The gun was reported stolen five years ago, from a home right there in your quaint little Brentwood neighborhood. Go check your computer. I've sent you all the information I have. You do know how to work a computer these days, don't you?"

"Brentwood? You sure?"

"Yup. Why?"

"Impenetrable fortresses of money. And crimes that get forgiven. Think O.J."

Chapter Fifty-Seven
More Worms

CARLY AND STERLING arranged for the intervention after calling me countless times, again, for a lunch or happy hour. I kept putting them off. I didn't want to lose my two best friends. Some may say I was either stubborn, or dim-witted, or ridiculously superstitious. I had a good excuse. I was working on the next cover article. Mostly, I didn't know what to say to them. And I didn't want them to die.

After much insistence, I met them for lunch at *La Luna Oro*. Only because I had news.

A report from the detective in Tucson. The cryptic email came in the middle of the night, but the brief communication read like a thesis.

He did not believe that Payton committed suicide. Finally, someone was on our side.

Both Carly and Sterling lectured me before I could share the news. Lauren Visconti is not cursed. People she loved had died. Poor little Lauren. Poor little rich girl.

"You're acting like a goddamn Kokopelli," Carly said.

"Excuse me?"

"You're the symbol of fertility. Lively. Vital. But you're motionless. You're framed in an archaic history."

"And you've given up on us," Sterling said.

"You're right. And you're all wrong," I said.

Drinks and salads arrived while puzzlement splayed across the faces of both Carly and Sterling.

I had copied the email Victor Romero had sent me. I shared my news. "He believes in us. He believes in Payton."

Carly said, "Now we have ammunition and we can get the sheriff's department to reopen their investigation."

"We can't rely on them. Not after they've closed the case once. I think we need to get our butts back to Tucson and find those three saguaro skeletons."

"Good god," Sterling said. "I have to admit. I was the one giving up on that. I thought it best if we all just move on."

Carly nodded, "Me, too. Lauren, if it weren't for you hiring this guy no one would ever get to the bottom of this."

"It's also digging up an old can of worms. Worms that none of us need," I said.

"It's the snakes that scare me," Sterling said.

"I'll make the reservations," Carly said.

Chapter Fifty-Seven
Foreign Grapes

ARRIVING LATE AT Tucson International Airport, we headed directly to Starr Pass, a resort near Saguaro National Park.

I called Victor Romero and confirmed breakfast the next morning. Perpetual party girl Sterling surprised us by saying she'd meet us at the outside bar later. She elected to plop herself down at the desk and set about getting her computer online.

Carly and I took seats overlooking the enormous meandering pool designed to flow like a river. The weather cooperated with a gentle breeze. Though decidedly cooler than our last visit, I still doubted we would be in need of the sweaters all three of us had packed.

"At least we aren't in Aspen, or Ruidoso," Carly said. "It could be snowing on us."

Carly. Always the one to find the silver lining on a cloud of rust, or the sugar rim on a glass of castor oil. I smiled and took in the warmth of the sun and the breathtaking views.

"What exactly is Sterling doing?" Carly asked.

"She's looking at the trail map again. And I think she's intent on talking to a forest ranger."

"I love her, but I swear I thought her only talent was in bobbing along with her baubles," Carly laughed.

The waitperson arrived with a wine stand, a chilling bottle, and three glasses.

"We didn't order this," I said.

"And you will love it," she said. "Compliments of another guest."

"Who?" I asked.

"I don't know. The order came from the inside lounge."

"Wait here," I said to Carly, and stumbled in my heels as I dashed toward where the waitperson had pointed. I didn't think of the practicality of wearing flip flops.

Wedging myself between patrons at the bar, I apologized and begged for the bartender's attention.

"Who sent this to us?"

"I wish I could tell you," he said. "Impossible. We have three conferences going on right now."

"But it must have been charged to a room. You must have records," I demanded.

"I'm pretty sure the guy paid cash. Said he didn't want to charge it to his room, at least."

"What did he look like?"

"Old guy. Dapper, I guess you could say. Seemed real friendly."

"That's all?" I asked.

He shrugged, turning to reach for the back cabinet and a bottle of Petron tequila as he poured the next order.

I forced myself to accept the situation. I apologized once again to the other guests and returned to the outside table.

The decanted wine now filled two of the three glasses.

Carly said, "Why are you freaking out? It's not the first time we've been offered a free drink. I find it charming."

No way was I anywhere near charmed.

"Look! It's produced locally," Carly said. "An Arizona vineyard. Didn't even know they could grow grapes in this dry heat. That's a foreign grape to me."

Where had I sipped an Arizona wine before? It didn't surprise me like it had Carly. Arizona had regions with vineyards. Whatever the nagging feeling, I had to agree it seemed out of the ordinary.

"Let me worry," I said. "A nice guy buys a bottle of wine for two women without evidence of male companions. A bottle? And why did he send three glasses over?"

"Good lord," Carly said. "He spent good money on a full bottle and hoped to join us and partake, but then you go into the bar and scare him away."

A bright flash of color headed our way. Sterling's halter dress popped with orange poppies. Her long blond hair caught the full attention of the breeze.

"This place is drop-dead gorgeous, but I gotta tell you, I think we're at the wrong resort," Sterling announced.

"What do you mean? We were lucky to get rooms here," Carly said.

Sterling swiftly filled the third wine stem. "Turns out I think we may be on the wrong side of town. There's a Saguaro Park West and it makes sense we're looking there. It's the larger of the parks and it's nearby Payton's home. But there's another one on the opposite edge of town. Saguaro Park East. And it has a trail named cactus-something or other."

"And you know this how?" I asked.

"Talked to a smooth-talking ranger named Jeremy. He's walked every square-inch of both parks."

I sat staring at the table. Maybe my vision seemed obscured by the glowing sunset evidenced by the light it shed on the mountains. Or Sterling's shiny attire. I winced and squinted, focusing on the sparkling glasses of wine.

Had our host ever intended to join us or did he know there were three of us?

Then it hit me.

The old man at Catrozzi's Restaurant. A gift of wine born from the fruit of an Arizona vineyard.

Chapter Fifty-Eight
Starr Pass

AS SELF-PROCLAIMED Trail Guide, Sterling was the first to awaken. The tantalizing aroma of brewing coffee forced me to open my eyes and roll off the bed. I tossed on my robe and joined her out on the patio.

For a long time and only as you can do with good friends, we sat in a sheltered silence.

"I do love it here," Sterling said after a slow sip on her coffee. "I loved the brilliant city lights last night. Not an L.A. glitz kind of brilliant, but beckoning. Sitting here now, I love how the sunlight begins to paint the mountains with strokes of inspiration. Kind of a da Vinci-inspired light."

I tilted my head and nodded in appreciation.

"Don't get me wrong. I'm a city girl all the way," Sterling said. "I don't like snakes."

Always a caveat with Sterling, but I loved her hidden qualities. Smart, for one. Computer savvy. And an appreciation for Mother Nature? These are things I didn't know about my childhood friend. Sterling? She grew up with that sterling spoon in her mouth.

She filled in my lack of words. "I'm only a ditzy blonde when I have an old man walk into the store. He doesn't know it when he enters through the door, but he's going to drop a wad of dough right into my lap for more diamonds than he wanted. Lots more. I even get away with charging them extra for gift-wrapping, but only if I play dumb enough.

"One customer came in and asked for two custom pieces. Mind you, his wife's name is in our files. He wanted gold dicks with Prince Albert diamonds on the heads, and not one was for the wifey."

"And you can accommodate that order?"

"Our business is custom. But this request? Well, it was extraordinarily custom. We have a gay goldsmith that was perfect for the job. He probably got a rise out of it.

"But get this. He wanted the same size gold dick for both of his girlfriends. But one got two carats and the other one got three."

"Wow. That's a hefty load for any dick to carry," I said, "given any Prince Alpert."

"That's Albert, with a *B*."

Funny girl, too. And now I would begin to take her for the smart and calculating blonde she was. She could even spell.

"So you think we should just pack up and drive to the east side?" I asked.

"That's what my lovely Ranger Jeremy suggests. Might as well, while we are here."

"We look for three saguaro spines, upright or felled. And then what?"

"Then we look for the secrets of the Sisterhood of Skeletons."

Carly stumbled out to the patio, with bleary eyes and a cup of coffee steadied by both hands. She flipped a sealed envelope onto the table.

"Where did that come from?" I asked.

"I opened the door to get the morning paper and the envelope fell out of it."

Studying my name printed in calligraphy on the front, I smoothed my fingers over the shaky but honorable old-style of formal writing.

"Come on! Open it!" Sterling said.

Having had more death threats circulating around me, I thought better of the idea. I passed the envelope over to Sterling.

She snatched it in midair and ripped the seal. Then she stopped.

"I'm too chicken. I don't play this game as well as I pretend," she said. She passed the envelope back to Carly.

Carly studied the writing. "It's difficult to decipher. The writing is horrible," she said.

"Okay. The message is plain and simple. She read it aloud:

"Good girls. It was no suicide."

Sterling withdrew deeper into her seat cushion and pulled her lanky legs up toward her chin. She drew a long breath. "You see! We have more friends on board with us, right?"

I scoured the note. And then each and every word. Every letter.

It was surely that from the old man that had sent me the reward of a few bucks after I returned his wallet. And that claim check for the stupid set of golf clubs. But how could that be?

"At least he's not scaring us away," Carly said, unable to understand where my deductions had taken me.

I wondered. Was he trying to scare us? At the very least, he was a stalker, if it was the same old man that had spied me dining alone in Cattrozzi's and now knew three of us had arrived in Tucson on an uninviting mission. It didn't feel, to me, that the unknown welcoming committee really welcomed us on our journey.

No. He wouldn't scare us away. But maybe he was inviting us into his web.

Chapter Fifty-Nine
On the Trail

WE CHECKED OUT OF Starr Pass without the luxury of enjoying the pool or the golf course. We made the drive to Saguaro National Park East.

"You didn't fail us, Sterling," Carly said. "I can't believe what you dug up."

The same kind of amazement I felt. Smart dumb blonde.

All three of us were a united front, if only words on any faded T-shirt. We told ourselves that if we had seen three saguaro skeletons in the west park we would have remembered such an unusual sight. Plus, we had photographs to back up our memories.

Sterling confirmed that no one outside of the forest ranger knew of our impending hike. Still, I watched the rearview all the way across town, down Tanque Verde Road, and even well into the park's parking lot. Be they friends or foes, it seemed that we were rich with persons interested in our pursuit.

Sterling navigated us toward our trailhead on to the Cactus Forest Trail. Equipped with hiking boots, heavy work gloves, and a couple of small hand trowels we'd picked up at yet another Tucson hardware store, we headed up the trail.

Once on the trail, Carly was the first to falter, but only after tripping twice and catching her fall with gloves that only protected her hands. Stickers shot up out of the skin on her arms.

"This is a waste of time," she said. "Why would Payton come all the way across Tucson to this park when she lived on the west side? It's not like there aren't plenty of hiding places there."

"Keep walking. Keep looking," Sterling said, with a sudden healthy outburst of a Boy Scout's attitude.

And we did.

A trio of troopers. Naïve in desert country and even more naïve about what the hell we were trying to accomplish.

Still, as all little troopers go, we marched forward like amorous dogs in search of tail. Any tail.

Sterling forged ahead on our ominous mission, sweeping branches and stickers out of our way, and even pointing out the horny toad taking shelter under a massive rock. Dust swirled around us and somehow we took relief in the hot breeze.

Carly grumbled something again about stumbling into three human skulls. We laughed and refueled on the water bottles with electrolytes we'd picked up at Trader Joe's. The water was warm. We didn't complain with the wet sensation on our dry mouths and tongues.

We continued for another mile or so. The trail wasn't steep. Carly and I took turns taking photographs. Of nothing. When we came upon a cluster of boulders it took no communication for all of us to decide it was time to rest. Drawing on our bottled water, we swung our necks at the sound of snapping twigs behind us.

"It's a public trail," I said, with water dribbling down my chin.

"Yes," Sterling mumbled, taking in the vista that surrounded us with ample viewing opportunities for anyone that may care to look. Or spy.

Carly forced a laugh. "We're paranoid. Look at us! We look like punk Desert Rats. Nobody gives a damn about what the three of us are up to."

Little doubt none of us believed our own words. We felt vulnerable. Exposed to both the desert sun and the juxtaposed danger of mankind, we remembered Victor Romero's warning.

We shared one question, for we knew we were being watched.

Friend or foe?

Chapter Sixty
Snake

COMMON SENSE DICTATED we stick to the trail. Carly had procured a walking stick from the desert brush and now took the lead. At the sound of castanets where no castanets should be in the middle of fricking nowhere, she froze.

The coiled rattlesnake sprung left, then right. He was near enough I could see the diamonds on his back and his forked tongue biting at the air.

Sterling neared me. With a low voice she demanded the potion.

"What?" I said.

"Don't mess with us now, Lauren. The voodoo potion. You have it in your backpack. Slowly pull it out and use it."

Both Carly and Sterling had given me plenty of crap about Geoff's crazy grandmother's potion. Sterling knew I had it when I'd long ago forgotten I'd tossed it into in my backpack to journey through the middle of the Sonoran Desert.

I slid the small vial from the stiff denier of the outer pocket on my backpack. I fondled it. I tried to recall Geoff's words when he gave it to me. I closed my eyes.

I placed one drop on my tongue, then spat it out. That is what Sterling and Carly told me later as I have no clear recall.

The snake's rattling grew fiercer.

Two drops dripped onto my tongue.

The snake reared its head, prepared to strike at any or all of us.

Something inside of me continued with *her* tongue sticking out of me, the vial of liquid catching glints from the high sun. I turned to Sterling and spat the liquid into her face. I turned to Carly and spat in her face.

I could hear myself. I had no control. I began to ululate in a voice more customary of ancient cultures, times, and places.

The snake uncoiled. Wary, watching; then turning to slither away.

"Let's go," I suddenly announced. I felt a lift of opaque fog that had clouded my memory, and maybe my judgment.

Carly and Sterling were still frozen in their hiking boots, but eager to get away.

Sterling backed up. Carly cowered.

"No," I said. "We have to follow it."

"You have to be out of your fucking mind," Sterling said.

"We follow it," I demanded.

The encounter is one I will not forget. I stood almost trancelike but fully cognizant, in the middle of the desert.

For me, it amounted to a trust that materialized out of the dust that day. A knowing trust.

We followed the snake as it winded away, and within minutes we stood before three fallen saguaro.

Other than Carly's shoulder twitching, we came to a still-stop in front of the skeletons. Once again, I took the vial of potion, stared at my friends, and placed four drops in the position of the four directions.

I said we must fall to our knees and bless the earth. Three city girls and with a rattlesnake nearby. But they did as I somehow instructed, in silence and with jaws dropped.

Chapter Sixty-One
Voodoo & Who

IN ONE MOMENT of eternity we watched the snake slither away.

I regained a sense of purpose. I pulled out the hand rake wedged into my belt. Sterling and Carly followed suit. None of us spoke about what had just occurred. Not one word.

It was I that pulled at the arm of the furthest skeleton. It shattered under my hard tug, and beneath it I could see the corner of a clear plastic bag.

Sterling dropped to the ground. "What is it?" she said in her own calm but upbeat voice.

"It's a flash stick," I said.

A severely damaged flash stick that looked like it had endured years on a populated railroad track.

It was then that I heard Geoff's words replaying in my mind when he handed me his magic potion: "My grandmother had one more message. You will sing and have no memory of it, and that will be a good thing."

WE DELIVERED THE bag and its contents to Victor Romero. It had not survived the elements in the plastic bag. The heat had melted what was left of the plastic surrounding the element. A creature had long ago ravished most of it, extracting what he could to make a nice comfy den somewhere nearby, Romero told us.

"Indeed," Romero said. "The treasures of the desert. I'll have to send it to a lab. See if we can get anything off of it. I can't promise you much."

We nodded.

"Do you mind telling me how you found it?"

I looked across at Sterling. Carly looked at me. Sterling looked at my backpack.

"Must have been voodoo magic," I said.

DETECTIVE WRAY MIGHT as well have been Denzel Washington, as he took over the halls of *CoverBoy*. He'd interviewed the entire staff at least twice, and they all loved him. He was still an annoying Columbo to me.

He positioned himself at my door, holding up a hand with the index finger raised. "Just one more question, today, Ms. Visconti. This won't take long."

I kept reminding myself his presence around our offices meant free additional security.

"Yes, Detective?"

"Do you know of a place called The Center?"

The lump in my throat wasn't going down. What was he up too, now?

"I'm just curious," he continued.

"Yes. I know of it."

"Now does that mean you know of it in the magazine publishing business, or is it a personal knowledge?"

THE LAWYER COAL HAD scrounged up along the way and so many years ago turned out to be his trump card. A coup to find the little esquire. Not so hot at getting him off the string of misdemeanor charges and warnings, but most excellent in handling the mishandling of estate law. It seemed the guy had found his niche acting as executor to the largest estates whose heirs were either MIA or otherwise mentally incapacitated. When Coal first met this fine attorney, the man was acting attorney and executor to twelve of the city's largest empirical fortunes.

Unfortunately, Coal put an end to that prosperous relationship when some of his carnal temptations made their way to the misguided and unforgiving press. Turns out that by some cruel act of fate one of Coal's conquests turned out to be the whiney attorney's ten-year old nephew.

Coal had learned his lessons. After the revocation of his license in New York, he headed off to the dusty highways of Arizona, where life promised him anonymity and, along with that, a certain absolution if only by omissions.

Coal was a master at patience. That discipline would unlock the larger-than-life pocket books, unsuspectingly hidden around the small city of Tucson. He was the only player in town. He'd hone in on the lonely and the depressed and especially, yes—the suicidal. Great companions. Better marks.

The next stage was the most delicate. Wait. As they turned to him more and more he'd start them out on a diet low in protein. Wait. Then love-bomb them again. And wait again. He'd deplete their bodies of nutrients, and then enrich their fragile minds in what he could do for them. And he would wait with a timing superior to the rising and falling sun.

This crazy runaway drifter kid he'd met in New York led him directly to Tucson and his even crazier sister. Payton Doukas was relatively low stakes, but her two friends were royal tickets. And the third friend from Chicago would be moving to California. He had every intention of setting up 'shop' long before her arrival.

He'd studied their profiles. Lauren Visconti would be the biggest mark he'd ever made. Poor little rich girl. Daddy died. Fiancé died. Everybody poor little Lauren loves seems to die.

It didn't hurt that Coal knew about the rape, too. Bad blood running in that girl. And Coal knew that idea of a bastard-seed left Visconti helpless. And Visconti had no idea that she and Coal shared the same blood. Poor little Lauren. She didn't stand a chance, especially because she believed it.

Armand was right. Two little problems with Visconti. She was smart and well connected. She was also messed up and vulnerable. And perfect for a take. Especially, given the fact that with every one of those tragic deaths Lauren's financial pot grew exponentially.

Sterling Falls would prove to be a bit more challenging. Oh, not getting her into bed. That would only be his problem if it came time to perform with a woman. Smallish boobs, and he didn't even like boobs. An outrageous personality, which Coal admitted fascinated him. Maybe that would prove to be the ultimate challenge. But she was dumb and dumber. With a very rich daddy.

She had no money to speak of, but all of that would change dramatically with the fatal fall of Old Man Falls. Coal would take care of those nasty details, and who knows? Maybe he had groomed Armand well enough to take the Falls girl in the sexual relations department. He'd seen Sterling fixate her eyes on any and every handsome foreign-looking man. God knows Armand would be up to the task, as long as he didn't beat her up. The thing is, and Coal was so good at this—he saw something in the bimbo no one else could perceive. Something. She'd be tricky to fully conquer. He'd have to go to work, research her a little more, and trust in his powers of persuasion.

Knowledge is power.

Chapter Sixty-Two

No Kissing Cousins

WHEN BAD THINGS happen to good people they either get tough or let go. Sometimes they die. *Que sera, sera.*

But when bad things happen to everyone you love, you give up. You quit loving.

The wedding dress turned to paper. The smoke and flames engulfed everyone but me, and yet I wore the tinder.

I sat straight up in my bed. The windows were open. The sea breeze had calmed to a gentle movement timed to the crashes of the tide. The rhythmic motion should have centered me. Instead, it made me further delve into the very notion of life's rhythms and the messages hidden in the dream.

There was a new twist to my Visconti Curse that gnawed at my stomach lining. I had adored the runway model. And I loved and respected Dhurra. They were both dead.

I deplored the ruthless and greedy plastic surgeon. I hated the pedophile priest. They, too, were dead.

What had changed? Was the curse now attaching itself to anyone I felt *any* emotion toward? Good or bad?

THE NEXT MORNING I asked Geoff to meet me at a local café. He had yet to sit down before I started drilling

229

him. What had I done out there with the snake in the middle of the desert and with his dead grandmother's voodoo potion in my hands? He hadn't exactly given me instructions on snake encounters and voodoo potions. Sure as hell didn't tell me anything about spitting in my friends' faces. I acted as if I'd rehearsed the scene twenty times before. I knew exactly what to do. Somehow.

He simply stated, "My grandmother. That's all you need to know. She journeyed with you."

WHILE TWO OF MY head writers had abandoned *CoverBoy*, three remained.

Gone was the electric charge of creative energy. Instead people shuffled into chairs, mumbled pleasantries. and closed their mouths.

"We have to ramp up our stories. It's either that or we might as well bail out right now," I told them.

They fidgeted in their chairs. I chose to nurse on a quad-shot of pure caffeine.

My junior writer spoke first. "The article on podiatrists and cut off toes got us lots of traffic. And no death threats. We're on the right track."

"That's great," I said. "Let's talk about traffic. The slave-trafficking entering America. The girls, the slaves being shipped into the cities hosting big sports events. Play-off games. March Madness. The Super Bowl. Thousands of sex slaves right here in America."

"Don't tell me we're back off to Afghanistan?" Sukie whined.

"I said America. And that means roundtrip tickets to Toledo."

GABRIELLE CRISCIONE steadied both her thoughts and her carving knife. The thick venison on her cutting board needed to be sliced razor thin, for her guests would expect nothing less of her.

She focused on the task at hand, with no remorse for the sick sonuva bitch. How many names had he burned through? Hell, he may be her second cousin, but he would always be a Judd. The Judd's and the Criscione's family tree intertwined the branches of wickedness cultivated by immorality and a vicious greed.

It made her sick.

Chapter Sixty-Three
The Fall of Falls

STERLING CALLED ME at 10:30 the following morning. Her voice rattled off in a distant stream of consciousness. Clearly, her throat sounded strangled as if wrapped in leather boot laces. One word and deep gasps. Another sentence, inaudible, with garbled words choked by tears.

"It's Dad. He's not in yet."

"He's not at the store?"

"No. I mean yes," she cried.

I knew instantly why panic registered. Her father always arrived at Falls & Falls at precisely 9:00 a.m., even though the jewelry store didn't open its doors for business until ten. That, and the fact he had undergone two major heart surgeries in the past eighteen months provoked good cause for alarm.

"Theresa said Dad wanted her in early to inventory some new loose diamonds."

Theresa ran as slow as the last smidgen of catsup oozing out of the bottom of a spent bottle. She'd also been an employee of Falls & Falls for some thirty years.

"Did you call his home? And his cell?" I asked.

"He doesn't pick up!"

"Who's there with you?"

"Theresa, Curtis, Kathleen, and me. We're all here."

"Sterling, it's Wednesday. Doesn't your dad play gin at his old tennis club today?"

"Not until 11:00. He should be here by now."

"He probably didn't charge his phone. You know how he is. And he's just running late. These things happen. The man likes to play his cards and he'll be there."

I didn't believe my own words. Something was wrong.

"What the hell do I do?" Sterling asked.

"You wait twenty minutes and then you call some of his gin buddies. If he's not there I'll meet you over at his house. In the meantime, if it will make you feel better, you call the police and see if he's been in an accident."

Silence.

"Just give them your dad's name and a description of his car. And the roads he takes to work. Okay?"

"Okay. But Lauren, I'm scared to death."

"I'm worried, too," I admitted, but we both knew he liked his nips of booze, too. Sometimes it didn't matter the time of day.

Fifteen minutes later I agreed to meet Sterling at her father's home. I was closer.

MY ROUTE TO Oliver Fall's house proved short and direct. I arrived well before Sterling. With the garage sealed up tight and no windows, I couldn't tell if his car was inside.

I rang the bell and used the heavy brass door knocker. I called out his name, always Mr. Falls to me.

Kicking off my heels, I sprinted across the lawn and the perimeter of the front. The window blinds were closed. I headed toward the side of the modest home when I heard the familiar engine purr of Sterling's car.

She wore an ashen gray face with the key fob shaking in her hand. I grabbed it from her and unlocked the front

233

door. Sterling had the presence of mind to disengage the alarm system.

Looking through to the family room, we could see Mr. Falls asleep on the sofa.

"Good grief," Sterling grumbled. "Daddy must have gotten into his gin bottle before his gin table today."

She stormed ahead of me. "Dad. Get the hell up. You blew off your meeting with Theresa and you had us all worried sick."

I knew what was happening. Mr. Falls always met his commitments, in spite of his penchant for a nip or a guzzle of liquor now and then. Concern and worry turn into anger before the next stage, which is usually truth. They say love is blind. This was that special beautiful bonding love between a father and daughter as I saw it unfolding in front of me.

And I knew this much was true. The loving daughter was blind to the reality she was facing.

Chapter Sixty-Four
Another Memorable Memorial

PARAMEDICS ARRIVED WITHIN ten minutes. They were about ten hours too late.

Falls died of massive coronary heart failure. Although my mom, dad, fiancé, best friend, and every other death I'd encountered were unexpected, Sterling knew in her heart that this day was inevitable.

I understood that grief is an equal opportunity employer.

THE MEMORIAL SERVICE displayed the dignity of the man we were honoring and remembering. Quiet. Respectable. Even Sterling toned down her glitz. Flowers overflowed. No one could prevent the mourners' arrival en masse, although the final wishes of Oliver Falls dictated cremation without pomp and circumstance.

Brock had an away game. Excused. But where was Carly?

Sterling and I hadn't really made any plans for afterward, but I presumed I would take what guests might linger on to a nice meal at an equally quiet restaurant. Sterling shocked me when she told me she was unavailable. She and Dr. Coal were leaving together. They had made other plans.

"I didn't realize you even knew Dr. Coal," I said.

"Daddy liked Harlan," Sterling said.

235

She must have seen the distress in my eyes. And maybe jealously, which is hardly an appropriate emotion at the conclusion of a memorial service.

"Daddy probably liked Harlan because he knew he's the only male friend I have that hasn't jumped my bones. That's a record for me, you know," Sterling said in defense.

"You're dating him?" I asked.

"A few times. If you can call no sex a date. He's not my shrink, Lauren. You can't go after him on ethic charges. And in case you haven't noticed he's a drop-dead hunk."

"Of course," I uttered, still unsure why it was a private affair between the two of them, and right after the service. Yes. Coal was my shrink, although after the invitation to buy the home on his compound I had neglected to schedule any further sessions with him. Somehow, I got the feeling Coal could be more persuasive than Gabri when it came to buying a home. Somehow, I didn't want a dead person's house. And I certainly didn't want to move away from the beach.

The timing was all wrong, but still I wanted to ask Sterling what Coal was like. The man and not the shrink. On a date. And I wondered why in the world, if he wasn't the seducer, had Sterling not yet seduced him—in totality.

The timing was wrong. I would wait.

CARLY WAS NO WHERE to be found. I kept phoning her studio and cell. Finally, I called Sterling.

"Oh, yeah," Sterling said. She took off for a few days. Gave her employees some time off, too. She was going to take some days for herself, and then go install some big design job. You know the one. The job that's going to cash flow her new antique store."

I knew. And I didn't. Honestly, my mind and time and efforts had been driven back to *CoverBoy*, and then to help Sterling handle her father's final goodbye. I had left the tumultuous affairs of Payton Doukas into the capable hands of Victor Romero. As for all the heinous stuff going on with the slayings that seemed to surface with every issue I printed, I guess I had left that to Detective Wray. It seemed to me there was some guy out there pulling a Robin Hood thing. Instead of robbing from the rich he was robbing the world of all evil.

"You haven't spoken to Carly?" I asked.

"She's not returned my calls, like I could care right now," Sterling said. "She's a big girl. Chasing her dream."

Chapter Sixty-Five
Fateful Decisions

ARMAND'S REGURGITATED memories could satisfy him for weeks. Occasionally, after an especially delightful encounter, he could go for months.

He was no killer but he loved blood. He obtained his fix with the brutality of his own hands. The burgeoning skin that instantly swelled under the force of those hands only caused him to want more. He preferred the screams that came with it, but he acquiesced to Coal and stuck with the Rohypnol. Sort of. Sometimes he cheated on that promise. When living in the desert he'd experimented with the abundant oleander foliage, and, later, he learned the wonders of camphor. Armand especially liked the convulsions when he used camphor. It beat the hell out of fucking a passed-out ragdoll on the roofies.

He abandoned the rohypnol all together after he had found the magic of the colorless, odorless, and tasteless scopolamine.

How stupid of him to waste time on the other drugs. Yes. So easy to get from his homeland in Bogota, scopolamine became his drug of choice.

Armand had long-known that he had two problems. One, rohypnol might cause a type of amnesia, but in recent court trials, clever attorneys had placed their poor little victims under hypnosis and their lost memories were not lost at all. They were there on the hidden transcripts of the brain all along.

Harlan Coal assured Armand that he could take care of any of those memories, claiming them as false, or even laying the fresh veil of a new memory over any reality. But that led Armand to his second problem. Coal had made himself indispensable to him.

Armand was quick to reclaim his roots. The *borrachero* tree. Scopolamine and its drunken pollen stopped any recorder in the brain. Not a pause. No record. Just STOPPED.

A few seeds and the drug could be lethal. Armand learned this to be true through trial and error. But pure and cheap scopolamine, easily acquired throughout Bogota and the harvested fields of Ecuador, allowed Armand to be in control of his own destiny. This secret, he owned.

I love my life, Armand thought. The Rohypnol and all the other drugs leave my conquests like splayed-out dolphins after the slaughter. How fun is that? With the *borrachero*, his little playmates were free to scream, slither, and slash back at him. Just the way he liked to come—good and hard.

He did enjoy the privacy of the Bel Air house. The huge walls afforded him more options, but, too many times Harlan Coal would ditch some of his boy toys inside. He'd have to keep them doped up, along with any of his bloody little whores.

The whole scene grew wearisome, even as he folded up his black leather gloves and folded them into his pocket. *Better than latex, should ever his memory-loss program fail him.* The gloves scared the shit out of his girls, Armand reminisced. Just like they had the Visconti woman.

CARLY LOVED BIG BEAR. She breathed in the cool pure mountain air and felt the pulse of time slowing down as she left the big city of angels behind in her rear-view mirror.

In time, she would ask Sterling for forgiveness, for even though she knew about Sterling's father's death, Carly had a business future to secure. Surely Sterling would understand. Sterling had been born with a sterling silver spoon in her mouth and Lauren's was golden, but they would both somehow remember Carly's splintered wooden one.

The cabin rested on the rim of the lake, protected by a cathedral of towering pines. Carly had never met the non-resident owner, but she'd been up to the property on four occasions to tour it, take measurements, and facilitate the deconstruction process that needed to occur prior to the magic of her design work, furnishings, and accessories.

Carly knew the scale of the job would match any king's castle. The income would be enough for her to place the phone call to Gabriella Criscione. Carly would finally secure her dream antique store.

The truck had delivered the first phase of furniture and accessories. Although they would be stripped of shipping containers and any wrapping, Carly would be lucky if the king-sized mattress set actually made it into the master bedroom.

The owner wouldn't arrive for another two months. His parameters proved to be vast. He didn't want too much cabin-like horse and cowboy crap, no contemporary look, and no Scandinavian. The left Carly's design palette wide open, fueled by an exorbitant budget.

With a bed she could put together herself, decorator towels and linens she could replace before the owner ever knew it, and a remote quiet, Big Bear beckoned her.

The hundred-mile drive had never been so easy. Carly needed time to think, oblivious to any verdict of fate.

Chapter Sixty-Six
Big Bear

JUMPING OUT OF the van, Carly stretched out her legs, took a deep breath of pine-laced air, then grabbed a load of the new linens from the cargo door.

A quick walk-through and Carly realized the delivery men did a better job than she expected. Even the beds had been put together. It pays three-fold to treat your people with respect and surprise bonuses, Carly thought. Some designers refused to treat their hired labor as humans, let alone give them tips.

She eagerly grabbed the August Horn linens and dressed the king bed for a good night of sleep. She'd already made the note to take what would now be used linens home with her and reorder new ones. Even at her cost, she would not be one to invest in them for herself, but this time was different. This time was special.

Carly would enjoy a great night or two of sleep. Maybe even three. She would work hard on the furniture, the art, the lighting, and accessories. And she would have time to relish and bless this design job that would launch her into her new career as proprietor of a world-class antique store.

After finishing making up her borrowed bed Carly toured the rest of the home. New tongue and groove flooring banished any sensation of the cold or damp. The leathered granite counters, installed in the kitchen, three bathrooms, and the wetbar offered a surface of milky-green perfection. Copia Designworks hardware adorned walls and cabinetry. Their bronze towel bars hung like pieces of art, cabinet knobs and pulls rose off the cherry wood panels, as if each one opened up a treasured jewelry box.

While firmly attached, Carly could feel the meaty weight of the bronze knobs as she opened up the cabinets. The empty cupboards would be filled with her ultimate kitchen package in another six weeks. She needed the time to lug the heavy pieces of furniture and art around without concern for breaking the new china and crystal.

Besides, her client wouldn't be there and expect complete perfection for another eight weeks.

Lala Corriere

Chapter Sixty-Seven
Beach Storm

RETURNING HOME FROM the sorrow of Oliver Falls' memorial service, I made several more calls to track down Carly.

Nothing. Maybe she really did need a great escape.

My car never got over twenty miles an hour, even though it felt like I'd been taking curves in a racing Shelby with no idea how to shift.

Traffic was crawling out to the beach communities. Rain pelted down hard as the wiper blades caught blowing grit and sand that scraped across the windshield.

When my cell rang the diversion startled me, so hard were my eyes focused on staying on the road.

"I'm worried about you out in this storm," Brock said.

"I'm a little worried about me, too," I admitted. "Are you home?"

"You bet I'm at home, and dry. You bolted from Oliver Falls' reception service before I could tell you the good news that I have a few days off for good behavior. You didn't even see me there."

I'm sorry I didn't see him. I could have used his shoulder. But this wasn't good news. Brock's old shoulder injury had never healed properly, but the pitcher refused to baby it the way it deserved and the coach, the team, and the league seemed to look the other way. For a while.

"Look, I didn't bolt. I just knew this storm would hit hard and I wanted to try and beat it. And you sound like you're in pain. Are you hurt?" I asked.

"I'm okay. I'll be back in the game soon."

"Did you see Carly there at the service?"

"Nope. And where are you by now?"

"I'm almost home. Ten minutes. I have a full tank of gas but I'm low on windshield solvent. I guess I'm sort of hoping it keeps pouring rather than have sand sticking to the glass."

"Swing into a station and get some solvent."

"Too lazy. And like I said, I'm ten minutes from home."

"The forecast is gloom and doom and it sounds like the coast is getting the brunt of it. You take twenty minutes, then call me."

I shut off my cell and drove another thirty minutes, sighing with relief when my car pulled into my drive and the garage door rolled open.

The wind gusts pushed the pelting rain into my damp but warm garage. Closing the overhead door before I exited the car, I listened as the wind moaned and the massive door heaved and creaked. Smell of salt and sand—a refreshing smell now, that I wasn't driving in it, permeated the air.

Windshield solvent, I remembered. I should put some in now, rather than forget it and risk muddy drive conditions in the morning.

I popped the release of my hood and pulled it up. When I turned toward the oak cabinet that housed my limited selection of auto supplies, the hood slammed shut.

A second attempt produced similar results.

Shit. Okay. Prop it up with something. No big deal.

The broomstick was too long to squeeze in, I deduced. The squeegee, and where the hell did I get that? It was too short, anyway.

Feeling like Goldilocks, I searched for just the right size of gadget that would hold the damn hood open. The roar of the wind urged me to go inside, but logic told me I was safe from any weather if I'd take the time to put the stupid solvent in my car. Hopefully, the storm would be gone before my morning commute, but just in case...

I opened the built-in closets to find them bare-to-empty. Then I spied the golf bag. The same one I had collected from the airport package service.

I unzipped the cover and pulled out one of the shorter clubs. Golf is not my game, but I know I used an iron. Just the right size. Goldilocks got it right.

Once again I popped the release button and lifted the hood, wedging the club into place. I had started pouring the solution into the funnel when the crash sounded and I jumped, losing control of both the solvent and the funnel.

As the golf bag careened over to the concrete floor, its contents splayed through the air. White golf balls toppled out and pinged across from wall to wall. Clubs spewed out of the bag with a harsh clanging noise, along with dozens of pieces of paper.

The solvent now poured onto my shoes and the surface under them, blazing a river of steely blue liquid toward the mess of golf clubs. Only then did I realize the papers were photographs.

Without thought, I collapsed to the floor and scrambled to retrieve the glossy images.

Revolting. My hands shook as I glanced at the photographs, wiping off the fluid where I could. Black and whites. Color. Sodomy. Fellatio. Naked boys of every size and color. I couldn't tell their ages, but if they were of

COVER BOYS AND CURSES

flesh and blood, they were all innocent children that had been violated.

I didn't want to look at them. I couldn't look away. One photo, then another and another. I scooped them up and dumped them into a garbage bag, bringing the uninvited nightmare into my home.

Why were the photographs in a golf bag?

Where did the golf bag come from?

Where were the kids' parents and how could they let their children fall victim to such atrocious evil?

I dumped the images onto my travertine floor. Nausea set in, an odd companion to an ever more disquieting sense of familiarity. A knowing sense, although of what—I did not know.

At first, it was just one photograph that captured my mind. A pillow on the floor. A pair of wire rim glasses, common enough. A Dhurrie rug. Again, common enough.

What was it that unsettled me?

I scoured more images and returned to the one that held my stomach captive.

The Dhurrie rug. It was a pattern I knew.

I sorted through the photographs again. A realm of familiarity engulfed me.

My eyes and my heart froze when I focused on the statue of the ivory elephant with a raised foot and in a boat, and perched on a blue slab of stone. Lapis lazuli.

It had been in *his* office. I saw it there on my first visit. Definitely, he had told me it was one of a kind.

Chapter Sixty-Eight
Perhaps Not Circumstantial

AS THE ROOM swirled to keep up with my stomach, I
snagged my cell phone and called the only person I could
think to call. Someone who had helped the bad things go
away, ever since grade school.

Brock was at my house within twenty minutes.

"Forty-two of these photographs," he counted out.
"That's not just one moment of indiscretion we're looking
at."

The photographs now lined the top of my dining room
table. The dimmer on my chandelier was set on high to
cast the maximum light on the disgusting exhibit.

Brock asked me to find a magnifying glass, which he
knew I often used to scour Sukie Fields' work.

"What should I do?" I asked.

"You're sure about this statue?"

"I've been told it's one of kind. And that one of a kind
is in Harlan Coal's office. Plus, I recognize other things,
including the rugs."

"You should call the police. That detective."

"I have to think about that. The man already believes,
and with every right, that I'm up to my eyeballs in
murder."

"Okay. Then think about this. How is it you ended up with these photographs?" Brock picked up the photo with the statue. It seemed eerily weighted in his hand.

"I have no idea. Coincidence?"

"Something stinks," Brock said. "Think back. We were together when we found the wallets. The day I picked you up at the airport and we ran into those would-be car thieves."

"So maybe they belong to you. You should have taken them."

I tried and failed to break a smile.

"You returned the wallets to their rightful owners. And then some guy sends you back a receipt and the receipt lead to these clubs. Did you save his name and address?"

"No. I remember I didn't use any tracking numbers. No insurance or return receipts. I just wanted them out of my possession and back to their owners."

The rain continued to pelt down against the glass panes of my windows. It would have hurt like peas flying out of a peashooter against raw flesh.

Bare flesh. Young boys. Dr. Coal?

I jumped up to close the plantation shutters. I suppose I tried to keep out the boogey-man.

Brock dropped the photograph back onto the table. "Do you think someone put those photos in the golf bag after it was already here at your house?"

"Now you're scaring me!"

"I'm not the one who wants to scare you. The obvious suspect would be that gloved maniac that threatened you at your doorstep. He wanted to scare the piss out of you. I think we need to call that detective friend of yours."

"He's not my friend, and wait, Brock. Please. Just you and me, for now. Let's keep playing detective ourselves. It's a gut instinct. Please."

249

"No telling how old these kids are," Brock said. "A lot of 'em look to be of age, but then we have ones like this and we're looking at a serious crime, Laurs."

He tossed over a photo of a skinny little boy pulling himself up out of a black Jacuzzi. He had the face of a cherub; the only puffy flesh on his body filled out his cheeks. He couldn't have been more than ten. Maybe eleven.

"Where are these kids now?" Why do you suppose not one of them has come forward or gotten any media attention?" I choked back tears.

"There's no crime without victims. And you and I have both seen your Doctor Coal in action. He's a fucking bona-fide bullshitter that could sell bicycles as transportation in the middle of the fucking Aegean Sea. You know what he does. He's the provider of verbal lobotomies!"

I nodded. Disdain filled my mind just as despondency laced my throat. "Through experience, I know a few things too many about the pathways of our legal system. Just because some of Coal's possessions seem to be in the photographs, he's not in them. He could claim it to be anyone. Especially with his no-locks-on-doors policy.

"And he wants me to move onto The Centre grounds."

"He fucking what?" Brock yelled. "Why didn't you tell me this? When?"

"It's no big deal. A home became available at The Centre and he asked if I wanted it."

"Bullshit. Coincidence, my ass."

"I know you're the poster boy of baseball on game days," I said, desperate to change the subject if only for a moment. "No drinking a few full hours in a row. But you're off the field right now. How about a brandy?"

"I bet my doctor would insist upon it. Help with my physical therapy. I'm sure somewhere in there I was told alcohol relaxes the muscles."

Brock foraged in my kitchen until he retrieved the coveted bag of popcorn.

"We do what we must to heal your shoulder," I said from the bar. "I've never understood how they can expect anyone to play as many games as you guys play. You give up over half of your year, and on the road."

"Way more than half, if we're lucky, babe. We can still make the post-season, if we keep at it. It's why I don't take on a serious relationship, remember?"

We retreated to my living room. As I had done in the dining room, I drew the plantation shutters closed to keep out the boogey-man.

"Yes. I remember. All you players with pent-up emotions and living in hotel penthouses. You poor boys have to resort to getting off with your groupies."

I turned on the gas fireplace to take the chill out of the air but the freeze penetrated my soul. *CoverBoy* had run the article on perverts, albeit only perverts in the priesthood. Could there be a connection there?

Ding. Dong. The priest was dead. No one was denying any connection there. At least not to me.

Brock chomped away on handfuls of the popcorn, spilling much to the floor.

"Something about those car thugs?"

His question was rhetorical in tone. I didn't attempt to answer. Brock waved his brandy snifter in the air, imploring a refill. I obliged.

He stuffed a final wad of popcorn carbs in his mouth. "Maybe that asshole Coal tried to hurt those kids, and somehow they knew you could help."

"No way. I didn't even know Coal then. And we've just established that we don't know when those photos were actually stuffed into the golf bag."

"Lauren. There are a couple things we keep sidestepping."

251

"We're sidestepping a lot for the moment, but I'll bite. What?"

I could call it whatever I wanted. Synchronicity. Coincidence.

Brock glided the basket of popcorn to the table beside him, as if he had a catcher's mitt and he was sliding with the prized ball to make a homerun. Safe. Home base.

I'd propped myself up against a chair, on the floor, preferring to stretch my legs out in front of me. Some tension eased out of my body with each stretch.

"Why are you so nervous?" he asked.

"Nervous?"

"Yeah. Whenever you're uptight, you pull on your ear and pop your neck."

"I've heard that before," I said, remembering Carly's comment to me. "Lucky I've never seen it."

"Sometimes you add a nervous giggle. You're not giggling tonight," he said.

"I'm thinking, Brock. You told me to think."

Brock remained quiet. The rain abated; the thunder provided regular and ominous booms, partnering with blazing bolts of lightning that penetrated the protection of the closed shutters.

I watched as the gas fire fought a few drops of rainwater that had fallen down the flue. The fire won.

"There've been a couple times I thought Coal was coming on to me," I said.

"Wishful thinking?" Brock asked.

"Damn you!"

"I'm just stating the obvious. If we're right, he's not into beautiful redheaded women."

Damn me. Once again, Brock got it right. At least, maybe.

"What kind of money are you paying him?" Brock asked in such a matter-of-fact manner the arrogance in his demand didn't even hit me before I proffered my response.

"Probably five times as much an hour as L.A.'s top psychiatrists. Ten times the daily rate of a day spa where you can buy eight hours and a sprout lunch and heal instantly."

Brock didn't back off now that he was reeling again. "How much? Are your bankers checking you into Mount Sinai for a brain scan? That kind of big?"

"Could've saved an entire third-world community rather than a Hollywood Hills bi-polar psycho-center. That kind of big."

"This is a circuitous set of circumstances. That Detective Wray is right, and we have to figure out why."

"Why what?"

"Why all roads lead back to you."

I smacked my glass down so hard on the table it should have shattered.

Brock looked at me, his beautiful eyes now only casting worry. "What?"

"Not all roads lead back to me. Where the hell is Carly? She lives at The Centre. Dr. Coal's center. No one has heard from her in days!"

253

Chapter Sixty-Nine
Missing

I CALLED AND TEXTED Sterling four times. Maybe my messages came off a bit terse, given the fact she had just buried her beloved father, but damn it! Carly was in trouble. I sensed it in every bone and in the structure of every cell in my body. Something was wrong.

When she did call, I felt remorse. She was worried about Carly, but still sinking in her own pool of deep grief, while saying her goodbyes to relatives and friends as they headed back out of town.

It occurred to me that with no other heirs, at least Sterling wouldn't be bogged down with estate affairs.

I wondered. If I had known Oliver Falls better, I would have feared my Visconti Curse. Maybe because I didn't have much of a relationship with him Sterling's father had lived a long and happy life, working well beyond his retirement years. Still, Sterling's voice resonated sadness from a week of trying to pick up the pieces. I had a relationship with sadness.

I proceeded with a cautionary voice, "Do you know where Carly's design job is?"

"I've been thinking. I'm not sure. I think she said Big Bear."

"Do you know where? No one at her studio seems to have a clue."

"There was something about privacy. I remember that."

"Sterling, think. What was the client's name?"

"For sure she never told me that, but just maybe I have the address at Dad's store."

Falls & Falls had always been *their* store. Now, upon her father's death, it became her Dad's store. That was the unselfish Sterling I knew.

But why would she have an address there? I wondered. Sterling had already disconnected.

THE NOISE CAME from a car coming up the remote dirt driveway. Carly then heard a door slam shut.

One of my guys, Carly thought. All of her helpers had keys to her projects. Never once had her trust been misplaced.

She attended to her task at hand, placing the leather-bound books onto the shelves in the library. Books that would likely never be read, Carly had to assume.

What she missed was the distinct purring from a luxury car's performance engine.

A loud voice demanded, "Who is here?"

From around the corner Carly smiled. "As if you can't tell by the van parked outside. Larry? Is that you?"

"You're trespassing," the voice boomed.

"Cut the bullshit, Larry. Mike?"

Silence.

Determined to end the cat-and-mouse game with her drapery installers, Carly stormed out of the library.

A smallish man stood firm ground at the door front. Actually, the gun in his hand stood all the ground.

"Oh my god," Carly whimpered as she caught her trembling fall against the new club chair.

"Carly Posh?" the man demanded.

Carly tried to stand. Disoriented. Trying to think while she stared down the barrel of a gun.

"Posh?"

"Yes. That's me. Are you A.J. Ehm? The owner?"

The man chortled something beneath his breath and replaced the gun into the deep pocket of black pants.

He's here early, Carly thought. Is it really him? Oh my god. I'm in his home. It's not ready. I've been sleeping in his bed. I'm going to lose this job and my antique store. She retreated further against the chair.

"Calm down, Ms. Posh." The man tilted his head, as if amused by the sight of her panic. A long black ponytail fell to his left shoulder.

"I'm sorry," Carly muttered. The man seemed familiar, she thought. *Probably just his voice. I have spoken to him on the phone.*

"I want to see what you've done with the place, but I've been driving for six hours. There's a place in town. You look like you could use a meal as much as me."

"But you weren't due in for a couple more—our contract says—"

"I didn't expect to find any work completed and I certainly didn't expect to find you here. Now come. Let's have some lunch and get to know one another.

"And you can call me Armand."

Chapter Seventy
To Encounter a Stranger

CARLY SLID INTO THE leather passenger seat of the polished black Jaguar. It was a magnificent machine, in spite of the stench of rancid cigar smoke. They headed toward the small area of commerce near the lake.

Carly was agreeable to the idea of lunch. It was drawing upon noon and she felt an uneasy gnawing in her stomach. Besides, he seemed like a gentleman. Not exactly gracious, but then again, he was the client.

She was at an unwelcome juncture in life. Burned out. In her career. Certainly in her private life. Somewhere along their drive in a brief moment of conversation, Armand mentioned he wanted to get rid of another home filled with antiques and English attitude, and that home he wanted to turn into a true contemporary. He told Carly he would exchange his valuable antiques for the new stuff, and she could cash in on the intrinsic value he didn't so much value. Of course, Carly very much liked the idea. The antique store she'd always wanted. But how could he know?

Armand made a couple of sharp turns. They drove another five minutes in complete silence. It was overwhelmingly awkward for Carly, and the longer they drove together in silence, the harder it became for her to initiate conversation.

257

Carly watched as Armand's eyes focused on the road. She decided the silence was fine with Armand. Maybe preferable. She had more time to think.

No matter how she fought it, she remained passionate about her work. She loved the freedom each canvas of space, room, nook, and cranny held for her. She loved it like a potter loved the feel of wet clay on her hands and under her fingernails. Creativity was a fiery experience when she was allowed total freedom. A bachelor usually had few rules, or even guidelines, and this job in Big Bear proved it. Maybe his other house would be an even better job, especially if it was stuffed with unwanted antiques.

They arrived at the restaurant and Armand pulled the sleek Jaguar under the tacky make-shift porte-cochere, lined with even tackier strings of lights. The doorman greeted him by name and Carly followed inside. In spite of clear state laws, the room permeated enough smoke that it distorted the dim lighting. Armand led the way past the bar and to a red leather booth in the back.

He grabbed a waitress and gave her a quick groping hug followed by a juicy kiss. Even before sitting down, he ordered a double Jack on-the-rocks from the girl. Carly asked for an iced tea, but Armand scowled at the notion, snapping at the waitress he had just groped. Ordering her to make it double-double Jacks.

Drinks came within minutes, and soon afterward, two plates arrived with pastrami on rye sandwiches. Carly never saw a menu and never asked for the pastrami. She hated pastrami.

Armand observed her hesitation. "I eat *only* pastrami and I only pay for pastrami, and the waitress damn well knows it."

Carly took a sip of the dark liquid on ice. Her father had taught her how to drink a scotch, but she had never tasted anything quite as awful as this thing called a Jack.

There was no way she could drink the whole thing, and never—*ever*, for lunch.

Armand devoured half of his sandwich and ordered another Jack for himself. He gulped it down, along with the side plate of fries. He announced it was time to get back to inspect the house. Guzzle and go.

Although alarmed that the home wasn't ready for any inspection, this suited Carly. She felt anxious to leave the stench of smoke, hard liquor, and pastrami. But she still had a nagging question burrowing inside her belly. How did he know she was interested in antiques?

Chapter Seventy-One
The Inspection

ARMAND'S BEHAVIOR changed. No surprise, Carly thought, considering all the lunchtime booze he consumed. He was much more talkative, narcissistically jabbering on about his fast life. And he was driving fast, too. Way too fast. Like a Jaguar fast.

Carly sighed with a quiet relief as they pulled up the familiar long drive of the Big Bear home.

Armand pulled his Jaguar up to the two huge moss rock pillars that announced the entrance. Carly's shoulder tension eased when he stopped the car and turned off the ignition key.

Once inside, Armand excused himself, briefcase in tow. "I'm going to change my clothes. Mind pouring me a Jack? Double." His voice commanded more than asked.

"Sure," Carly said."But—"

"You know where the bar is," he chortled. "There's a box of booze on the counter."

"There is?"

"I brought it in when you went for your purse. And you might as well pour yourself something, too."

"I think I'll pass," Carly said.

"Nonsense! I have the finest stocked bar in all of Los Angeles and I plan to have one here. Fix yourself a damn drink."

Armand disappeared up the stairs and Carly turned toward the bar. Familiar with her surroundings, spying the liquor box already on the counter startled her. And where had his clothes come from? Why was he changing? And would he see that she had slept in his new bed and on his new sheets?

The ice cubes were out in a bucket, slightly melted and stuck together, requiring her to test her skills with the ice pick. Where had he found an ice bucket, let alone ice and a pick?

It was only two in the afternoon, but unnerved from Armand's reckless driving and the imminent client inspection still facing her, Carly declared her father an angel for teaching her how to drink a *real man's* drink. After filling each glass with ice, she poured a stiff drink for Armand, then poured about two fingers of a single malt scotch for herself. Her daddy would have frowned but she topped hers off with plenty of water.

She glanced around the room and its furnishings. True to what Armand seemed to want, the room already held the distinct ambience of luxury mountain living. Richly upholstered wing chairs, club chairs, and a sofa framed with solid wood and nail-head trim offset the pattern of the tapestry rug. Ornately carved bookshelves gave the room depth. Distinct. Handsome. And then she remembered her client had had a few of his personal antiques delivered. They were supposed to be out in the garage.

Carly took a quick look around the garage and found a desk and two tables crowded into a dark corner. She looked closely through the smoldering light of a single dim bulb. Good enough light, though. She could see they weren't antiques. Fine reproductions, but not saleable in the antiquity market.

Had she been had?

An itsy bitsy spider began crawling and creeping around the lining of her stomach.

Chapter Seventy-Two

Taste is for Sale

ARMAND WALTZED BACK into the room, just after Carly had returned. He'd exchanged his sweater and black pants for black sweat pants and a flowing black tunic.

Snatching the glass of Jack waiting for him at the bar, he took a slug of it, then turned to the sound system left behind by the previous owner. He selected Rachmaninoff. The high ceilings amplified the somber notes, yet still Armand turned the volume higher. He downed more bourbon, then slid into one of his new wing chairs.

Was he agitated? Why?

Carly, left standing alone by the bar, couldn't endure more discomfort in the absence of conversation. She struggled for words, fearful that her naiveté would reveal itself in each one, and fearful her naiveté, too, would appear through the cracks of any silence.

She had a job to do. A talented designer, she knew her stuff. She certainly knew those antiques in the garage weren't worth taking on in any trade. But right now, she had to get through this job. This was the only project that mattered.

Anxious to get on with her work and get home to her Pugs and her home at The Centre, she pressed herself. "I have some catalogs in my van. The lighting that's not all in yet. Stuff I've ordered. I'd like you to see how your home will look in another few weeks."

"It's fine right now," Armand said. He smirked, scooting a misplaced ottoman over to prop his feet up.

Carly felt his taking pleasure in her dumbfounded expression. He hadn't really even looked around. Not that she knew.

"Yes, of course," she said. "Give me a few more weeks." I had two months, she thought.

Carly diverted her eyes to the center of the cocktail table and the thick spines of the art books she had carelessly splayed across it.

"Taste really is for sale, if you can afford the price," Armand said.

Carly braced herself against the bar. She wasn't sure what he saying anymore, but she understood the warning bells in her gut. At any cost, she still selected her words with care. "Perhaps you aren't in any further need of my services. Maybe my skills aren't quite right for you.

"I'm sure your skills are exactly what I need."

She watched him watch her. He enjoyed her frayed nerves. Her apprehension. Her inability to digest the situation. She realized she was fidgeting and he relished in it. She felt her neck tighten and she swallowed hard, and he watched her.

"I'd like you to show me my bedroom now."

She had no response. Did he delight in that?

He pushed the ottoman aside and sprang to his feet. At her side. He caught her off-guard. Instinctively she stepped back, far against the backbar.

"Forget the goddamned bedroom. We don't need it. You really didn't think this was about your stupid design services, did you, Ms. Posh?

"You are the posh possession. The first time I saw you I knew you would be a challenge. You aren't like all the other sluts."

When? When had he seen her?

Chapter Seventy-Three
The Violation

SECONDS BECAME MOURNFUL eternities. Carly slowly reached for her purse, but maybe only in her mind. She wasn't sure. It really didn't matter. Stupid her. Stupid. Keys. No good keys. Her van, the keys dropped somewhere as she unloaded goods. Stupid her.

"You don't want to do this, Armand." She raised her head high, summoning a false sense of fierceness. But her shaking, rasping voice betrayed her fear.

Armand put his hands to her face. He touched her cheeks with his fingers as if she were a treasured old high school sweetheart.

"I do want to do this."

She had to get out. How? She could run. Stupid. Stupid her. Stupid feet that stuck fast to the wood floor and wouldn't give.

Armand pushed her farther into the corner of the backbar, sealing off any last means of escape. He moved fast. Jaguar fast.

He cuffed his leg against the back of Carly's calf, causing her to buckle. Her last sense of balance crumbled. She fell hard against the polished wood floor.

Armand was all over her. He had a small frame but his muscular strength yielded hardened evil. He ripped open Carly's cherished silk blouse. He yanked at the navy slacks. He tore into her pretty ivory panties.

265

Carly tried to move. Any way. Left or right. Up, if only she could. Cornered behind the surrounds of the bar, she was no match for the forceful hands now yanking at the short tresses of her dark hair.

She begged him to stop. Screams became shrieks.

He didn't even try to silence her. It was as if he got off on hearing her yelp for justice.

No neighbors nearby. Every resident, part-time or full, lived well out of ear shot. She knew that. Stupid her.

Too late. No options. Her hand had been dealt.

Armand reeked of alcohol, and the last thing Carly saw before squeezing her eyes shut was the white powder up inside his flaring nostrils.

She would not be delivered from his madness. The pain was excruciating. He ripped at her. He tore and slashed at her with his manhood. He pierced through her virginity.

Her virginity. Yes. She had saved it. For someone special. Someone she could love. Forever. It was supposed to be a good thing.

Carly couldn't cope any longer. So scared she neared insanity, she didn't want to be there any longer.

Her only escape route would be that through her own mind. She didn't want to be behind that beautiful bar anymore. With him. She couldn't and she wouldn't.

She allowed herself to fade into that hidden darkness. Somewhere hidden in the caverns of her subconscious, Carly slipped away, deep into hiding. She waited there, somewhere away from her body and into a surreal existence of protection. She waited there, patiently. She waited to see if her body would survive this violent sexual attack. She waited to see if ever she could return to her suffering body and get out, with it, alive. If not, she would be content to stay where she was. It would be okay.

"You wanted it, you whore. Maybe you won't admit it now, but you wanted it. I'm your ticket to a new life and you like it." Armand chuckled with a shrill and giggling falsetto voice.

One cell at a time. One second more ticked off the clock. Carly finally returned to the violated human body that lay in a crumbled heap on the floor. Time to get out. Not too late.

She slowly pulled herself up off the hard surface of the cold wood and rose to her knees, grabbing at her shredded clothing.

Unfortunately for Carly, Armand was there to lunge at her once again.

"I don't think I have your attention, bitch," he raged. "You gotta prove to me you aren't talking. You gotta prove to me you want my offer. We can be a team. I can use a class-act like you around me, and I can pay for you beyond your wildest, fucking-ass dreams. I can buy every fucking antique you want, and fifty times more. I can set you up for life, but you aren't leaving here, bitch, until I *know you're taking my deal* and that you're *not talking!*"

Her head burst with fireballs of rage. *Quick.* She painstakingly tried to assess her options, but she had to be quick. *Okay, be real. No options.* He would never let her go because she would never take his deal. Never. She didn't want his ticket to paradise.

Barely standing, she reached to steady herself against the bar. Her hand felt the cold metal of the instrument and she grabbed it like the wild animal her attacker had forced her to become.

Armand's eyes betrayed his shock. The ice pick penetrated his main artery and blood squirted out of his neck in bursts like a frozen garden spigot. He grabbed at his neck, foolishly pulling out the silver ice pick. Not a good thing to do. The blood now gushed through the deep hole in his jugular vein, spurting rivers of red everywhere. He held the ice pick up and attempted to lurch at her again, but instead he blacked out, hitting his head hard against the green marble bar-top and then collapsing to the floor. His glass of Jack Daniel's, left behind on the bar, was now topped off with a streaming sea of red blood. Carly watched as Armand's blood poured onto the wood, mixing with that of her own. That blood of a virgin.

Curled up in the corner behind the bar, she tried to move but her body became a puddle of nightmares. She tried to scream but she had no voice. She tried to move away, but had no limbs. She tried to see but had no vision.

If she had, she would have seen Armand's last bit of life energy as he reached for the Glock tucked under the waistband of his sweat pants and said, "Yours is an inconvenient death."

Chapter Seventy-Four

Unfinished Business

STERLING HANDED ME the piece of paper with an address scribbled on it.

"Big Bear," I read. "It's not like I can call their police department on a vague whim of a bad feeling and a photograph of an elephant statue."

"But you can already prove some sort of child-sexual abuse. From someone!"

"And how will that tie into Carly? We need to find her, first. How did you get this address?"

"Some guy came in here wanting to sell loose diamonds. He said he was a friend of The Centre and that Carly was doing a big design job for him."

"You saw him?"

"No. Dad took care of it. Later he asked me about The Centre. I told him I really didn't know much, but for Harlan. He liked Harlan. We're normally not a street buyer but Dad quickly deduced that they were good quality stones with legitimate papers. Still, we take our time. Dad's insistent on following his procedures to make sure we aren't peddling blood diamonds."

"Did your dad end up buying them?"

"He never finished the paperwork. I remember one thing Dad said was that the guy wouldn't give him a local address—only this one in Big Bear. That bugged him. And his name was practically nothing but initials."

'Initials?"

"Look for yourself," Sterling said, pointing back to the slip of paper she'd handed me.

"A. J. Ehmm," I read. "And did anyone else around here see this guy?"

"Nope. I've asked. And I have a bad feeling."

"So do I," I said. *A feeling as nervous as a stick in a beaver pond.*

Chapter Seventy-Five
No Ambulance Required

HARLAN COAL PHONED Gabriella Criscione.
"Our relationship is over," Coal said in a measured and hushed voice, as the dutiful new servant provided his morning cocktail.

"We're family. We'll always be relatives and we'll always be the family with the secrets," Gabri replied.

"Not if someone digs deep enough," Coal said.

"I think they're digging our graves, good doctor."

"I'm sick and tired of cleaning up other peoples messes."

"I forked over several million dollars in leads to you," Gabri warned.

"And you've made as much in those leads," he warned.

While still listening to his angry outburst, Gabri decided she would host an intimate dinner party that night. Even for a few guests. She sharpened the knives and then began tackling the venison, with the phone cocked between her ear and shoulder and listening to the rants coming from the other end.

It mattered not what Coal had to say.

As always, she would cut her own meat. Her servants would prepare and serve and take no credit.

271

STERLING REGRETTED THAT she couldn't leave the store. She protested too much. She almost rambled in her graveling. I knew she was bone-dry scared.

Again Brock came to the rescue. He'd be a handful on the 100-mile drive to Big Bear, loathing his aching shoulder all the way. Loathing the fact he was benched. Still, he proved to be the better driver.

The navigational device led us straight to the driveway of what I'd call a mansion-cabin. Like none other I'd seen. Carly's van was at front. I sighed with relief. A black jaguar had pulled in behind the van. All good. Given the late hour, maybe Carly had finally found her Romeo. I felt better. I made myself feel better. I'd already been calculating how to ask Carly for her forgiveness that we interrupted her private time.

After ringing the bell and knocking on the door and having no answer, Brock turned the doorknob to find it unlocked.

My concerns over any apology careened to the porch stoop.

I guess Brock moved in ahead of me. I remember both of us calling out for Carly. I remember thinking all about me. I've just entered a stranger's home. Breaking and entering. And I remember thinking about the Visconti Curse. My very own curse. And I thought it was time for me to be a savior, damn it!

Brock grabbed my arm. Of this, I am certain. He shoved me back toward the front door and I resisted all the way. And I was glad I lost.

"Get out of here. Call 911. Tell them two people are down and we need ambulances."

I obeyed. I had hoped for the adrenaline rush we all see in the movies but instead I got a slow-motion film. And no cell phone reception.

Brock appeared out on the front porch. After understanding my shock and inability to place the call, he tried from his phone.

Now he didn't ask for any ambulances. Only for the local police.

ANOTHER LOVED ONE had died. We were four girlfriends, then three, and now two.

Brock escorted me to the front pew. After all, Carly was his grade-school friend, too. Carly had long ago abandoned the notion of making amends with her family. No representative of the family appeared.

Sterling showed up for the service in a draping black dress that covered her arms, legs, and even her lacking cleavage, usually trumped up with jewels. Perhaps death was getting to her, too. We were morphing into God knows what. My world had already spiraled down from down.

We'd all noticed Detective Wray at the back of the church. As the service drew to an end he stood still in the same spot. Only the slightest nod indicated he wanted a word with me. Sterling and Brock followed.

"I know my timing stinks," he said.

"Good. That's one thing you got straight," I said.

"No good time for these things. I understand you knew the deceased male," he said.

"It depends on your definition of the word *knew*."

"Ms. Visconti, I need some answers."

"Not here, Detective Wray. Please."

Wray thumped on his unopened writing pad. "I thought this was one of your best friends. And you found her. I mean, if that's true, wouldn't you want to tell me everything you know, and as quickly as possible. Our killer may be catching a jet to Malaysia by now."

273

I backed into the corner of the church. Wray, Brock, and Sterling all followed.

"Wait a minute. What killer? I thought you had this one figured out. The man raped Carly, she stabbed him with the only weapon she could find, and then he shot her dead. Am I missing something?"

"I want to know about the man."

I gulped. I held my breath. I bit my bottom lip to keep it from quivering. I couldn't hide my eyes refilling with another stream of tears.

"Ms. Visconti, you've yet to tell me what you know about this place called a center. You've left me flying and flitting around like a bat without sonar."

"But these deaths and their causes are explained, right?"

"Yes. But we still have no ID on the male. No driver's license. The Jaguar turned up as stolen. Did you know this man?"

Brock tightened his grip on my arm. He whispered in my ear that maybe it was time for me to get my lawyer involved.

"I don't know him, but I think I've seen him."

I turned to ask for Sterling's help, since she had the Big Bear address. She had disappeared from sight.

As if reading my mind Brock said, "We got the address from Sterling Falls. She has all the information on this guy."

"All false. A phony name. Probably heisted diamonds. And that address at Big Bear? It's tied up in an estate probate. The owner died almost a year ago."

I swallowed dry air. "I think the man has a beach house near mine. At least someone strongly resembling him does."

I was afraid to say more. Harlan Coal had told me his assistant occupied the house. He told me that the night of the storm when the lights had gone out. Not mine. The man with the braid. His lights.

"Anything else?" Detective Wray hammered.

Brock nodded to me.

"I can't be certain, but it's possible I've seen him around at The Centre." I spelled it out. *C.E.N.T.R.E.*

"Where Carly Posh lived?"

"Yes, Ace. Couldn't you have put that together on your own?"

"I like confirming things here and there. Now tell me one more thing. Who is in charge of this"—he spelled it out, *"C.E.N.T.R.E.?"*

Again Brock nodded.

"His name is Dr. Harlan Coal. He's a psychologist."

"Okay. Good enough. I want you in my office first thing in the morning."

"Should I bring my lawyer or more black mourning clothes?"

Detective Wray stared me down with his chocolate-glazed eyes. "I'd tell you to bring a helluva gun for self-protection, but they wouldn't let you through security."

275

Chapter Seventy-Six
VICAP

AND WITH THAT night came another dream. My own personal nightcap.

Wedding dress. Paper. Burning—everyone burning alive but me.

Except, maybe? Did I see Payton very much alive? And now Carly?

BROCK DROVE ME to the police station. On our way, I told him I would not mention the photographs.

"Why the hell not?" he asked.

"Call it that same gut feeling."

"Stop with this."

"I'm serious. I think for damn sure I take all this more seriously than anyone else, including the detective. If Coal is involved he might as well have raped me, too."

"But apparently Coal prefers little boys."

Brock's humor only fueled my heated position. "You're along for moral support. And I appreciate it. But let me play this my way. It's my life on the line. And just maybe this whole thing has to do with that creepy man wearing a braid and not Coal."

"You're too damn loyal," Brock said.

"Like a Labrador. And I'm too damn stubborn."

"Stay away from him, Lauren. He may like his sex from little boys but he wants something else from you."

DETECTIVE WRAY SAT us down on two sticks of chairs in front of his desk. His office didn't exactly offer the deep-seating chairs mine did. He was playing on his turf now.

"The Centre, Ms Visconti?"

I told him everything I knew. Almost. Carly had been his patient and suggested I go. I did. Harlan Coal helped me. Carly moved onto his compound to be nearer Coal's work. She seemed happy. She was embarking on a new career with a brand new energized dream.

"And this deceased male, Armand?" Wray asked.

"You know his name?"

"Give some credit where credit is due," Wray laughed. "We found a hefty set of keys on his body. Any idea what locks those keys might fit?"

"I don't know any more than what I told you yesterday. Not about any keys. Not even anything about the man. He moves with the shadows, and—"

I broke to think back to the man that I saw taking photos of me, then disappearing. At the hotel bungalow. The warning calls and notes and hellish leather grip around my throat. Was it this man? I thought yes.

"Ms. Visconti?"

"I don't know. The man killed Carly after raping her. We all know that. Maybe he's the one that's been after everyone—"

"Yes. Everyone you love and loved. The Visconti Curse," the detective whined.

A knock sounded at the door and it opened. Detective Wray jumped to his feet.

"Excellent timing," Wray said. He made the introductions to an FBI agent in VICAP, reminding both me and Brock it stood for the Violent Criminals Apprehension Program.

277

Wray said to me, "You like *quid pro quo*, so let's get started."

The agent said, "Ms. Visconti, I'm a case-profiler. I'm here to share a few things we know about this case."

"And it's not to leave this room," Detective Wray interjected.

"Agreed," Brock and I both said in unison.

"Let's start with the multitude of multiple stabbings. Clearly all events relate to you and your magazine. Specifically, the articles."

"You're spawning hatred," Wray said.

The VICAP man shook his head.

"Slow down," I said. "I printed nothing derogatory about the runway model. I portrayed her as the victim she was. And the same with Dhurra Solayman. A female victim in Afghanistan."

"Exactly," the man said, "but we feel it's possible we're dealing with one person. Someone who suffers from deep-seated resentment. That resentment has festered into fury."

I rolled my eyes to the ceiling of the dank and gloomy office.

"Let me back up. The first two stabbings were rather crude. Almost as if there were no planning, but, in fact, we know by the removal and insertion of certain objects that this isn't at all the case. It's then possible to deduce, in plain English, our killer was getting his feet wet. Operating on a low level of motive. That original resentment stage.

"It's possible the first two killings fulfilled certain fantasies. And generated desire. Our killer developed a real taste for the kill. His resentment then escalated into rage. You see, multiple stab wounds like we've seen here indicate overkill. Your magazine articles fueled this rage and gave the killer, in his mind, a vehicle for justified release. Do you follow me?"

"Yes."

"We have a person that is planning his every move. And yours. Maybe in a sick way, this person even cares for you, Ms. Visconti. He thinks he's helping you by bringing down your bad guys. It's almost like you have your own personal vigilante working for you."

Lala Corriere

Chapter Seventy-Seven
Forgiveness, Firepits, & Farming

WE DROVE FOR fifteen minutes in quiet. It suited me well.

"Okay," Brock finally said. "You're driving me crazy. Let's start by you telling me exactly why you didn't mention those pervert photos to Detective Wray."

"Because maybe I'm wrong about that statue," I defended myself. "We already know Coal blows hot air, so why not tell me it's an original? It's just one more little prevarication on his part. So where does that leave us?"

"I give up. I'm driving. What the fuck?"

"It leaves us with no evidence. Nothing. Everything in my life is a big nothing."

"Tell me what you're really thinking."

I didn't pause for thought. "I'm thinking that *CoverBoy* is evil. Or at least creating evil. I'm thinking my dream to incorporate serious investigative reporting into the folds of a fun magazine with all the glitz and glamour of glossy pages and gorgeous specimens of men has failed. I wanted people to learn something about what is going on in their backyards. Instead it's inciting hatred."

"Did you kill any of those people?" Brock asked.

"Of course not."

"Did any of your staff kill those people?"

"No."

280

"Then it's beyond your control. You write the truth in order to cause awareness with hopes that these evil truths have a chance to be righted."

"I'm all mixed up right now, Brock. The magazine is one thing. That meeting in there with the detective and the fancy agent didn't even begin to explain to me what happened to Carly, and why. And I still don't know what happened to Payton."

"I'm going to get you home and I want you to make yourself a cup of tea or pour yourself a couple shots of tequila, and go stare at that ocean. That's your backyard and you're damn lucky, so enjoy it. Go back and wish upon a star with the belief and full expectation that your dreams will come true."

"It's daylight. No stars," I said.

"A good point that makes my point all the stronger. They're there, all right. You just can't see them for the sun. Go back to that child that tossed a knotted tennis shoe-lace into her mother's lap, then went out to play. That little girl knew. She trusted that the knot would disappear when she came back for it. And it did. And it will."

"Who would have taken you for some sage old soul?" I said.

"Not my mother. She was too busy unknotting shoelaces."

"By the way," I added, "Sterling is researching that damn elephant statue as we speak. If anyone can figure it out, she can. We'll know if it's an original."

MOON BLADE CIRCLED around the blazing firepit, stomping out ashes and scattering others while concentrating on the unfathomable task at hand. Out of control. The situation was out of control. Time for action.

281

THE FARM NEEDED Coal's attention, but he didn't even remember it until four kids brought in the weekly truckload of vegetables and home-baked pies. Key on his mind was that he held the key. Or keys, as it were. He had the only other set of keys to the cells on the farm. The little bad ants would be getting food and water, but they hadn't been outside the cells for—a very long time.

Something else bothered him, but he refused to entertain the insult of thought. Armand had the original set of keys. And like any prison cell, those keys were quite unique. Where were they?

Chapter Seventy-Eight
Nailed

AFTER A MOST DISMAL but mandatory meeting at *CoverBoy,* I headed straight for the beach. Brock was right, after all. I needed to enjoy my own backyard.

I drove down the street in front of my house and stomped on the brakes. Fear shackled my hands and feet. I froze in place.

My garage door was open. Not all the way. Maybe twelve inches.

I could call the police. Sure. Detective Wray or the locals in Malibu. Either way, what? I'd say, "Hey, I have an emergency. My garage door is open. Well, no, ummm, not exactly open. But it's a whole foot off the floor."

They'd come running. Sure.

It would be impossible for me to peek inside my garage before whatever, if anything, would see me approaching. I drove past my home, then parked two doors away. Grabbing my cell phone and my keys, I also retrieved the trusty can of mace I carried with me in spite of the fact it was at least five-years old.

I scampered between homes to make my way to the beach, an activity my neighbors would abhor if they saw me. Let them be the ones to call the police!

Once on the beach, I yanked off my heels, leaping past the two homes until I approached mine, and I came to an abrupt stop. What the hell was I doing? I should have

283

opened up the garage door and checked it out from the safety of my locked car.

Now what? I looked around. A couple of guys on the beach, possibly within ear-shot, if things didn't go well. A rabid looking dog, too. Not the wolf-dog I had encountered at my front door, but mean looking, nonetheless.

I steadied my keys and unlocked the sliding patio door. I tried to remove the keys from my lock. They stuck. Sliding the door open on its track, I left the unyielding keys behind.

Not hearing or seeing anything unusual, I slinked through the door into my own home.

I'm being ridiculous. This is my sanctuary. My safe haven.

My heart pounded.

This is my old paranoia, stemming out of nowhere but mindless threats.

Geoff had asked me to hire security. That seemed like a really good idea right now.

It's nothing.

It's something!

I stepped into the room, bringing up the can of mace.

It was *nothing*. Why didn't it feel like nothing?

I neared the kitchen, looking at my cell phone and wondering if I should make a fool out of myself and call for the police. Or the guys on the beach. Or the rabid dog.

I looked across to my front door. Intact. The alarm system flashed green; I must have forgotten to arm it. But my silver coffee service sat undisturbed on the buffet in my dining room. Nothing had been touched. Nothing was out of order.

I'm a paranoid idiot.

Relieved, I tossed my phone onto the kitchen counter just as I heard the clamor of steel from the garage. The door to the garage stood slightly ajar.

I fingered the release on the mace and brought it up to my chest when the door flew open and a crowbar met me in the eyes.

"Jesus, A-Bubba, girl!"

I was still trying to spray the mace into his eyes, but rather a stream of the aged chemical dribbled down my fingers.

"What the hell are you doing here?" He yelled.

"I think that should be my question since it's my house."

Brock dropped the crowbar onto the floor and took the spewing can of mace from my hands.

"You best wash that stuff off of you. Anyway, I asked first. You were supposed be to meeting Sterling for lunch and a movie."

"She's too busy. I'm too busy. And I can use the sabbatical on the beach you told me to take."

Brock fired me a look, well aware that was now certain I was the Angel of Death.

"What are you doing in my house?"

"I'll show you," Brock led me to the garage. "This, Ms. Visconti, is a garage. A real garage."

"Wow. Look at all these gadgets and gizmos," I said.

"They're called tools. And I hope this takes me off the hook for breaking and entering with the key you gave me."

New pegboard lined two walls with hammers, tape, wire, and screwdrivers—even a staple gun, all hanging from red clips. Admittedly, some objects were unidentifiable by me.

"Why all this?"

"Because you think you have to be so damned independent, Laurs, but real men don't hold a car hood up

285

with a golf club," he teased. "Besides, I figured you needed your nails now. I've got a game coming up and it will be too late for my help."

"I thought you were benched to rest up your shoulder?"

"Back in the game next week. All patched up."

"Where's your car?"

"That's my bad timing. My car's being detailed. The kid should be bringing it back in an hour or so. Meanwhile, you're sort of stuck with me."

"Okay. Come on, real man of real garages. I'll cut you some slack," I said, leading him back inside my house. "Can you drink?"

"Got any beer?"

"White wine."

"Close enough. But watch me. Don't try and get me drunk when I'm this close to getting back in the park."

I pulled a bottle of *Far Niente* Chardonnay out of refrigerator. Brock had already located two wine stems and moved fast. I obliged.

He led me by my hand to the bedroom. The short distance down the hall took us twenty minutes to negotiate. My silk blouse bellowed to the hickory wood floor like a white cloud of angels. Next my shoes. His shoes. His jeans. My hosiery. My skirt. Somewhere along the way, Brock's denim shirt surrounded me as he nailed me to the hall wall.

I wanted to caress and kiss each dimple, then move to his bounty of carved-out abs. I wanted to lick the sweet salty taste in the hallows of his muscled thighs. And I wanted all of him. Inside of me. I wanted all of Brock Townsend.

His smooth hands stroked my cheeks, my ears, and then my chin. They moved down to cup my bare breasts, and then drew teasing circles around my navel.

Downward, Brocks fingers traced my inner thighs, teasing me until he saw me quiver under his touch.

We made it to the recamier in my bedroom. Brock retrieved our wine glasses. I raised mine to meet his. Neither of us spoke. The glasses clinked with the sound of a crystal symphony—instruments in harmony for the first time. We both took just one sip and returned the glasses to the nearby table.

With still no words spoken, Brock took me into his strong arms. He held me close to him, looking into my eyes and pressing closer and closer against my naked flesh.

This kiss was different. The passion ran deep and intoxicating. Unbridled.

He didn't stop with my lips. He kissed my fingers, my hands, my arms, and moving my long red hair to one side, he then kissed and sucked at my neck. He twirled me around and kissed my back, starting at the nape of my neck and slowly nibbling down the length of my back and toward the curves of my hips.

My body ached and throbbed. Accepting his hand, we both fell onto the floor. I pressed against him as he pressed even closer to me, both our bodies now singing in symphony with mutual desire.

He moved slowly, teasingly, lovingly, then fervently and madly, and then lovingly again. When he finally entered my inner sanctum, I felt a ripple through my entire body, surging ever upward where I felt a titillating sensation in the back of my throat.

He rode my body rhythmically. Soft and hard. Passionate and patient.

I finally succumbed to the ecstasy, my body trembling. I threw back my head and cried out a final surrender into total fulfillment.

Lauren Visconti is alive and well, I told myself.

287

My knees were still weak when my mind finally became engaged, and I thought I should rise up from the floor. Brock sprung to his feet and crossed to my mahogany armoire where he knew I had two Turkish bathrobes. His gaze never left mine but to retrieve our wine.

He offered me his hand and I accepted it as he lifted me to my feet. He embraced me for a small eternity.

We did make it to the bed, finally, but only as a collapsed tangle of human flesh.

I can remember falling off to sleep and thinking, *oh to be human. To experience life. To experience great love.*

In the pre-dawn glow of promised sunlight, I felt only fire. I awakened to my dream of imminent danger.

My paper wedding dress was burning.

Chapter Seventy-Nine
Listen to Me

BROCK STIRRED THE MOMENT I sat upright in bed. I wiped the tears from my eyes before his eyes could focus in the dim light.

"We both have an early day," he said. "How about I whip you up one of my special omelets?"

"I don't have any eggs," I said.

"Okay. How about pancakes?"

"No pancake mix, no syrup, no eggs."

"Toast?"

"Sure. I think I have a toaster. And the coffee is in the fridge," I said, wanting him to leave my bed.

I'm not certain, but I think Brock sensed my distance. It was far better that than for him to know my sadness and fears.

I quickly showered and donned yet another bleak business suit. On some days they suited me well, I thought.

As I walked out of the bedroom Brock pulled me against the wall in the same hall where we had left our ripped-off clothes from the night before.

"We need to talk," he said.

I pushed him out of my way.

"I'll grab some toast but I need to run. Like you said, we both have an early day." I scurried to the kitchen.

289

"Shit. The sun is barely up and we have time. I need you to know that I'm not the bachelor baseball playing hunk-of-the-year most people think I am."

My eyes rolled and Brock must have seen the smirk that crossed my face, spreading as fast and long as the tracks left in the snow by a team of Iditarod dogs.

His face turned to a crimson red. I could see the pulsing of blood at his temples.

"Listen to me! I can't be celibate but I sure as hell am the best candidate to be monogamous. With you. I love you."

I fell back toward the toaster, trying to disengage any connection, I suppose.

I said, "You love me as a childhood pal, but all grown up. Yesterday, you thought I should have nails in my garage and get nailed. That's what friends are for."

"Damn it again! I love you. I always have and I always will."

His eyes pierced my heart but it didn't sting too much.

"Damn it again! Say it or, I swear, I'll walk right out of here and this time I won't come back. I can't take it anymore."

I wanted to say it. I knew it was true. But I also knew if I spoke those three words aloud, Brock Townsend would be my next loved one to die.

Chapter Eighty
Choices

VICTOR ROMERO HELD his face five inches from the computer monitor. He studied the images over and over again. Dr. Nathan Judd, New York City. Dr. Judd Harlan. Tucson. Dr. Harlan Coal. Los Angeles.

They were one and the same.

Romero grabbed the phone.

"You sitting down, Wray?"

"Hell no! I don't have the luxury. Not like your retired fat ass."

"For your information, I'm working my ass off on your investigation."

"What do you have?"

Romero told Detective Wray all he had found, then sent the images over to Wray's computer.

"Sonuva bitch!" Wray yelled. "Did you hear? I'm working on a double homicide that somehow must be connected to that scum ball?"

"Timing is everything," Romero said.

"You've got that right. We can't place Coal anywhere near the scene. Airtight alibi. And he's playing all nicey-nice with us. Full cooperation and all that shit."

"Get him in for a polygraph, if he's so damn helpful."

"Already scheduled."

BROCK STOOD IN FRONT of me, regaining his composure or at least the tawny color in his face, until he turned away.

"Brock?"

"About that self-proclaimed sabbatical from your best friends."

"What about it?"

"You're making choices, Lauren."

This time I was the one fuming.

"You're damn right I am. My loved ones don't get pissed off at me. They don't move away to Mozambique. They die! Last time I took inventory I was down to one girlfriend!"

"Life is about choices. Sure, God gives us our starting ground. We're born rich, poor, beautiful, ugly, or even diseased from the get-go."

Brock had a younger brother born with Spinal Muscular Atrophy. Ninety percent of children born with this affliction don't make it past two years. Brock's little brother made it to ten, and long enough to see his older brother have talent scouts come knocking at the door after watching him pitch a few games.

"You've made choices, Lauren," Brock continued. "You decided to go to university. You decided to major in journalism. You decided to go it alone and start up your first magazine, sell it for a fortune, then move here and start up another one."

"It's not exactly like heading west in a horse and buggy with Indian arrows flying at my back."

"But somewhere along the way you decided to become a victim."

"No. That word is not in my vocabulary."

"Maybe not. But it's in your mind."

"The deaths of my mother, father, fiancé, and two good friends are not in my mind."

"But you're allowing those events to come in and take up residence. You're making a decision. Every decision we make come from one of two roots. It's either a love based decision, or it's one that's fear based."

I felt my rage escalate. "When did you become so all fucking mighty? God knows you sleep around with any pussy you can have for a night, you drink too much, and smoke rancid cigars."

"Touché. So I guess you and a whole lot of other folks would call me a hypocrite because we wild bachelors choose to call that behavior all part of the human experience," he laughed.

A hypocrite and a sleaze ball. You bet! And now with the audacity to try and lecture me from some spiritual pulpit, I thought.

"You might as well be oozing a snout full of snot. It would be preferable to the verbiage coming out of your mouth."

"Slanderous. Even coming from you. Don't you think I hurt like hell when my little brother died?" Brock's voice cracked. "Hell, I had to see him on the sidelines, in a wheelchair, and we all knew I had a real chance at making it to the big leagues. This was my little brother, Lauren, and I felt sorry for him, but all he did was clap and cheer and whistle when I made a good play. And it killed me when Payton died. Maybe we don't know how she died, but it doesn't take away or alter the pain or the fact. And then Carly. Dear sweet Carly. Reconnect with the people who love you. Your disavowing their friendship is hurting them."

"Okay, already," I yelled. "Anything else you have to cram down my throat? Maybe a baseball with porcupine quills on it?"

"As a matter of fact, yes. Let's nail this sonuva bitch so-called doctor."

293

Lala Corriere

Chapter Eighty-One
The Professionals

Brock made one call and cancelled his physical therapy appointment. He implored me to do the same with my first meeting.

"I have an idea about how to get what we need from Coal so that you can and will get your sweet butt to the police. With everything."

Once again his eyes penetrated mine and I closed my lids tight. There was no denying I trusted him.

I acquiesced and called my office and cancelled my morning plans. All of them. Then I closed my eyes again and held onto the countertop to stabilize both my body and my mind.

"Let's take our coffees and go down to the beach. I need to feel the sand in my toes. It makes for a great pedicure for you," Brock said.

We walked in a slow silence along the shoreline—the waves our only steady conversation. We slopped along the water's edge, the sparkles of sand and foamy bubbles forming new patterns with each step we took.

"We need to get into that locked room at The Centre," Brock whispered, barely audible above the sound of the waves crashing.

"I agree. I think."

295

"We have to have something to tie this creep to those photos. And whatever he's hiding, it's probably behind the only locked door on his entire so-called free grounds."

We sat down a few feet from the surf. "Have you really got a plan?" I asked.

"I have the start of a plan. We have a fireworks home-game coming up, and I've got clubroom passes, all the V.I.P. perks we want. We invite Coal and make it an event for him and some of his boys he has in that cult of his."

"Wait a minute. I never said it was a cult."

"No protein in their diets, Laurs. It breaks the body down, and fast. Physically, and mentally, too. The chanting going on. No privacy."

"Call it what you like," I said.

"He knows he'd look like a fool or the fraud that he is if he turned down the free offer for his favorite boys."

The thought sickened me. Who would watch those little boys?

"Okay. Suppose we get the good doctor out to your ballgame. If you're playing, that leaves me to do the breaking in?"

"I said I have the start of a plan. Not a printed manual."

"So we come up with one. They buy into it. Then what?"

"I'll have security keep an extra eye on them at the game. It's going to be up to you to get into that room."

"Breaking and entering charges all on me."

Brock grinned. "You did say they don't believe in locks. You might have to plead your innocence in that you were just trying to help them stick to their own damned communal laws."

We made the turn on the beach and headed back toward my house. I turned to check out the beach home formerly occupied by Coal's assistant. The window coverings were closed tight. There was no sign of life. Literally.

"Hey, last night when you came home—what the hell were you thinking by attacking a burglar with a can of old mace?" Brock asked.

"You want me to become a burglar, but you come down on me for not protecting myself correctly?"

"First, I didn't say we'd steal anything."

"Glad to hear you use the word 'we'," I said.

Brock broke off our conversation to make a call. "That's it. Geoff will take care of everything.

"And just so you know, Geoff and I talked about it yesterday. The security company that guards your office building will be out here starting tomorrow at your house. Full-time. And Geoff will be with you when you go in to get a look at that wall."

"You figured out all of that just now?"

"Like I said. We've been talking."

I should have thanked him. Instead I said, "Brock, just what would you have done if you'd come into my house today and heard me in the bedroom?"

"You mean like 'heard' heard?"

"Exactly."

"Wouldn't have gamboled into your bedroom, I guess."

We didn't talk about those three little words, but with Brock's new plan in play, I knew he would come back to me without me speaking them. Maybe.

ALONE, I TUCKED MY head toward my knees and closed my eyes. My hands both fisted as I accepted the call from Detective Wray.

"What about Dr. Coal?" I asked.

Detective Wray's response came quickly, "He's a person of interest. Turns out Carly Posh had two real estate holdings and Coal seems to think he's the new owner of both. For now he's happy as a cold clam belly and willing to go the extra mile to help us. He's coming in tomorrow for a polygraph.

"In the meantime, don't do anything stupid. You got that?"

DO YOU EVER GET that dichotomous sensation that things seem to slow down and speed up at the same time? That's how I felt.

I made the call from my car while finding a coveted parking space. Harlan Coal's voicemail answered, thank god. I left the message for him that I'd been swamped with a new *CoverBoy* issue. I told him it would be another week or so and then hoped we'd find some quality session time together. I prayed he didn't hear what felt like magpies pecking on the back of my larynx.

With my schedule tied up, Coal might be more inclined to accept the baseball passes. It's not like I could be that important to him. But Coal would be up for a game of sticking anything to Brock Townsend during one of his games. And both games, I now deduced, were being played by professionals.

Chapter Eighty-Two
The Plan

I SAT WITH BROCK at the Santa Monica Pier, where devouring fish tacos became my number one goal.

Brock couldn't wait to tell me. In the time I had hung up my phone, parked, and walked to restaurant at the end of the pier, Harlan Coal had confirmed his tickets for the baseball game.

"Are you sure you're up to this? You're doing that thing with your neck and pulling at your ears," Brock said.

"Just tell me when," I said. We waited for our favorite table. Brock bought us a couple of Corona's at the bar.

"Next Thursday's divisional game. My first home game since I was benched. Coal and six of his little resident boyfriends. They're confirmed to come early and stay late for tours and to meet some of the players."

"How do we know he'll show?"

"Oh, he'll show. They have private passes reserved with all the V.I.P. perks: a luxury box, the Adelphia Stadium Club for all the food and drink they can put away, Dodger Dollars for souvenirs, and locker room passes for after the game."

"Wow! I'll take you up on those locker room passes," I said.

"There's my old girlfriend, back again. More important, we're in control of their comings and goings. I

299

got them transportation in the form of a stretch Hummer. Told Coal it was part of the deal."

I managed a wry grin with pursed lips sealed so tight I felt like a gator. I could close my mouth shut but there was little strength to open it again.

I managed, "Isn't he going to wonder why you're being so generous with him all of the sudden?"

"He thinks it's all because of you. So our war continues. We'll be like two gladiators fighting over our princess's love."

I didn't go there with him.

Geoff had told me he'd help anytime. What I didn't know was that he was an old pro at jimmying locks. I updated Brock, who said he already knew.

"Everything is set to go. So then, what's wrong? Something is, honey. What is it?" Brock asked.

"Besides breaking and entering?"

"Shit. That ain't nothing for you," he teased, but his penetrating eyes revealed his concern.

"I'm missing a set of keys to my house."

"Did you tell the security company?"

"Nah. The guy watching my house is a moron with muscles. And I'm not about to switch out every lock, then find them in the bottom of a purse somewhere."

"They're not with your car keys?"

"I keep a set separate for when I valet park."

"I seem to remember teaching you to do that."

"Then you get the credit that I lost them."

The hostess led the way and we slipped into the cheesy white plastic chairs that adorned the funky deck. The moist sea breeze immediately began tangling my hair, feeling like a spa treatment in comparison to the city's intense heat and smog.

"You know, I think it just pisses me off. There I was putting out an entire issue filled with articles on perverts, and I had no idea Harlan Coal could have been my lead story."

"Quit beating yourself up. Let me ask you one more time. Are you ready to roll next Thursday?"

"Yes. I'm more than ready."

"I'll call you on your cell when I'm positive both Coal and his bevy of boys are at the ballpark. Then, only then, you and Geoff go and do your thing. And be quick about it, Laurs, even though I said you'll have plenty of time. You're there to get photographs. If you start feeling spooked, that's it. You get out."

The waitress arrived and without a glance at the menu I order the large plate of fish tacos.

Brock ordered another beer.

"Aren't you going to eat anything?" I asked.

"Didn't I tell you? I'm going out tonight. Saving my appetite."

So Brock took some bimbo out to dinner, then probably screwed her brains out, assuming she had any. One way or the other I had no doubt he had sated his appetite.

That next morning my doorbell rang. A locksmith had orders to change out every lock on every door. Brock Townsend had prepaid for it.

The arrangement, our relationship, suited me just fine.

FIVE DAYS LATER THE Dodgers were suiting up to play the Atlanta Braves. Geoff and I sipped on iced Frappuccinos from the front seat of his oh-so-obvious bright green P.T. Cruiser, parked several blocks away from The Centre. We were as ready as we'd ever be when my phone rang.

"Our guests of honor are in full attendance, at their box and ready to belt out the *National Anthem* on a

301

Chamber of Commerce day here at Dodger Stadium," Brock announced.

"Perfect," I said with a lump in my throat.

I tossed my cell back into my purse and pulled out the camera. Within minutes we had scrambled to the front gate of The Centre. The halls that once beckoned me, and the walls of the inner sanctum that once coddled me, now scared the living crap out of me.

Geoff turned his dark-brown eyes to me. "It's not too late. You could go back to the car and let me take care of this."

"No way."

My mind fissured and leaked like a cold egg, spewing its contents into the middle of a boiling pot of water.

Chapter Eighty-Three
Breaking & Entering

GEOFF AND I WALKED around the compound as if we belonged to the community. Actually, Geoff strolled around as if he owned the joint. I felt more conspicuous than when I sat on Coal's office floor with the short skirt.

Plenty of people meandered around the gardens. Open doors revealed others gathered on floors of both homes and community spaces. No locks and no clocks. I saw a buffet line under a covered patio. No protein that I could observe. Small circles of meditative spirits spread out under the shade of the trees. I noticed the play equipment at the far end. No children. Not one.

Why hadn't I seen how weird this whole thing was?

"You okay?" Geoff asked.

"Why does everyone keep asking me that?"

"Just answer me!"

"We have to walk right past Carly's house. I think now would be a good time to really meander. Like to the far left."

I wanted to make a dashing beeline to Coal's inner chamber, but I still had a mind working for me. We continued to meander.

"I'm into those funky lotus ponds, anyway," Geoff said, nodding toward the landscaping to the left of us.

The flowers blossomed in fragrant grandeur. Masses of purple-coned Echinacea and rich lavender burst with

303

color. Manicured rows of herbs rounded out the enthralling blends of sweetness and spice. I had to admit the grounds permitted an experience equal to any botanical garden. And I had to admit my dollars helped pay for the experience.

"The coast is clear. No sign of anyone I recognize," I whispered.

"Which means hopefully no one recognizes you," Geoff said. "If you ask me everyone around here looks like they're mostly into themselves. No one's paying us the slightest bit of attention."

"That's Coal's house over there," I pointed.

"Duh. It's a subliminal standout."

True. The structure marked the far point of the triangle that comprised the compound. Massive, but the architecture subtracted rather than amplified the otherwise blatant capaciousness.

I panicked. "Geoff, I think after you get us in you should come back out here and be the lookout. I know what I'm looking for in there." At least I thought I did.

"No way, Sweets. I'm used to standing out in a crowd, sometimes for being so damn pretty, and sometimes for my fairy black ass. They may not be looking at me now, but if I hang around out here the neon lights are bound to start flashing around me."

"Then let's get the hell inside."

We slipped into the unlocked section of Harlan Coal's so-called residence, opening the creaking screen door. Beyond it was his Hall of Records, but for now, the space in front of us seemed safe. Public. Pure.

Geoff tried to lighten up the gravity heavy in the air. "You have me confused. Here you are, a girl who grew up with everything, and yet you thought that a man with a wooden kitchen table and a futon as his sole possessions could show you the light?"

"I thought money might be the root of all evil. I thought he was a happy minimalist. And I guess I thought he'd at least appreciate a Van Gogh."

"More like Van Gogh's ear."

Or his penis, I thought. I glanced over toward the photographs at the far corner of the room. Nothing we could use.

"And what do we have behind door number one?" Geoff touched the massive teak door centered amidst the wall of solid rock.

I had already snapped photographs of the outer room just in case there might be something I had overlooked, and to be certain. Certain of what? I wasn't certain at all.

Geoff pulled out a leather case from his deep cargo pants' pocket and zipped it open.

"What's all that?"

"Your everyday tumbler picks," he said.

"You know how to use them? You own them?"

"I've got more talents than you've ever imagined, and this is one of my finest specialties. This takes a queen's sensitivity, light fingers, plus visual acumen and an analytical mind."

The lock turned and the large teak door opened. We both stood back and gazed into the narrow chamber in front of us.

"Come on. Let's get inside and get this door shut. Just in case."

Sure. Just in case, we can die sealed up in a vault rather than out in plain sight.

Geoff fumbled for the light switch and closed the door.

"Would you look at this place," I whispered. "Some Hall of Records." Old video tapes, DVDs and CDs framed the walls of the galley shaped room from floor to ceiling. I could also see three boxes full of flash drives behind the glass doors. All locked.

"A goddamn librarian lined these shelves. Take photos. I can't pick those locks without busting something obvious," Geoff said. He had already spied the second locked door.

I took twenty or so quick photographs. The light was dim but doable.

Geoff groaned, "This lock is a little more challenging. I need to get my gun."

"Gun? What the hell are you doing with a gun?"

Geoff pursed his fingers to his lips, shushing me. "A snap gun. A fancy lock pick, that's all. Chill out. Don't get all freaky on me now."

"Right." I used the zoom to take more photos.

"Holy mother of shit!" Geoff wailed as the second door flew open.

"What is it?"

"Let's just say your guy isn't exactly a minimalist," Geoff said, stepping aside.

"Holy shit is right," I mumbled. "Look at this place. There's more fine art and collectibles in here than at The Louvre."

Geoff began pushing buttons on a remote control he found atop a stainless steel cocktail table. Music came on, lights dimmed, and skylights opened.

"Just get some photos and let's get out of here," Geoff said with a new warble in his throat. "I'll take a quick look through some of these closets and drawers."

Baffled by the sheer opulence in our surroundings, neither one of us heard the screen from the outer door creak open.

Chapter Eighty-Four
Move! Fast!

Following closely behind Geoff's lead, I snapped photo after photo. I stopped focusing on any one thing, relying on the memory of the camera.

"Get a load of this body vat," Geoff said, rubbing his hand on the polished obsidian walls of an oversized jetted bathtub.

"Okay, now I'm freaking out and you can't stop me. I took the guy for a sitz bath in holy water or dipping into a horse trough. Anything but this."

"And this," Geoff squealed with the distinct sound of delight.

"I don't get it," I said. I saw a fountain filled with crushed ice.

"This be a urinal, sweetie," Geoff said. "There's some restaurant around here that's had something like it for years. Guess their male customers get a kick out of causing their own meltdowns. Even your very own Queen Geoff enjoyed pissing in it."

"Let's check out the bedroom, then get the hell out of here. I don't want to be around when the fresh ice arrives."

I could just imagine Armand replenishing any yellow ice as part of his daily duties. And who would do it now?

"It makes me sick, but I guess it's hardly criminal," I said, taking more and more photographs.

307

"Yeah, but this is," Geoff said from across the silk leopard printed bedspread. He held up a medicine bottle from the top drawer of a nightstand.

"What are they?"

"Most certain they are roofies. You know. The date-rape drug. And why I'm guessing no victims are coming forward. They don't remember a damn thing."

"What the hell is going on here?" the voice screamed from behind me. I was so startled I dropped my camera down the plunging basin of the bathtub.

"What are you guys doing in here?" the vituperative voice demanded.

"Just calm down," Geoff warned. "All we're doing is taking a little look."

I felt the instant release of warm liquid streaming down my right pant leg. I will forever know the meaning of the phrase "it scared the piss out of me".

Panic rushed across my face, but not as much as the horror that painted the face of Sterling.

"What is this place?" Sterling gasped. She held a book in her hand that had Coal's name written across the cover.

"This is our Doctor Coal's private domain. Cozy, isn't it?" I answered.

I had climbed down into the bathtub to retrieve the camera, but now I wanted out of there, even with the embarrassment of the wet pant leg.

"No, really. What the hell is this place?" Sterling whispered.

Geoff paced his words, "What Lauren is saying is true. We obtained some information that maybe everything isn't so cool over here so we came to check it out. Dr. Coal is a fraud. More than a fraud."

Sterling's eyes devoured the sights in front of her, in one swift gulp of too much information. She recognized the signs of wealth and she was standing amidst pure luxury. I didn't know if she was dating Coal, or more than that. It didn't matter.

On the shiny stainless table, she spied one of her prized Faberge Eggs she had acquired from the Forbes estate. She didn't even realize it was missing from the store.

And that is exactly when I spied the rare elephant statue sailing on his sea of blue lapis lazuli. The one I had seen in his office. I took several photos but I didn't dare touch it.

How did it get there? Maybe it wasn't one of a kind. Maybe there were thousands of them.

"We need to leave. Now," I said.

It didn't take another word of instruction. Geoff threw the bottle of pills inside his fanny pack, I tossed the camera into my bag and grabbed Sterling's rigor mortis-like arm. She cradled the egg with her other one, unable to turn away from the affluent abyss that was Dr. Coal's private *paradisio*.

The inner door closed automatically behind us. The tampered locks showed a few scratches, but you would have to look close. Geoff closed both doors and the lock snapped shut.

"We've got to move fast," Geoff said.

"You go home, Sterling. Forget about all of this," I said.

"Bullshit, girlfriend. I'm going with you. I can't stay around here and I don't want to go home."

"She's right," Geoff said. "Just look at her. She'll break down the moment anyone walks up to her. We have to stick together."

"Okay. But once we see these photos, we need to get some help."

"You're not talking about that dufus Detective Wray?" Sterling scowled.

"He's all we have."

The three of us scurried into Geoff's car. Sterling broke down and started to whimper, clutching her treasured Faberge. "I thought he was a good man," she said. "Daddy liked him. He never went after me like all the other guys."

It dawned on me she had no idea what was really going on, about the same time I became embarrassed when I remembered my urine soaked pants pressed against Geoff's leather passenger seat.

And then my mind's eye flooded me with memories. The guys with the camera at the hotel. When I had first arrived. One of them had a long braid. The guys at my gala. One of them wore dark sunglasses. It was Harlan Coal!

Chapter Eighty-Five
Thick with Blood & Money

Detective Wray sat studying the polygraph report while biting his lower lip and thumping his heavy thumb on the final page. Harlan Coal, in spite of all his brainwave-psycho-babble garbage therapy, and from behind his perfect veneered teeth and his handsome manners, failed the polygraph. At a negative nineteen it was damning. But inadmissible.

He called Victor Romero.

"Any word on that flash drive our girls found out there in the desert?"

Romero chuckled. "Hell, no. No way could our forensics team do anything with it. They sent it up to the big guys at Quantico. That means it might be months."

"Nothing else?"

"Just sent you an email," Romero said.

"Give it to me the old-fashioned way. Talk to me, buddy."

"I've done a little more homework and there's something you should know. Your Dr. Coal has a cousin."

"So?"

"So they go way back. Thick and tight. Big money going back and forth between them. The cousin was some hotshot New York real estate tycoon but somehow ended up in your fair city. Looks to me like this cousin set Coal up in that compound of his."

"Come on. Families run thick with blood and money. So what?"

"If you'd done your homework with that fancy-schmancy department of yours you would know that this cousin is the one who reported the gun stolen. The gun that was used for the suicide—or murder—of our Tucson's Payton Doukas."

"Damn! Give me his name," Wray said.

"*Her* name is Gabriella Judd Criscione."

STERLING TOOK OVER the research, trying to find the artist of the elephant sculpture or any evidence that is was mass produced. Without that we knew the drill. We were stuck with rumors, libel, false accusations or whatever else they called it in a court of law.

We all knew what was behind those locked cabinets but I wasn't going to the police without hard evidence, in spite of the insistence from my new team of Sterling and Brock. And Queen Geoff.

"He loves you, you know," Sterling said.

"Who?"

"Brock. You're a fool if you let him get away."

"He's helped me out a lot. Who'd have figured him for the good guy?" I said.

"You blind woman. He loves you but you just won't let him in."

TWO DAYS LATER my cell rang, even after I'd gone through the hassle of changing the number in order to avoid talking to Harlan Coal.

"You didn't listen to me. You stayed. You snooped. You saw. Now it's all up to you. You better watch your back or you won't get out alive."

THE MORE HARLAN COAL thought about it the more his blood pressure surged.

"That stupid bastard," he said aloud. And his soliloquy continued.

"We had Carly Posh in our hands. We have Sterling Falls and all of her inheritance. What the fuck?"

He had to go to the farm. That pissed him off, but he had the only other keys to the ant cells. A long drive, and doing Armand's job.

Furious at a dead Armand for fueling his dick where it didn't belong, Coal would make the best of it. While he was at the farm he might as well have a little fun.

Chapter Eighty-Six
The Black Sheep

STERLING LEFT ME a voicemail. She first told me that she found nothing on the elephant sculpture. Perhaps it was an artist from a third-world country or something. Nonetheless, it didn't appear to be mass produced. Sterling pointed out that even if we did find it to be a true original we couldn't possibly know when or how Coal acquired it. And then her voice took a blunt turn toward sadness. She reminded me that she had lost, too. Her mother had died during childbirth. *Her* birth. And now her father. And two of her best friends, too. More or less she was telling me once again to get over myself and leave my pity party behind.

DETECTIVE WRAY JUST happened to be in the neighborhood. Old line that I was fond of using. No matter. I knew Brock had sent him. I knew he wanted the photographs. I had delivered him the originals of those I had found in the golf bag. I kept copies.

"I hear you just might have some others," Wray said. "Not saying I know how you got them. None of my business."

"There's a problem with those," I said. My camera was missing. I know I left it on my kitchen counter. I know it! "It seems I've lost them."

"You're kidding me," Wray said. "You broke into the man's home, took photographs, and lost them? Don't you have a decent photographer on your staff?"

A whole lab, I thought. I couldn't explain it.

And then I remembered. I had a missing set of keys. But the locks had been changed. And I had an alarm system. No. I had simply misplaced the damn camera.

I called Geoff into my office as Detective Wray walked out. "Do you think Sukie somehow got her hands on my camera?"

"Like *the camera* we used to risk our lives and take those photographs inside The Centre?"

"Yeah. That one."

Geoff slumped into the sofa in front of my desk, plopping his legs up on the cocktail table. That always meant I was in for an earful.

"*Brujeria*," he said.

"More voodoo?"

"It's not just voodoo. The Catholics adapted many of our beliefs and rituals. *Brujeria* is a blockage. It's negative energy prohibiting good energy. You don't need pendants and talisman and potions anymore, Lauren. You need to find *Ohbeahman*. This is balance. This is karma."

DETECTIVE WRAY CALLED Harlan Coal in for a second polygraph and interview. Coal refused, citing his busy calendar. He was out of the city and unavailable. He also cited his previous cooperation and something called rights. Wray cited something about a missing mental health worker that just turned up slashed to death. Coal didn't seem to know anything about that.

I ACCEPTED THE lunch invitation. I'm not certain why. The caller said he was a friend of my family's. He said we had met once a long time ago. And he invited me to join him at one of my favorite restaurants—Catrozzi's. And there was something familiar about his voice.

After almost finishing one glass of Chardonnay and pissed I was stood up by some stranger, I summoned the waiter for my check, and then the old man with a cane and a fedora joined me at my table, removing his hat as he took his seat.

"Do I know you?" I asked.

"I imagine you've seen me around," he said, after ordering another glass of wine for me, one for himself, and their famous platter of antipasto. "It was very good of you to meet me today. And very brave."

The voice registered with me. But when? Where? Who was this elderly man that called me brave?

The wine arrived promptly and he gestured a toast. I acquiesced and returned the civil gesture.

"My late wife had magnificent red hair just like yours," he said.

"Thank you. Now will you please tell me why I am here?"

The man shuffled his napkin into his lap and dived into the olives and salami.

"It's about family. A good family you need to know about."

"Go on," I said.

He swirled his wine glass, pausing as if gathering both his breath and his words.

"Would you agree with me that all families have a black sheep?"

Maybe I nodded. Maybe I sat motionless.

"We do, you know. You and me."

"I don't know what you mean, but it's time for me to go." I reached for my purse.

He moved his liver-spotted hand toward mine, but not touching.

"Please. Indulge an old man, just for a short while and an even shorter story."

He seemed harmless enough but his voice haunted my soul. And he was wasting my time.

Recognizing my reluctance he said, "Let me start with an admission. One of several I've come to deliver. I am the person that has been warning you to stay away. Go away. And above all, to be careful."

"You've been threatening me?"

"No. Just warning you."

"You call a chokehold and a rabid wolf-dog at my door a harmless warning?"

"I know nothing of that. Only a couple of notes. And a few phone calls. Oh. And the golf clubs along with its content."

I felt like an Etch-A-Sketch. I had just been shaken and it left me with nothing. I had no orientation. No map to where I was or where I was going. "You sent me that claim ticket for the golf clubs?"

"I didn't know your plane was late. I planned, somehow, to meet you and give you those photos. Had a bag of clubs in my car and checked them. Then I went out looking for your friend's Jaguar. I had just spotted it when those street thugs jumped me. They smacked me around, broke my hip, and stole my wallet."

"The wallet with the receipt in it," I said.

I paused. "Did you call me just the other day?"

"Only then did I realize you are so much like my wife. She called herself piss and vinegar and she was proud of it. I realized you have a strong heart and determined mind, not to mention the testicles of both the matador and the bull."

317

His warbled voice and mastery of the simile caused me to smile and ease up on the tension.

"I had my helpers make certain of your welfare."

Threats. My safety. Nonsensical.

"The geriatric doctor on your tenth floor. He's my very best friend."

"He's watching me?"

"Yes."

"And who the hell are you?" I asked.

"Ah. My last confession. I don't think this will be easy for you, Lauren, but I am your grandfather. My name is Nathaniel Judd."

Nathan Judd. The bad seed. The Visconti Curse. The very bad seed. The rapist. *Senior?*

Nathaniel Judd paced his words again, but they came across as bullets from a semi-automatic rifle. I fell lifeless as I listened to his story.

Nathaniel Judd and his red-haired wife bore four children. One died a hero in military battle. One died only a few years ago, a victim of cancer, and a third continued to lead a quiet and fruitful life in Chicago. But his first-born—

The black sheep that raped my mother. Nathan Judd.

"What I'm trying to tell you is that you come from good stock. An honorable family with honorable lineage. Those seeds of greatness are in you."

"Who is this man that fathered me? Your black sheep?" I got up to leave. For good.

His tone of voice, mired by the ages, sparked with a fresh nervousness, "I've given you enough to digest for one day. We'll meet again soon. Just know you have more family that loves you and cares about you. You have good

blood in those veins of yours."

Chapter Eighty-Six
Polished & Sharpened

VICTOR ROMERO ALMOST knocked over his prized Mexican beer as he fumbled to answer his new smart phone.

"Damn this thing! Whatever happened to a fucking phone you just pick up and talk into?"

His old friend, Detective Tom Wray, roared from inside his jiggle-belly.

"What do you want? I don't want to be crying over my spilt beer because of you."

"Shoot me later," Wray said. "For now, I have something you're gonna want to hear."

"I'm listening. And drinking. And getting ready to light up a fresh Cuban cigar."

"You retired rat. Good thing you have a friend like me that has a better friend over at VICAP."

"That special agent?"

"He put a rush on that flash stick you came up with. You know the one your sorry ass department couldn't read?"

"Yeah. Yeah. What'd you get?"

"That Payton Doukas was smarter than both of us combined. The stick has everything on it. Nude porno shots of little boys and a man I know here as Dr. Harlan Coal. Newspaper clippings, quit claim deeds, false identity

319

documents, plus a dirty Excel spreadsheet file that's bigger than my first computer."

"Okay, then. Nail the bastard," Romero said. "Hey, one more thing. What about that stolen gun we still have over here as evidence? "

"Keep that thing locked-up tighter than your girlfriend's liberty hole. I don't have all the pieces but you and I both know you're dealing with a murder. Looks like your so-called suicide broad knew too much for her own good."

DR. COAL SLLIPPED onto the farm largely unnoticed, despite his flowing white robes and dark sunglasses.

He reached his sanctuary. Not as welcoming as his quarters on the compound, of course. But private. Very private.

He practiced. He observed his moves in the one mirror on the farm and listened to his voice. It was not really the words which were memorized, but his inflection. Perfect inflection.

And then, with a couple commands, his stage was prepared, his audience waited, and he walked on stage.

Also, a little bit of chemicals were provided with the beverages. Just a little. Control.

He appeared before his masses—his ants—from behind the wispy white stage curtains.

"We're gathered here to learn together. We want to learn to laugh and cry. Both, we need. We want to learn tenderness and forgiveness. Both we need.

"I'm not here to convert your thinking. I'm here to give you permission to begin to think. For many of you, it will be the first time."

Sixty, maybe eighty people had gathered across the freshly blanketed lawn. Young people in their twenties or so. Blue-hairs well into their eighties. Children. Plenty of children.

"The world is not what it seems. Our lives certainly aren't about time-clocks and paychecks. You are here because you understand this. You understand the true origins of our world and life itself."

Coal positioned himself onto the great chair. He held his arms wide open with the fabric of the sleeves now billowing with the breezes.

"Let's talk about anger. Who are you angry with?"

Coals words quickened as he felt he owned his audience in the palm of his hand.

"Are you angry with your spouse? Your mother or father? Your child? Are you angry with yourself? Are you angry with me that I have sent our less-learned members into detention?

"I am here today to free our young men into your welcome arms. I am here to trust that you will show them the way. The only way. Take care of the young boys I entrust back into your care. We will need their youth and spirit as the future unfolds before us."

Coal tossed the keys to the cells into the audience with a final caveat.

"Do not be fooled by their rhetoric. Do not listen to their delusional stories. You are only here to heal their souls.

"We shall all prosper or die in purity and goodness."

The chanting began. Drugged, somewhat.

His people would weep and then they would sleep. No harm done. They would awaken by dawn and remember the keys to the cells and release all the little bastard ants. And their guru would be a couple thousand miles away. A new name he disfavored for its lack of strength. William Clark seemed so egalitarian to him. But the name and the identity of a dead man cost him only a couple nickels. And

321

maybe his new boring name would do him well, hidden in the moneyed communities where no one would think to look.

Yes. William Clark of Wichita, Kansas.

He could give a rat's ass about the farm land and The Centre. He had more than enough hard cash in his bank account. Or William Clark's account, that is.

MOON BLADE KNEW there would be no turning back. But maybe—just maybe—there could be an end to the madness.

Removing the macarta knife from its treasured hidden resting place from inside the left leg of the suit of armor, Moon Blade stationed it on the kitchen counter.

Polished, sharpened, and ready to slice and dice. Just the way it should be. One more time.

Chapter Eighty-Seven
Mrs. Teller Tells

MY TENANT ON THE TENTH floor wanted to meet with me. My geriatric doctor tenant and apparently the friend to my biological grandfather.

In less than fifteen minutes he sat before me. No introductions were necessary, nor were further clarifications needed as to who he was and why he stubbornly held onto his lease rights in my building.

"I know you have reason not to like me much, Ms. Visconti, but you can't argue that I've been a good tenant."

I could argue with him. I could use his floor for expansion. And good or bad, he was a fucking spy.

The man twisted and turned in his chair, like a *dreidel* on a highly polished wood floor and spinning with the same game of chance.

"The thing is I've stumbled upon some information I think you might want to know."

Although tolerance was no virtue of mine I told him I would listen.

"I have a good practice. Lots of patients. Seniors, you know."

He started popping his knuckles. He did a better job of popping than Orville Redenbacher. I had no idea why he would be nervous.

"Yes, you are a busy doctor." And I'm well aware of all your senile patients crawling into my elevators with their bulky walkers and canes and using my paid security guards as personal ambulatory attendants, I thought.

"I have a patient. Mrs. Teller. She's a good woman. She's been my patient for years and sometimes—most times—I seem to always feel better after my visit with her more than I think I helped her."

My new heels were killing me. Should have cut off my little toes but rather I would take them back to the retailer. I wanted to confirm an important luncheon date. I wanted to be away from this new friend of my new family.

"Ms. Visconti, are you listening to me?"

"Go on."

"Well the thing is Mrs. Teller is just a part-time resident. She spends most of her time on her family ranch in Kansas."

Good god, I thought. Who is screening my appointments?

"Mrs. Teller is still active in her community. She struggles with her speech but she's as sound of mind as they come. And she has good friends. Reliable connections. People in the know about sales of properties and such.

"I know that you know that I'm a friend of your grandfather, like it or not. I just wanted to make sure you were okay in any way I could. Staying out of your way, too. But this lady, this patient, she brought his name up!"

"Who?"

"That Coal. Dr. Harlan Coal."

I rolled my taught fingers through my hair and away from my face. I wanted to see the old man. I wished I had the habit of popping knuckles.

"Seems he's managed to get himself on the title to a large ranch just outside of Wichita. A very large ranch. Over a thousand acres, Mrs. Teller says. And the scary thing, well—this is conjecture—but one young man owned the whole shebang. No one seems to know what happened to him, not that I'm any alarmist. Just seems odd, though. I'm out of the loop these days with all these new therapies, I suppose, but I know this name. I guess you know that. Judd. Then Coal. I know he's doing very well in town. Seemed odd enough that this man would pull up stakes in L.A. and want to go to Kansas, but then he went and quickly quit-claimed the deed over to some other fellow. Some man named Clark.

I had that same Etch-A-Sketch feeling. Shaken down to nothing but a blank screen.

The geriatric doctor reached for his wallet and pulled out his business card. He told me to call him if I ever needed anything, and he said it with genuine concern, his eyes penetrating mine as if roots had intertwined the two of us.

The door closed and I sat back down at my desk. Palming his card, something called to me. Plain black raised lettering. Nothing fancy on a doctor's card, of course. Name. Address. Phone number. And his specialty. Geriatric Psychiatrist.

I kicked off my too-tight heels and ran to the old-fashioned box that housed my collection of business cards. And there it was. Dr. Coal's raised black ink.

The Centre
Dr. Harlan Coal
Therapist
Therapist
The
The rapist
I left the information on Detective Wray's voicemail.

Chapter Eighty-Eight
Thin to Win

WHILE ONLY A simple dinner invitation, Gabri's voice sounded both sad and tired. And urgent for company. I felt obliged.

I crossed the moat that declared the entrance into Gabriella Criscione's fortress. After both ringing the bell and knocking, I turned the unlocked doorknob.

She's immersed in her culinary skills, I thought.

I hadn't seen her for some time. Rumor had it she was having problems with her legs. A complication from diabetes. Fact had it that she didn't attend the memorial services of both Oliver Falls and Carly Posh. Both, two huge clients of hers. She was conspicuous by her absence.

"Gabri? I'm following the aroma of your cooking. I hope it's okay," I said.

Her gourmet kitchen boasted the finest of every appointment, and yet every time I saw it I failed to see anything, so overcome with the tantalizing aromas of a caramelized onions, sautéed garlic, and always—ripe tomatoes. This occasion was no different.

"It smells divine, my friend," I said as I walked in.

"*Costolette di Vitello* and *Fava al Guanciale*. Veal cutlets and fava beans with bacon."

And then I finally saw her, less about forty pounds.

"My god, Gabri. You look terrific!"

"I've always been strong as a rabid pit bull on steroids, but only my upper body. Diabetes came knocking at my door so I took some drastic measures. The kind you get on a doctor's table, but still, it's working. You gotta be thin to win in this world."

She stirred the inside of a giant stock pot and offered me a glass of Chianti.

Only when I sat down did I notice the large painting hanging above the archway. The hideous painting of her fat former self, unveiled at that fateful dinner party.

She caught my stare. My uneasiness. "Darling, don't worry. I've come to find it quite humorous. We all need to quit taking ourselves so seriously."

"Indeed," I managed with surprise.

"Actually, I've learned to like that painting. It encouraged me to lose the weight more than the diabetes scared me into it. And I think he's a rather talented artist, don't you?"

She said *he*. "Do you still think Brock Townsend painted that?"

"Oh, heaven's no. I was too quick to judge. I just think the painter meant no real harm and ended up helping me in the long run."

Gabri changed the conversation. She wanted to know all about the final goodbyes to both Oliver Falls and Carly. She regretted personal matters prevented her attendance.

"So much death," she surmised. "It's like it's the devil himself."

My reactions slowed to the beat of a dried-up turnip. Nothing. I had nothing. My emotions grew slight.

"You still worry you've done something wrong, don't you, dear? "

I didn't remember ever telling Gabri about any of my personal affairs, although there had been plenty of press on the *CoverBoy* articles and the subsequent deaths.

BROCK TURNED UP AT Falls & Falls, and he wasn't buying jewelry.

"Where the hell is Lauren? She's not answering her cell, her home phone, and she's not at work."

"I haven't heard from her. Did you check in with Sukie or Geoff? Sometimes she takes off with them."

"Geoff was with her last night. She asked him for more of that voodoo potion crap. Damned if I know what that means but he hasn't seen her since. Sukie is on assignment in Toledo, of all places. Nothing makes sense anymore."

Brock called Detective Wray.

"Technically she's not missing. My hands are tied," Wray said.

"Sonuva bitch," Brock screamed. "Give me something!"

Wray let out an audible sigh. "Is there any chance she might be with Gabriella Criscione? Maybe shopping for a new home, income property—something?"

"What's that supposed to mean? What aren't you telling me?"

"Calm down. I'm just curious," Wray said.

Chapter Eighty-Nine
Buon Appetito

GABRI PULLED A HUNK of veal from her simmering pot. She carved it masterfully, reminding me she was the daughter of a gifted surgeon. She layered our two plates with the stock vegetables and beef over a bed of mashed potatoes, then poured a special sauce into a small carafe.

"*Buon appetito,*" she said.

Taking my seat at her kitchen table, I said, "Gabri, I'm not sure why I am receiving the honors. You're a very busy woman and frankly, I guess, I need to make it clear that I'm not a prospect for you. Not in the near future."

"You think this is about money?"

Her raised voice alarmed me. "I didn't mean to imply that. I'm truly honored."

"I don't like to eat alone and these days I'm not throwing many lavish dinner parties," she huffed as she passed me the warm sauce.

We sat in a hush for a few moments with the fabulous sounds of an Italian aria playing in the background.

"This is delicious. No restaurant on this earth has a dish like this," I said, spooning up the rich broth I had poured over the main dish.

While not a very good cook I couldn't resist asking, "What have you done to make this sauce so divine?"

"It's brain matter," she answered.

"You mean brain food. Mega nutrients," I said.

"Both."

We laughed. I guess we laughed. We talked about the real estate market. We talked about the magazine. Such small talk. I kept thinking she was going to hit me up for some donation or something.

"Have some more of my sauce, Lauren."

I gladly took a few more tablespoons of it.

"Good girl," Gabri said as I finished my last morsels of meat. "Seems like brain matter agrees with you."

I laughed, but as odd as this sounds I can't remember hearing any laughter.

I cleared my throat. It didn't work.

"Take a sip of wine, my dear. You look pale," Gabri said.

I reached for the stemware. My hand trembled so fiercely the red wine sprinkled across my white blouse.

Gabri lifted the wine glass from my hand and then took me by my arm. Strong. She pulled me from the chair and lifted me to her sofa. I remember she wrapped an afghan over my trembling arms and legs.

"I think I need a doctor," I moaned.

"Yes, of course you do. How about I call your good friend, Dr. Coal?"

I shook my head.

"All good things must come to pass," she said. "As for me and my cousin, boy, did we ever have one helluva good ride."

I tried to reach for my face to wipe away tears that weren't there. My arms didn't move.

"He's quite a talent, you know. A great therapist, a great artist."

She nodded toward the kitchen painting of her grotesque nude body. "If you look closely at the painting Nathan's signature is plain and clear. But he's such a trickster. I mean, he knew no one would dare look too closely.

"And he's an all around great cousin. Second cousin, to be honest.

"I understand you've met Gramps. That can't be good."

Lala Corriere

Chapter Ninety
Friends

"COAL?" I CROAKED the word. His name.

"Oh darling. Yes. Harlan Coal, and before that something else and before that, something else. I can't keep track anymore. I've always known him as my Nathan."

Nathan Judd. Harlan Coal. All spinning words.

"Armand's the one who got us into trouble, you know. That idiot couldn't keep his dick in his pants. He was nothing but a dogsbody. Great journalist that you are, do you know what that means?"

I tried to shake my head but only shuddered.

"I didn't think so. Armand was the guy that did the dirty work. The grunge work. The shit work, really. He did clean up some messes. Big ones. That girlfriend of yours in Tucson. Smart cookie, that one. She found out what was going on and Armand took over to—well—clean up the mess.

"And he was a great toxicologist. I've borrowed some of his tricks, as you can see."

That was a great problem. I couldn't see anything but a kaleidoscope of color. It reminded me of the rainbow wrapping on the gift I thought Geoff had sent me. The gift that proved to be a decoy to my attention.

Geoff. I needed him. I needed his Obeah Voodoo grandmother and I called for her in my mind. My eyes fell

332

to the floor and then I did see clearly. I saw the tattoo on Gabri's left ankle. It was the same Chinese symbol of friendship Carly, Sterling and I wore on our left ankles.

Gabri caught my stare, I think. She continued with what was her soliloquy; her back now turned to me. "I wanted to be your friend, Lauren. Your good friend. I was so jealous of all you girls. You're all so bubbly and pretty and smart. Well, except Carly. I don't think that one was so smart. You inspired me. I hated the vermin of people you wrote about. Sometimes I think I hated them more than you.

"Don't you see that's why I did it? That's why I had to do all of it. I took up your causes. I got rid of the bad guys for you."

I heard new words as if they were coming from inside my throat. Since my lips could barely mouth words any more I knew this not to be true.

The potion is in you. You took it. It lives in you. It resides in your heart. You will live, and tomorrow you will awaken with a new dream that is forever yours.

The imagined voice faded. I felt it fade.

Gabri whipped around holding a large knife. Large enough to be a sword, I thought. The glare from its bright surface further blinded me.

"Armand is gone. Nathan will disappear again, and that leaves just you and me. It's time for my fairytale to end and for your nightmare to begin. You see, the only way to end this is to end you. By ending your life, I can put an end to my madness.

"My name is Moon Blade. At least it is in my beloved fairytale. Oh, to tell you more. Jacob and Wilhelm Grimm weren't even close to penning a real *grim* fairytale. I own that market; not that little children should read my fairytale."

333

Moon Blade? Grimm's fairytales? My body collapsed to the floor, kneaded and knotted like a pretzel yet to bake. A puddle of twisted dough.

Gabriella used my weakness to her advantage. From her pocket she wielded a roll of duct tape. She carved off a piece with the knife and secured it around my mouth. Pulling more from the roll, she then bound my wrists together.

"I'd ask you if you have any more questions, because you deserve to know, but I guess you can't ask," she cackled.

"All good things must come to an end. You, my dear, are a very good thing. Now don't mind me, if you have a mind left at all. I just want to start by whacking off that pretty red hair of yours."

Chapter Ninety-One
Fairytales

MY LEGS REMAINED free, if only they could rise up and kick or even move. They failed me. I saw the gleaming blade coming at me from all sides as Gabriella yanked at my hair and slashed at the roots. She seemed to squeal a few times when she took a chunk of scalp with her cuttings.

"Oh, and don't let's forget that cute little belly piercing of yours," Gabri said. "I know. Real diamonds. That Sterling is some good friend of yours. Only in L.A. would a woman hide four carats of diamonds under her clothes.

"I suppose I could get one. My stomach has shrunk but the skin is folded over like some kind of origami. Folds and folds of it—" Gabri's voice fell into a hushing lullaby.

And then she screamed.

"It's ludicrous. Wasteful. Do you know how many starving children those diamonds in your flat belly could feed? Why the hell didn't you write about yourself and your wastefulness? Your selfishness?"

She pulled at my arms until I lay flat on my back. She yanked at my blouse, tearing at the buttons, and then she yielded her weapon again, carving out the jewelry with precision. Almost as if with care.

I writhed in pain and only a muffled moan but this time I heard it. I heard me dying.

335

"Come on," Gabri puffed. "I can't leave you here to bloody up my beautiful living room. No good home can sell with blood on the damn floor. Get to your feet," she yelled.

My raw pretzel body didn't obey.

"I told you I was strong. I'll fucking drag you by the stubs of hair you have left," she yelled. 'We're going to try the moat for you. I've let my beloved Shubunkin fish go to the new piranhas. An experiment that worked beautifully. If my piranhas don't take care of you in time, the acid bath will."

My hair lay in puddles of color beside me. Red hair and red blood. And Gabri couldn't get a grip. She had nothing to drag me by until she finally grabbed my bound arms.

Together those arms had energy. I thrashed at her. I tried to knock her off balance.

She held tight and brought me up to my wobbling knees.

"Stupid bitch," she said. "I'll just have to clean up after you."

The doors burst open. Gabri's sentry—her suit of armor—was no match for the fury in Detective Wray's eyes and no match for the Glock pointed at Gabri's heart.

"Gabriella Criscione. It's over. Toss that knife to the ground or you're a dead woman."

Gabri froze, not moving the knife now in carving position at my neck.

"You've miscalculated me and my motives," she said. "I think I'm good and gone and most ready to die."

She looked down at me and said, "It's the end of my fairytale, right, Lauren?"

Detective Wray didn't fire. He moved in, but not before the knife slashed at his face.

The blow came from behind me. I saw the knife careen to the floor, but Gabri had told me my nightmare would only begin. I saw the black leather gloves.

The man at my front porch with the wolf-dog! He had come to finish me off.

Gabri slumped to the floor, her head cracking as it hit the top of her nautiloid cocktail table.

Detective Wray, now with only a whisper, "I should have known you'd be stupid enough to show up here."

The gloved hand reached for my mouth, pulling my body into his wrath.

"Shhhh. It's over. It's all over," Brock said as he gently removed the duct tape from my mouth and hands, and then cradled me forever.

I collapsed in his arms, and I slept.

Chapter Ninety-Two
Priorities

BUZZING AND BELLS and even voices tried to enter my dream, but they were not allowed.

I am running through a jungle. The hungry tiger is chasing me. I scream. I cry. I run faster. I pray and scream aloud to God to spare my life but God doesn't answer me.

After grueling hours of pain and loss of limbs and vision, I asked of God, "Where were you? I needed you. You almost let me die!"

The Higher Power, or whatever it was, cast hurt eyes upon me and spoke.

"You were looking for me to be somewhere out there in front of you. You were calling for me from outside of your being. If you'd only come looking for me where I reside inside your heart, think how much faster I could have arrived for I was with you all the time."

The nurse gently pulled at my arm. "You're awake, Ms. Visconti."

Brock stirred from the nearby chair where he was sleeping. His old injured shoulder and now his arm, bandaged.

"Is everything okay?" I asked.

The nurse responded to me. "You're in the hospital. We admitted you overnight for observation. You took some good gashes to the head but you'll be fine. There's no sign of any concussion. As soon as we can get the paperwork ready you can leave this joint."

DETECTIVE WRAY HAD his cops all over LAX and all flights going to Wichita, direct or indirect. He even advised the authorities to cover John Wayne International, just in case. All highway patrolmen had a headshot and a make and model of a car. A name was useless, Wray deduced. He could be anyone today and someone new tomorrow.

The call came in at four o'clock that afternoon. Nathan Judd, a.k.a. Dr. Harlan Coal, had been apprehended at the bus station.

Still hooked up to machines in the E.R., Wray began his own discharge by pulling out the I.V. and shimmying into his khaki pants.

Brock and I pulled the curtains surrounding his bed in time to see him zipping up his privates.

"Where do you think you're going?" I asked.

"Well, look at you and your new do," Wray said, responding to the sight of my now shaved head wrapped in bandages.

"Lauren's going to bring the turban look back into style," Brock said as he held his own bandaged shoulder near to his chest.

"Seriously," I said. "You can't just leave here."

"The hell I can't," Wray retorted. "I only took two slashes to the face, right next to the old ones. The nurses tell me if I can get me one more I could have myself a W branded on my face in keloid scars."

"Will that stand for *Wray, or wrangler, or just weird?*" I joked.

Detective Wray laughed and reached for his shirt. "I gotta get myself down to the station. Seems I have a half-assed would-be psycho-shrink taking a room there

339

courtesy of us tax-payers. The fucking bus station. Clever little bastard thought he could slip his royal ass out in a bus."

"We've heard. It's all over the news," Brock said. "I can't talk Lauren out of going down and seeing the schmuck for herself."

"Well, damn it! I sure can!" Wray said. "She has something far bigger and better to do."

"What's that?" I asked.

Wray gestured to the bed table as he tucked his shirt in and fiddled with his belt. "Grab that yellow note pad. Take a look at the second page."

I found a name and an address. *Anthony S. Find of Mount Laguna, California.*

"It's about an hour or so east of San Diego. Last time I knew anything the population was at about sixty people," Wray said.

"I don't understand," I said. I handed the notepad to Brock who shrugged with his one good shoulder.

"Your old Hollywood producer buddy, Jack Helms, came through for you. That's the name and address of Payton Doukas's missing brother. The kid got away from the fucking cult, changed his identity, and lives down there with his wife and three kids," Wray said.

"He must have wanted to be found," I said.

Brock said, "Let's go find Mr. Find. It is a bigger and better thing to do than go visit a jail cell."

Chapter Ninety-Three
All About the Diamonds

HEARING BROCK PULL up the driveway, I ran out to greet him. He'd told me to plan for a long afternoon. I understood. Mount Laguna was about a three and a half hour drive and he said he couldn't pick me up until after eleven. He also told me to pack an overnighter, "just in case."

"What's all this?" I said, climbing into the high front seats of the white Range Rover.

"This is the makings for one fine gourmet picnic."

"We'll never get there in time," I said.

"They're not expecting us until after six, and that's when Sterling figures she'll be arriving."

"Brock, why didn't you tell me? I could have worked for another couple of hours, and besides, we'll never make it back tonight."

"I thought you said you were all-clear on the work front."

"I'm not sure I'll ever use those words for *CoverBoy*, but things are pretty quiet. Geoff and Sukie flew up to Victoria to get some model shots. I'd rather run with more skin than more of those damn investigative reports. Still, I didn't think we'd actually be gone the night."

Brock turned down the music, my favorite Sheryl Crow CD. "Mike—now Anthony Find, owns a small bed and breakfast. Actually, just a few cabins. They've made

341

them up for us. They're really excited to meet you, Lauren."

"They're excited to meet all of us," I said.

We headed toward The Hollywood Hills. I guessed that Brock planned to picnic at Griffith Park. Alarm set in as we neared the old Centre.

"I hope this isn't some sick joke," I said, as Brock drove around the backside of the all too familiar grounds.

He pulled around the corner to what was the main entrance to the compound, and then shut off the engine.

"Now what?" I asked, forcing my voice to sound stable.

"I was at the dealers, ready to order myself a Mercedes Maybach. Then I got to thinking. It just made no sense to me."

"What are you talking about?"

"All that money for four tires. Money that could be put to good use. Come on," he said, pulling the blanket and basket out of the back seat, along with a set of architectural plans.

I felt panic. And I felt trust.

We walked to the heart of the grounds and I admit I felt saddened at the sight of once tended gardens, already succumbed to the heat. The lawn hadn't been mowed. It now looked more like wheat than grass.

Brock spread out the blanket and set about pulling food from the basket.

"What's this?" I said. "You call this gourmet?"

He unwrapped two hot dogs and then opened a large bag of potato chips.

"This is prime property, you know. Prime and perfect. It's going to make a great baseball park. There's a lot to work to do, but every owner in here will get more than an equitable price for their lot. My new Realtor has talked to all of them and you can bet all of them want to move. And I've already been assured by Detective Wray that most of the proceeds can go to the Victim's Assistance Fund they're setting up."

He unrolled the blueprints. Although rough, three baseball diamonds had been sketched, along with the much needed parking lot and even some concession stands.

Brock said, "There's no decent baseball park around here because the dirt is too damn expensive. And you and I both know poverty isn't too far away from all these white mansions around the block."

"When did you have time to do all this? It looks like you've been planning it for years," I said.

"Because I have been planning. I just never found the right property. But it has to be good with you, Lauren. I don't want to do it if you feel this property is stigmatized."

"You mean with my curse?"

He shrugged, but again with only one shoulder.

"That's it, isn't it? Your shoulder? You're not going back next season?"

I watched his face carefully for signs of regret, anger, and even pain. Instead Brock flashed me a full dimpled smile with his chin dribbled in yellow mustard.

"I don't want to just own the dirt and a fancy sign with my name on it. I want to be out here with the kids, giving them something of me," he said.

"Hell, we all know it's my shoulder. But I've been ready to give up the groupies throwing their panties at me for a long time."

He laid out flat on his back and stared straight up, then he turned to me, "Are you okay with this?"

I nodded. A nod with a smile.

"Great!" He jumped up. "Reach into that basket. We need a drink to wash all this junk down."

I pulled out the bottle of chilled champagne and two plastic glasses. Inside the bottom of one was a miniature leather catcher's mitt.

"I hope I'm not supposed to catch little tiny balls with this," I said.

He laughed and held the glove out for me to see. "You don't have to catch anything unless you want it. But you need to know my plans always called for diamonds."

"You were lucky to get three on this parcel."

"I didn't say you had to catch anything because that mitt already has done the catching."

I grabbed the tiny hand-stitched leather mitt, pulling back the fingers one at a time until I found the fourth diamond. Brilliant. Dazzling.

Brock pulled out his phone and turned up the tune. *Take Me Out to the Ballgame* began filling my ears.

"Don't worry. It doesn't have to be our wedding song.

Exclusive Excerpt

Evil Cries

Coming Summer, 2013

Is he crying for you?

The sociopath notices the panties lying on the floor next to his motionless victim. He picks them up, wads them in his hands, delighted at the prospect. He shudders with delight and maybe apprehension. Should he keep them? Yes, he should. Trophies. But what will he do with them? Where should he hide them where they will live on forever?

The psychopath snatches the panties from the dead. Once in his hands he gently folds them, starting from the left, then center to the right, then up from the bottom to meet the top. He tucks them inside the silk case he has in his left breast pocket. He's been adding to his collection for years. And like all new trophies, he knows exactly where this newest pair of intimates will go.
And all should cry.

Chapter One
Not the Welcome Wagon

SHE SMELLED LIKE Hell's testicles. Rotten teeth. Bleeding gums and grimy hair in a rat's nest of wiry mesh. And *urine?*

We hadn't even officially opened our new second store and Bag Lady decides she can stagger right through the front door.

I should have kept the door locked but all of our jewelry pieces were sealed in the vault until I had the security alarm fully functioning and we were open for business.

Bag Lady stumbled toward the center of the store. I slid behind the counter but in full stance, which is a pretty tall drink. She didn't scare me. She reeked.

"Can I help you?" I asked. I tried to be patient. This was not the first customer in Tucson I had imagined for *Falls & Falls.* Jeweler to the stars in Beverly Hills and all that.

She turned around. Her grubby hands braced against my beautifully polished glass display cases awaiting their shiny treasure chest of gold, platinum, and gems.

"I don't think I have anything here you want," I said.

She remained silent. Her eyes searched mine.

"I don't even have any food. Look, I can give you bottled water and maybe twenty bucks, but then you need to promise you won't come back. Do you understand?"

Bag Lady nodded. A speechless beggar. I expected to encounter some language barriers living so close to the border but this woman was lily white. Except for the grunge.

She followed me to the back of the store. When I entered the office I asked her to wait in the small alcove.

Turning my back to retrieve the water and my purse, I heard the tumultuous blast of sound along with the shattering of glass.

Bag Lady reeled around and pulled something from her purse with her right hand. A blow to my shoulder with her left hand pushed me further into the office.

The sound of bullets blasted out from the front of the store. Someone was shooting Bag Lady.

Bag Lady fired a single shot and hollered at me to dial 911.

Chapter Two
A shot not in the dark.

VICTOR ROMERO HEARD it on his home police scanner. Shots fired. Northwest side address.

Nice part of town, he thought. Upscale shopping. Decadent restaurants with more decadent tabs.

It hit him as hard as a kick to his nuts. "Sonuvabitch," he yelled out to no one. Romero grabbed his keys and rolled down Catalina Highway in his treasured lime green P.T. Cruiser.

BAG LADY PULLED off her crumpled coat and wrapped it around me. I had fallen against a wall and pulled my legs up to my body tighter and harder than a neutron star.

"Stay put," she said. "I gotta go check on him."

Now I was the one speechless and nodding. Thinking that a neutron star is ten billion times stronger than steel. In other words, I wasn't really thinking about anything pertinent to what was happening *out there*. Something so stupid I'd learned when I was certified as a gemologist when they told me diamonds were not the hardest substance in our universe.

Time lost its fourth dimension. It was like the inviting white light of the tunnel and the flames of hell all emerged into one infinite space, and both were incomprehensible.

"You okay, honey?" Bag Lady called out from our main salon.

"Like a neutron star," I said. I peered around the corner and into the alcove, then to the shattered glass sprayed across my new store. How okay could I be? A man splayed out in pooling blood on the pearl travertine floor.

The woman crouched over him and applied pressure to his chest wound.

"He did it," the injured man said.

"Did what? Who did what?"

And in a gasping voice the man said, "Trouble coming."

I could see him collapse into his own blood which now ceased to pump. I could see his last laugh at life as he urinated, the colors of a golden yellow slowly seeping away from his pants and mingling with the red liquid of death.

The woman now stood and began taking photographs, using a fancy camera with a huge zoom. Her subject? Blood and guts and a dead man missing some.

My voice trembled but I forced the words out hard and loud and demanded, "Who the hell are you?"

She smiled. A genuine smile of black teeth and green gum lines.

Two policemen came from two directions, weapons drawn.

"10-4," Bag Lady said.

One cop: "Well look at Ms. Shirley. Should have known you would be here. And aren't you looking simply marvelous today?"

Second cop: "I don't know. I like her better as a two-dollar whore."

Bag Lady hugged Cop One and shook her head at Cop Two. "That would be a twenty-dollar whore," she corrected him.

349

"Will someone please tell me what's going on?" I pleaded.

"We'll take it from here," Cop One said. "You have some answering—"

Cop Two, "And in walks the devil, himself."

I recognized the man instantly. Victor Romero. I was living in Los Angeles when my Tucson friend was killed. But nobody believed it. They ruled it a suicide. Victor Romero, a retired cop working as a private detective, believed it. He believed me. He believed in the honor of my friend.

He turned to embrace me. A gargantuan bone-breaking hug. "Good to see you, Sterling. But like they say, maybe not under these circumstances."

He looked back to the policemen with a 'let's all stay put' clench of the hands, then again to me. "These cameras working?"

Six were newly installed on the high interior walls. Three, outside. "Two of them," I said.

Romero, back to the cops, "Evidence. Get it." Back to me, "You can help them get the video, can't you?"

"Only after you tell me what's going on," I said.

Cop Two rolled the dead man over. "Crap. It's Manuel Perez. A.K.A. anyone you want him to be," he said, pulling out the wallet from the bloodied pants that held about six fake I.D.'s and none that bared his real name.

"Yeah," Romero said, looking at me. "Good old Manny. He has a rap sheet that could line the walls of The Louvre."

"I don't need to be introduced to a dead man, Victor. Who is she?" I pointed at Bag Lady.

Bag Lady shrugged, but with an odd shrug and glimmer hidden somewhere in her eyes.

"I'm retired, Ms. Falls. This time for good. Not here officially, but I listen to my scanner and I knew the address. I knew you were coming to town. This here is Ms. Shirley. She's one hell of an undercover.

"Come on, Shirley. Give her a little of the real you," he said. "With a dead man's guts on Ms. Fall's new pretty floor, and you scaring the B-Jesus out of her, she might just pack up and move out of Dodge before she's even unpacked."

Bag Lady stood erect. Tall. Almost as tall as me. She removed the outer clothes and the padding from underneath them. Slender. She tossed two plastic bags at Romero. He ducked. They fell to the bloody floor.

"Messing up the crime scene, Shirley. Come on. Keep going," Romero said.

The wig came off next. Underneath that rat nest was a coifed French bun. Mostly silver hair. Maybe some blond. She retrieved a plastic box from her large bag, then popped out two mouthpieces. Her teeth now sparkled white and brilliant.

"It's why I don't talk much when I'm wearing these things," she said as if annoyed. She dropped the fakes with the blackened teeth, missing teeth, and green gum lines into the box and snapped it shut. 'Hell, I can't mumble with these damn things."

I turned back to Romero. Digesting. Thinking. My body was fully charged but my brain lagged behind. "What is she doing here?"

"I guess she was trying to drum up some business," Romero said. "And it looks like she found some."

A wretched smell began to pierce through the already coppery stink of blood in the air.

Bag Lady, now Shirley, looked at me with another one of her shrugs. "Sorry, honey. Vic was supposed to catch those little bags. He used to be a catcher, you know."

Romero laughed, looking at the two plastic bags that had started oozing out some liquid onto the floor, mixing in with the pools of blood and urine. It wasn't exactly champagne laced with Chambord.

"Modern day stink bombs," Romero explained. "Squeeze them a little bit and you get your smell du jour. Whatever you want. Some urine. Some feces. Sometimes even the smell of money. Guess they landed on the floor a little too hard."

"You're a lousy catcher these days," Bag Lady laughed at Romero. And to me, "The smell goes away in about five minutes. I promise."

The medical examiner arrived, did his thing, and removed what he could of the remains of the would-be thief. Another pair of cops boarded up the storefront's windows and door. They shook hands with Romero and told him that their work was done. They mentioned a Detective Taylor would be arriving in a 'few' and Victor Romero let out a huge sigh and a big, "Yes!"

I fell back into one of the new jeweler's chairs, still covered with the protective plastic wrapping.

"They're done?" I gasped, looking at the blood and the guts and the oozing stinky bags.

Romero and Shirley told me we needed to wait for this Detective Taylor. She pulled out a cell phone from the same old bag. "We know who to call, Sterling. You're going to have to pay some big bucks, but she'll be here within the hour and by morning you'll never know or *feel* like anything happened here tonight." She handed me a card as she used speed dialing to make the call.

The card, plain as it was, said it all. *Scene Clean. Crime Scene Specialists. Zoey Lane: Sole Proprietress.*

About the author:
Since early childhood, Lala has been passionate about all the arts. She is a painter and a former stage performer. The extension of the arts, the written word, turned into a full-time passion in 2001.

- Endorsement and long-term mentorship by the late **Sidney Sheldon.**

- Published in regional magazines, newspapers, writer's guides and journals.

- Award winning poetry.

- Endorsements from Andrew Neiderman [author of the *Devil's Advocate*], Paris Afton Bonds, and many others remarkable authors.

- Her first novel, **Widow's Row**, became number 1 in Amazon Mystery. Released in November, 2010. Now available as an e-Book, trade paperback, and audio book.

- **Evil Cries**, coming summer, 2013. **Kiss and Kill**, coming fall, 2011

Lala is a desert rat. She nestles there with her husband of over 25 years along with a Ragdoll, an American Curl, and Finnigan, a 5-pound Teacup Yorkie.

Lala Corriere

If you'd like to learn more about the author or contact her you can find her!

www.lalacorriere.com

Facebook author page:
https://www.facebook.com/pages/Lala-Corriere-Author-Page

Amazon author page: http://www.amazon.com/Lala-Corriere/e/B004FLFUKA/ref=sr_tc_2_0?qid=137245714 5&sr=1-2-ent

Or use her QR Code:
PO Box 69194, Tucson, AZ 85755

Kiss and Kill
Coming Fall, 2013

Available Now:
Widow's Row
eBook, trade paperback, and audio

23997172R00196

Made in the USA
Charleston, SC
09 November 2013